HOW TO LOSE AN EARL IN 10 WEEKS

JENNI FLETCHER

PENGUIN BOOKS

PENGUIN BOOKS

UK | USA | Canada | Ireland | Australia
India | New Zealand | South Africa

Penguin Books is part of the Penguin Random House group of companies
whose addresses can be found at global.penguinrandomhouse.com

www.penguin.co.uk
www.puffin.co.uk
www.ladybird.co.uk

Penguin
Random House
UK

First published as an ebook 2021
Published in paperback 2022

001

Text copyright © Jenni Fletcher, 2021
Cover image © Lee Avison / Trevillion Images

The moral right of the author has been asserted

Set in 12.5/14.75pt Garamond MT Std
Typeset by Jouve (UK), Milton Keynes
Printed and bound in Great Britain by Clays Ltd, Elcograf S.p.A.

The authorized representative in the EEA is Penguin Random House Ireland,
Morrison Chambers, 32 Nassau Street, Dublin D02 YH68

A CIP catalogue record for this book is available from the British Library

ISBN: 978–0–241–62695–5

All correspondence to:
Penguin Books, Penguin Random House Children's
One Embassy Gardens, 8 Viaduct Gardens, London SW11 7BW

MIX
Paper from
responsible sources
FSC® C018179
www.fsc.org

Penguin Random House is committed to a
sustainable future for our business, our readers
and our planet. This book is made from Forest
Stewardship Council® certified paper.

For Andy

LONDON BOROUGH OF WANDSWORTH	
9030 00007 9737 8	
Askews & Holts	
AF	
	WW22007667

Dearest, if you're reading this then it means that my plan has worked. You'll have already guessed where I've gone and who with. Please believe that I've agonized long and hard over this decision and I hope that you of all people will understand. I wish I had time to write more, but the carriage is waiting and I have to go. I beg you not to think ill of me, but if you do, know that I remain

Your loving cousin,
  Always, C

14th May 1816

PLAN A: ASK NICELY

Dear Diary,
Today was wretched. The Earl of Something and his wife came to visit and brought their horrible son with them. He is the most disagreeable, loathsome boy in THE WHOLE WORLD! I wanted to play in the woods, but he insisted on shuttlecock so I said that he wasn't a gentleman and he said that I wasn't a lady because ladies ought to be obliging! OBLIGING!!! He sounded so much like Father, I wanted to hit him with my racquet. Then he ate the last piece of seed cake. I hate him, I hate him, I hate him! Fortunately, he's gone now and I hope I never see him again in my life. At least I can enjoy my birthday tomorrow.'
Also, I lost a tooth. That makes eight.

Essie Craven to herself, 28th February 1806

Chapter One

(Twelve Weeks until the Wedding of
Miss Essie Craven to the Earl of Denholm)

When the Honourable Essie Craven made up her mind, she didn't look back.

Essie was, in the words of her Aunt Emmeline, the most headstrong, obstreperous, downright impetuous girl in the whole of England. Unfortunately, these were all tendencies apt to cause problems, so when it came to really big decisions, she forced herself to be patient and consider. Birthdays, however, had a way of clarifying matters. Sometimes all it took was one additional year and ten solid hours of sleep for the world suddenly to make sense. And so it was that when Essie awoke on the morning of her eighteenth birthday, she came to one momentous, life-altering decision: that she would never marry her fiancé.

Now that the matter was settled, in her own mind at least, she acknowledged that the seeds of rebellion had been sown a long time before, on another, much earlier birthday, when her entire future had been mapped out before her horrified

3

eyes like some kind of military campaign. If her father had defeated Napoleon in hand-to-hand combat he could hardly have looked any more proud of himself than when he'd told her who she was going to marry – Aidan Ravell, the future Earl of Denholm. The very worst person she could possibly have been betrothed to.

And when she'd turned to her mother for help . . . At eight years old she'd already come to recognize that look of defeat. Her mother had been so overpowered by the whole thing that she hadn't even put up a fight when she'd caught a mild chill in the rain a week later. She'd simply kissed Essie goodnight one evening, retreated to her bedchamber and promptly died.

Motherless and confused, Essie had loathed the idea of her future marriage then almost as much as she hated it now. It was only on this numerically significant morning, however, that resentment and rebellion finally crystallized into resolve. She would end her nineteenth year as she'd just begun it, as *Miss* Essie Craven, no 'madam' or 'your ladyship' or 'Countess'. She would find some way to thwart her father's social-climbing scheme. Exactly *how* she would do it without being disowned, disinherited and thrown out on to the street for good measure was another, somewhat more challenging matter, but determination was the one virtue she didn't lack. It was all the others she had problems with.

'Determined to do what?' Her cousin Caro in the neighbouring bed peeled back her quilt like a butterfly emerging from a custard-coloured cocoon. 'You're thinking out loud again.'

'Sorry . . . It's nothing, just my birthday.'

4

'That's not nothing. Happy birthday.' Caro heaved herself up on her elbows, bleary-eyed and yet as radiantly lovely as ever. 'I know you're not excited about today, but I'm sure it won't be so bad.'

'I wish time could have stopped at midnight.' Essie glowered up at the ceiling. 'Then we could have stayed seventeen together forever.'

'But then I'd never have my birthday in two weeks or get a coming-out *or* Season, which doesn't seem very fair when you're already engaged to an earl.'

'An earl I never asked for, an engagement I didn't agree to, and a future I don't want.' Essie's brows contracted into a thick, dark line. 'And he'll be here before nightfall, Aunt Emmeline says. He might have given me a few days to get used to the idea.'

'You've had ten years to get used to it, Essie. And I think it's romantic – like he couldn't wait to see you.'

'Inspect me, more like. *And* he's bringing his mother. There's nothing romantic about that.'

'No-o, but it's not as if you're getting married today. This is only a meeting.'

'It's a farce! Nobody cares whether or not we actually like each other. It's just so we can all pretend this is more than a business arrangement.' Essie tossed her bedcovers back in frustration. 'If you ask me, it's barbaric to betroth a pair of children in the nursery without any concern for how they might feel about it when they grow up. And why?' she scoffed. 'All because my father is obsessed with the idea of making his only child a countess!'

'Mmm.'

'Are you going back to sleep?'

'Yes.'

'*Caro!*'

'I'm sorry. It's just that I've heard this rant so many times before and it's never made the slightest bit of sense to me. He's young, rich and an earl! Mama's heard that he's handsome too. You know, most girls would give an arm or leg to be in your position. I know I would.'

'Which is exactly why you ought to marry him instead.' Essie leaped to her feet, stalking across to the window and wrenching the curtains apart. The sky outside was a pale oyster-grey, streaked with whispery streamers of pink, marred only by a bank of fluffy white clouds gathering on the horizon. Nice enough now, but it seemed the earl was bringing bad weather with him. *Of course* he was. 'I'm sure he'll prefer you anyway. You're much prettier. Everyone thinks so.' She caught a glimpse of her own chestnut curls, wide forehead and too-big, brown eyes in the glass and dropped the curtain again. 'He'll probably wish *you* were his fiancée when he sees you – I'm only tolerable.' She kicked at the edges of a tasselled rug with her bare toes. 'That's what your mother says.'

'What?' Caro sat up indignantly. 'When?'

'The other night to your father. I overheard them talking in the library. Oh, don't give me that look! I had no option but to hide under the desk. I didn't want another lecture about reading. She's already threatened to keep the door locked if she finds me in there again.'

'Oh dear.' Caro looked sympathetic. 'I'm sorry.'

'It's not your fault.' Essie scampered back across the room, clambering on to the end of her cousin's bed and clutching at her hands. 'Just swear to me that you won't ever turn into your mother because I don't think I could bear *two* people criticizing my every move.'

'I won't, I promise, and *I* think you're very lovely.'

'Not like you.' Essie trailed her fingers down the long braid draped over her cousin's shoulder. It was gold shot through with amber lights, like sunshine itself. 'You'd make a much better countess than I ever could. You're beautiful and elegant and accomplished, you can speak French and play the harp and paint screens and you never look even the slightest bit bored doing embroidery.'

'That's not the point. *You're* the heiress and you're the one he's engaged to.' Caro lifted her shoulders. 'I know it's not what you want to hear, but maybe you should try to accept it.'

'That's not what Anne Boleyn would have done.'

'Oh, not Anne Boleyn again!' Caro threw herself backwards, grabbing her pillow and hauling it over her ears. 'You're only interested in reading about the bad women throughout history.'

'Because they're the only interesting ones! They show what's possible when a woman puts her mind to something. Besides, Anne Boleyn wasn't bad. She just had a bad husband.'

'She got her head chopped off.'

'That's what happens when you marry the wrong man.'

'I really don't think the Earl of Denholm is going to chop your head off.'

'Who knows what he'll do? I don't know anything about him except that he's an earl.'

'You know he's two years older than you.'

'All right, I know *that*.'

'And he inherited the title a year ago. And you even know what he looks like. You've met him before.'

'Once, when we were children! And he acted *just* like Henry the Eighth. All haughty and superior, looking at the world as if he owned it.' She scrunched up her mouth at the memory. 'You'll be sorry when he does unspeakable things to me.'

'Fine. If he cuts your head off then I'll put a notice in *The Times* saying you were right.'

'Don't forget my eulogy. Fortunately, I've no intention of losing my head.'

'Essie?' A flicker of alarm crossed her cousin's features. 'I know that face. What are you planning?'

'I'm not certain yet, but you'll be the first to know.' Essie smiled mischievously. 'Now, I can't believe we're ten minutes into my birthday and you still haven't given me a present!'

'It's right there on your bedside table. You would have seen it if you hadn't been so busy complaining.'

'*Emma*!' Essie gave a squeal of delight as she tore open the muslin-wrapped parcel and hugged the contents to her chest. 'How on earth did you get hold of the latest Jane Austen?'

'With a great deal of subterfuge and bribery, so for goodness sake, don't let Mama see it. You know the only novels she allows in the house are the ones she reads in secret. Hide it under the bed with all your other books.' Caro looked exceedingly pleased with herself. 'And, since Jane Austen doesn't write plays, I got you another copy of *Much Ado about Nothing* as well. Your old one is practically in tatters.'

'Oh, you're the dearest, best cousin in the whole world!'

'I know. And in case all that isn't enough, I have one more gift for you. I heard Mama telling her lady's maid they were going to start getting you ready as soon as you woke up.'

'But the earl's not arriving until this afternoon.' Essie wrinkled her nose. 'How is that a present?'

'Because I'm warning you, aren't I? If you hurry, then you can get out of the house before either of them gets their hands on you. If you think one hundred brush-strokes is bad, just wait for what they have planned for today. Scrubbing and polishing and squeezing and –'

'*Squeezing?*'

'Corset.'

'Eurgh! Thank you!' Essie sprang off the bed, wrenching her nightdress over her head before wriggling her way into a fresh chemise and riding habit.

'No stockings?' Caro looked faintly scandalized.

'No time.' She reached for a pair of boots and a jacket on her way to the door, pausing briefly to blow her cousin a kiss. 'I'll be back in time for breakfast.'

'No you won't, but I'll tell Mama you're too nervous to eat. That ought to stall her for a little while.' Caro waved before burrowing back under her covers. 'Happy birthday!'

Essie escaped with only seconds to spare. Amelie, her aunt's lady's maid, was just sweeping around the end of the corridor when Essie caught a glimpse of her skirts and dived quickly into an alcove, concealing herself behind a marble statue of a barely dressed maiden who was inexplicably holding a doe. A few seconds later and she was hurtling down the main staircase, past two surprised-looking maids and out of the front door, heading for the stables where Boudica, her grey mare, was already saddled and waiting – Thomas, the head groom, obviously knew her a hundred times better than her aunt did. Five minutes after that and she was pelting up the hill behind Redcliffe Hall as if the hounds of hell, each one of them bearing a striking resemblance to her aunt, were snapping at her heels.

Once at a safe distance, she stopped, heaving a sigh of relief as she gazed out over the rolling green and tawny-coloured hills of the Cleveland countryside, past the folly of a ruined castle her uncle had commissioned the previous summer, all the way to a sliver of blue sea in the distance.

She loved this view with its wide open spaces and big skies. She even loved the hall, with its columned Palladian frontage and perfectly symmetrical windows, despite it belonging to her overly critical aunt and surprisingly placid uncle. It was home – or at least it had been for the past nine years and eleven months, ever since her mother had withered away and her widowed father, Alfred Craven, the Right Honourable Lord Makepeace, had decided he had neither the time nor inclination for something as tedious as raising his own daughter. Having found himself a suitable future son-in-law, he'd concluded that it would be far better for everyone, but mostly himself, for her to be raised as part of his sister's family alongside her two cousins, Caroline and Felix, until her wedding day.

When she was younger, Essie had tried her absolute hardest to view this decision as a touching paternal sacrifice, but it was hard to believe that from a man who hadn't displayed even the tiniest flicker of emotion at her departure, no more than he'd demonstrated at her mother's funeral two weeks before. Instead, he'd sent her away with strict instructions to be modest and dutiful and virtuous and – what was the other one? – oh yes, quiet. After which, ostensibly, he'd forgotten all about her. Not once in the intervening years had he felt it necessary to visit, or even to suggest that she make the journey to see him. After this long, it was becoming hard to remember what he actually looked like, and trying to remember only cast a grey pall over her mood.

She turned her face up to the sky, looking for shapes in the clouds to distract herself. Sometimes this feeling of deep-rooted sadness came at her unawares, accompanied by a pounding heartbeat and a hot, constricting sensation as if her skin were too tight for her body. At other times she could feel it gradually building, like a deep, dark pool inside her chest, threatening to burst its banks and drag her down if she didn't take care to turn her thoughts in another direction.

A red kite streaked through the sky above her head and she watched its progress jealously. If only she could be as free! Free to swoop, to glide, to soar, even to fall. Most of all, to follow her own path. There was a whole world out there, a world beyond Cleveland or her childhood home in Norfolk, or even Hampshire, where the Earl of Denholm had his estates, and she wanted to explore it all, not to be shackled the very moment she was finally allowed out of the school-room.

The blunt truth that her father failed to appreciate, and that the earl was soon to discover, was that she simply wasn't countess material. It didn't matter how many lessons in etiquette and deportment she was subjected to – she didn't care about being ladylike. What she wanted more than anything was to be on the stage, her cherished dream ever since she'd discovered the *Complete Works of Shakespeare* on her mother's bedside cabinet the day after her funeral. She'd picked it up in amazement, marvelling with every turn of the page. It had seemed like such an unlikely work for her mother to own. To Essie's memory, she'd never even seen her open a book and yet there it had been, like a message left specially for her.

She'd devoured the tome repeatedly over the years, finding enthusiastic collaborators in her cousins. They'd put on their very first production the summer after her arrival at Redcliffe, a heavily abridged adaptation of *Hamlet*, in which she'd played the title role, Caro had played Ophelia, and Felix everyone else. Over the years, their performances had become increasingly ambitious, expanding to include some of Felix's school friends when they came to stay in the holidays, and gathering an enthusiastic audience amidst the local gentry. On stage, she could leave all of her resentment and dread about the future behind. She could become somebody else, somebody free and not completely miscast.

Unfortunately, like most other professions for women, acting wasn't considered remotely respectable. She already knew that her father wouldn't approve, and just the prospect of asking him led her thoughts back to disowning and disinheritance again, but if she could just get started somehow, without his knowledge . . . She could be the next Sarah Siddons or Elizabeth Inchbald, women she'd only heard of thanks to Felix, but whose lives sounded *so* much more interesting and exciting than her own. She had no idea how to begin, but just because an answer wasn't obvious didn't mean that it didn't exist. If she could only find that answer, and save enough money to support herself before her father found out, then she could be free. It would mean scandal and sacrifice and the loss of a great deal of creature comforts, but at least she'd be living life on her own terms, ideally without a single earl in sight.

Before she could do any of that, however, she needed to get rid of her fiancé.

Besides, if she ever married then she wanted it to be for love, an emotion she was certainly never going to feel for the hoity-toity, black-haired boy with the too-intense blue eyes she remembered from their one disastrous meeting as children. He'd called her unladylike and she'd called him something that would have given her aunt a fit of the vapours if she'd heard it, but had only caused him to laugh. Which had made Essie all the more furious.

Gazing out at the far-off waters of the North Sea, she seemed to hear that laugh all over again, taunting her and yet paradoxically strengthening her resolve. Fortunately, the fresh air had cleared her mind enough to give her an idea. A simple one really. The Earl of Denholm was on his way to meet her, probably to laugh at her again. If she wanted to end their engagement then maybe all she needed to do was put on a sweet-tempered face, pretend that she didn't loathe the very sight of him and simply ask. She would call it Plan A.

A for Ask nicely.

Chapter Two

Time, Essie reflected, had a way of working differently when she was out riding on Boudica. Hours could fly past in minutes and she could forget everything else, including the fact that her stomach was grumbling like a ravenous wolf and her ears and nose were turning numb in the frigid spring air. Which was why, when she saw Thomas riding hell for leather towards her, she realized that she'd obviously stayed out for too long.

'Apologies, miss.' The head groom was panting so hard when he reached her it sounded as if he was the one who'd been galloping. 'Your aunt sent me to find you.'

'Oh, bother. I really did intend to be back for breakfast.' Her heart sank all the way to her almost frozen toes. 'Is she on the warpath?'

'No more than usual, but it's not just that. It's the earl too. She says he'll be here within the hour.'

'What? But it's still morning!' Essie swung her horse around and then stopped, frowning. 'Isn't it?'

'Barely, but one of his men just rode ahead with a message. They're arriving early.'

'Drat!' She flicked on her reins and charged headlong down the hill as tiny flakes of snow began to fall all around them, twisting and twirling through the air like miniature ballerinas. By the time they reached the stables, a light dusting had turned into a moderate blizzard and she dismounted with relief, throwing her reins to Thomas with a grateful smile before running into the house and up the back stairs, bursting through the door to her bedchamber, scarlet-cheeked and out of breath.

'Where have you been?' Aunt Emmeline looked on the verge of hysterics, her golden ringlets bouncing around her head like a cluster of angry snakes. At six and thirty, she'd retained enough of her youthful good looks that in a favourable light she might almost have been mistaken for Caro's older sister instead of her mother. They had the same blond and blue colouring, the same willowy figure, the same pert nose and the same enviably flawless complexion. Only their mouths were different, and there was no mistaking Aunt Emmeline's perpetual pout for Caro's warm-hearted smile.

'Sorry, Aunt.' Essie fought her way out of her riding habit and dropped on to the stool in front of her dressing table. 'I wanted some fresh air.'

'So you can look all windblown for your future husband, I suppose?' Her aunt inhaled audibly. 'Where are your stockings?'

'Um . . .' She exchanged a quick glance with Caro. 'I forgot?'

'Just look at this bird's nest. So many knots and tangles.' Her aunt clutched a handful of hair and yanked it towards Amelie. 'There's no time for a bath now, but do what you can. Caro, keep a watch by the window. As for *you*.' She narrowed her eyes at Essie in the mirror. 'I expressly forbade you from going riding this morning!'

'Did you?'

'Yes! Last night after dinner.'

'Oh. Sorry. It's just that you forbid so many things. It makes it impossible to remember them all.'

'Give me patience!' Her aunt squeezed her eyes shut as if she were looking inside herself for strength. Either that or she was soothing a burst of palpitations. 'It's a good thing your father's already arranged a match because I'd despair of finding another poor man to marry you. You're reckless, disobedient, stubborn, and now insolent to boot! You get this from your mother's side of the family because it's certainly not from mine. Your father would be horrified if he could hear you.'

Essie clenched her jaw, wondering whether her aunt had forgotten that it was her birthday or if she simply didn't care about her feelings. She strongly suspected the latter. As for her father, it was hard to imagine him paying sufficient attention to have *any* feelings regarding her, but she supposed horror was better than nothing.

'You certainly don't deserve your good fortune,' her aunt concluded eventually, her expression so sanctimonious that Essie couldn't resist responding.

'How is it good fortune if I don't want it?'

A look of panic flitted across her aunt's face, succeeded by a sharp hiss. 'For pity's sake, girl, think of the family and use your common sense for once. Don't do anything foolish!'

For a relatively small woman, her aunt had a surprisingly powerful grip, Essie thought, wincing as she and Caro were bundled out of the hall and down the front steps, just as a black carriage, emblazoned with a gold coat of arms and accompanied by a baggage cart and half a dozen liveried riders, rolled down the drive.

After thirty minutes of vigorous grooming, her cheeks were now rosy pink rather than violently red, her hair was twisted into an elegant chignon held in place by an entire boxful of pins, and her ability to breathe was severely hampered by the constricting presence of a corset. She felt like a doll, dressed up in an expensive cream-coloured silk gown embroidered with pink butterflies that her aunt said made her look pretty and modest – the word *rich* was implied – but which was woefully inadequate for the wintry conditions. The snow had dwindled to a few stray flakes, but the temperature was still glacial. Any actual butterflies would have frozen the moment they opened their wings.

'Well, don't you both look charming?' Uncle Charles was already waiting on the steps, smiling his usual jovial smile. 'Just in time too. Here they come.'

'Can I pleeeease wear a jacket?' Essie threw a longing glance at Caro's lace shawl. It wasn't much, but it was still better than her own bare and probably-soon-to-turn-blue arms. 'It's so c-cold!'

'No! A lady remains poised whatever the temperature, and you want him to think you're making an effort.' One of her aunt's bony fingers jabbed into her lower back. 'Now stand up straight, keep your shoulders back, remember to curtsey and stop shivering.' She looked away and then back again. 'And say as little as possible.'

Essie rolled her eyes, deliberately slumping her shoulders and huddling against Caro for warmth as the carriage rolled to a halt in front of them. Honestly, it would be hard to speak even if she wanted to with her teeth chattering so violently, but right now, all she needed to do was smile nicely and act as though her first meeting with the earl had never happened.

'Lady Denholm, how delightful to see you. How was your journey?' Aunt Emmeline was the first to speak, dipping into a curtsey as a dignified-looking lady with grey-streaked hair and a humourless face descended the carriage steps and looked around with the expression of someone whose low expectations had just been fulfilled.

'Long.' The countess's tone implied that she was already bored by the conversation. 'Do forgive our premature arrival. I was informed that the weather was likely to worsen so I insisted on our setting out earlier than intended. Snow in March. Intolerable.'

'Oh, I agree, quite appalling.'

The countess's gaze fell on Caro, her thin lips contorting as if she were attempting a smile. 'You must be my future daughter-in-law?'

'Me?' Caro's cheeks flamed as she turned to her mother for help.

'Ah, this is my own daughter, your ladyship. Miss Caroline Foyle.' Her aunt gave an embarrassed burble of laughter. '*This* is my niece, Miss Essie Craven.'

Essie dropped into a dutiful curtsey, aware of the other woman's smile fading at the same moment as a man dismounted from a chestnut stallion behind her. He must have been hidden by the carriage before, but now, from her low position, she could see that his legs were encased in a pair of tall black boots so highly polished she wouldn't have been surprised to find her own reflection staring back at her. Stealing a glance upwards, she found that the rest of his clothes were equally spotless and shiny. Thigh-hugging buff-coloured breeches, an ankle-length greatcoat, navy blue waistcoat and a cravat so luminously white she felt almost blinded. He looked as if he'd just put them on, not ridden halfway across the north of England. She'd probably got more dirt on herself just coming downstairs. He looked as distinguished as a prince. Henry V or Troilus or Hamlet. Or maybe a pantomime villain.

She gulped, feeling as though the temperature had just dropped by several more degrees. Frankly, it was a good thing she was already crouched down because her knees felt decidedly wobbly too. There was only one person it could be. Her fiancé. Her future. Her earl.

Not if she could help it.

'Lord Denholm.' Aunt Emmeline stepped in front of her, blocking her view before she had an opportunity to lift her eyes any higher. 'My husband and I are honoured to welcome you to Redcliffe.'

'The honour is all mine, I assure you.' His voice was deep and strong, without any trace of ten-year-old whininess.

Newly impatient, Essie leaned to one side to catch a glimpse of his face, almost toppling over in the process. To her intense irritation, he was just as handsome as her aunt had said, although still as hateful and haughty as she remembered, with an aquiline nose and cheekbones sharp enough to cut her fingers on. Only his eyes looked as grey as the snow clouds rolling towards them, rather than blue as they had once appeared. It was as if any warmth had drained away over the years. And there hadn't been a great deal to begin with.

'Miss Craven.' He turned abruptly, as if sensing her scrutiny, causing her to start. 'It's been a long time. I believe that birthday wishes are in order?'

'Your lordship.' She clamped her chattering teeth together and bobbed another small curtsey as he walked towards her. He had a lean build and a graceful, almost fluid way of moving. It reminded her of a cat, all sleek elegance and poise, which was typical since she was really more of a dog person.

'Call me Aidan.' He reached for her hand, brushing his lips so lightly across the backs of her knuckles that she wasn't entirely convinced they touched at all. 'You look –' his brows contracted slightly – 'cold.'

'*Is* it cold?' She couldn't resist the urge to throw a pointed look at her aunt. 'I'm sure I hadn't noticed.'

'Humour me.' His grey gaze roamed over her face for a few seconds before he removed his greatcoat and draped it around her shoulders.

'Oh . . .' She blinked, hardly knowing how to respond. She didn't want his greatcoat, not in principle anyway, but she had to admit it felt deliciously warm. 'Thank you, my lord . . . *Aidan* . . . but I'm really not cold.'

'Indeed?' His gaze dropped to one of her arms. It was practically blue and carpeted with goosebumps.

'Are we going to freeze out here all day?' the countess snapped, drawing an expensive-looking purple cloak, complete with plush trim, tighter around her shoulders. 'Or might we be permitted a cup of tea?'

'Of course, your ladyship.' Uncle Charles extended his arm. 'Do come this way.'

'Would you care for some tea as well?' Essie gave a tight smile, wondering if the earl had noticed his mother's rudeness or whether he expected to be fawned over too. If he did, then she wouldn't be able to act nicely for long.

'I'd be most obliged.' He inclined his head, his expression utterly unreadable, before offering an arm to her aunt. 'Shall we?'

❧

One interminable luncheon later, during which the countess expounded at length about the abominable northern weather and even more abominable state of the northern roads, followed by one long and tedious afternoon in the drawing room while the countess laboriously described her plans for redecorating her future dower house, and Essie was starting to suspect that she wasn't the only person in the house with a plan.

She'd spent the time while being combed and coiffed that morning to compose a speech, working out the nicest possible way to ask nicely, but instead of being granted a private interview with the earl as she'd expected, she'd found herself unable to exchange more than the barest of civilities without her aunt descending like a beady-eyed hawk on a particularly juicy rabbit. On one occasion, Aunt Emmeline had interrupted simply to observe how well the earl's waistcoat matched her curtains. On another, she'd launched into a five-minute account of a recent, uneventful shopping trip to Guisborough, while on a third she'd asked his favourite colour. At dinner, Essie's suspicion that her aunt was trying to prevent her from saying anything rebellious – or worse, *honest* – was finally confirmed when she was seated on the opposite side of the table to her fiancé, next to her prospective mother-in-law, who seized the opportunity to both inspect and lecture her.

'The efficient management of an earldom is no small feat.' The countess's gaze burned with ardour about her subject. 'It requires a strong partnership, not to mention a sense of duty and dedication, but for the right girl, one capable of following instruction –' here she paused, as if questioning whether that description applied to Essie – 'there is no greater honour.'

Essie, who could think of at least a dozen higher ones just off the top of her head, remained silent, biting her tongue as she studied her mostly silent fiancé. It was becoming harder and harder to act nicely when his aloof, reserved manner seemed almost calculated to provoke all her old feelings of rage and resentment. Annoyingly, he appeared to have aged more in the ten years since they'd last met, so that now he had an air of maturity that made her feel frustratingly young and gauche by comparison. He was also immaculately attired in a black evening suit with yet another dazzlingly white cravat, this time arranged in an elaborate knot with a sapphire pin at the throat. The effect was undeniably impressive, exacerbating his haughty demeanour even further, but then maybe haughty was just the way earls were supposed to look. Maybe he couldn't help it and it was a veneer that came as a kind of birthright. Maybe he didn't even know he was doing it. Maybe she ought to tell him.

She tilted her head to one side, wondering what would happen if she did just that, then asked to end their engagement right then and there across the table. There would be horror on her aunt's face, offence mixed with possible, *probable* relief on his mother's, polite dismay on her uncle's and Caro's and . . . she had no idea what on his.

No sooner had the thought crossed her mind than he looked towards her, his pale gaze locking with hers in a way that made her breath snag unexpectedly in her throat. For a fleeting moment, she thought she saw a flicker of speculation, followed by amusement, as if he'd just read her mind, before a shutter descended and both were gone.

She was left with the distinct, highly irritating impression that he was laughing at her again.

Chapter Three

'I can't get anywhere near him. There's nothing else to be done.' Essie stood up from the bed where she'd been sitting for the past half hour, considering and reconsidering and re-reconsidering her options until she thought that her head might explode.

'You can't!' Caro grabbed hold of her arm as she made for the door, panic etched on her pretty, heart-shaped face. 'You really can't!'

'I have to. I can't pretend to be sweetness and light any longer and it's the only way I'm going to be able to speak with him privately.'

'But if anyone catches you visiting a man's bedroom at night, you'll be ruined!'

'It's a risk I'll have to take.'

'Can't you just wait and speak with him in London? Mama says he's going to be there for the Season.'

'I can't wait that long.'

'But are you absolutely hand-on-heart certain that you *don't* want to marry him?'

'Positive! I've never wanted to marry him, not since the first moment I was told about it. Only my father and your parents won't listen, so all I can do is appeal to him directly.'

'What if he says no?'

'I refuse to acknowledge that possibility. But if he does then it's on to Plan B.'

'Which is?' Caro sounded exasperated.

'I don't know yet, but I'll think of one, and Plans C, D and E if necessary. There are twenty-six letters in the alphabet. One of them has to work.'

Her cousin let out a shuddering breath. 'I still think you're making a terrible mistake, but I can't stop you.'

'Thank you.' Essie unpeeled her cousin's fingers from around her wrist, giving them a quick squeeze before creeping out into the darkened corridor, candle in hand. She knew that the earl's suite was in the east wing, which meant passing both her uncle and aunt's bedchambers on the way, but thankfully, she knew all of the best hiding places. As it turned out, however, she didn't need them. The house was eerily quiet, the only sounds being her own footsteps, the occasional, unfortunate creak of a floorboard and the rapid pounding of her heartbeat as she tiptoed along the gallery.

She slowed as she reached the east wing, ignoring the disapproving expressions on the portraits of her uncle's ancestors until she reached the right door. It led to the best and largest guest chamber, the unimaginatively entitled Blue Room, a place where she and Caro had played hide-and-seek as children until her aunt had found out and had conniptions. She hadn't been inside since.

Until now.

She closed her eyes, sucked in a deep, fortifying breath, lifted a hand and then froze, realizing that she didn't have the faintest clue about what to do next. She hadn't considered this part. If she knocked, it might draw the attention of the countess around the corner, but she could hardly just walk in without announcing herself.

Could she?

She looked swiftly up and down the corridor, reached for the handle and turned it.

The room beyond the door was blissfully warm and thankfully not entirely dark. A pair of candles were still burning on top of a cabinet, which meant that the earl hadn't yet retired for the night. But there was no sign of him either.

Perplexed, she put her own candle down and peered deeper into the shadows. The old four-poster bed was just as large and lofty as she remembered, with royal-blue velvet drapes that perfectly matched those at the windows. The chaise longue was still there in one corner too, as was the large mahogany wardrobe that Felix had once leaped out of while she'd been searching for Caro. She narrowed her eyes and took a few cautious steps towards it. Not that she really expected a peer of the realm to be hiding inside a wardrobe, but now that the idea had occurred to her she couldn't just ignore it . . .

'Can I help you?'

She jumped almost a foot into the air and swung about with a quickly muffled yelp to find her fiancé sprawled in one of the leather wingback chairs by the fireplace, his long legs stretched out in front of him and his feet propped up on a coal scuttle. He was still dressed, but only just. His shoes had been discarded along with his evening jacket, waistcoat and cravat, leaving only his breeches and a gaping white shirt as if he'd started undressing and then couldn't be bothered to finish.

'Miss Craven, this is an unexpected honour.' He didn't get up, quirking an eyebrow as if he were perfectly accustomed to women creeping into his bedchamber at night. Which maybe he was. 'I'd ask if you were lost, but since this is your home, that seems rather unlikely.'

'I'm not remotely lost.' She tipped her chin up, feeling her cheeks flush as his eyes took in her nightgown and bare feet. The whole room felt warmer suddenly, as if his gaze were having some strange effect on her body temperature.

Even stranger, however, was the fact that he appeared to have changed into a completely different man since dinner, one with chest hair and an expression she could only describe as sardonic. The impeccably dressed, impeccably mannered, haughty example of earldom she'd seen earlier hadn't seemed capable of either sprawling or sardonic-ness ... sardony? Whatever it was, it definitely hadn't been there a few hours before. If it hadn't been for those pale eyes, she might have thought she'd walked into the wrong room, after all. Although there had been that one fleeting look at dinner ...

She cleared her throat, aware that his eyebrow had been raised for several seconds while she'd been staring. 'I need to talk to you. It's important.'

'Sounds intriguing.' He gestured towards the chair opposite. 'Take a seat. I presume that your aunt doesn't know you're here? She might not consider it quite –' he twirled a hand in the air as if he were searching for the right word – 'proper.'

'She wouldn't care about that.' Essie snorted as she sat down. '*That's* not what she's worried about. She'd only use it to force us to marry sooner.'

'Indeed? Then what *is* she worried about?'

'This. Us talking. You must have noticed she hasn't allowed us a minute alone together since you arrived?'

'Yes, I did wonder about that.'

'She says it's to stop me from saying something foolish, but it needs to be said.' Essie smoothed her hands over her nightgown, straightened her spine, opened her mouth and then snapped it shut again, noticing some charcoals and a pile of papers with sketches scattered on the floor beside him. Which wouldn't have been remotely shocking if one of the sketches hadn't looked a lot like . . . 'Is that *me*?'

'What?' Aidan frowned instantly. 'Yes, I was drawing to pass the time.' He reached down and flipped the paper over. 'You were saying? About something that needs to be said?'

'Right.' She smoothed her hands over her nightgown a second time. 'I'll get straight to the point. This engagement is completely unfair.'

There was a long pause, so drawn out that she was starting to think he wasn't going to respond at all, when he swung his feet to the floor abruptly.

'I agree.'

'What?' She gasped, taken aback by the flare of colour in his pale eyes.

'I absolutely agree. I think it's a terrible idea. I always have.'

'Really?' She was briefly offended before remembering to be thrilled instead. 'Oh, you don't know how happy I am to hear you say that. What a relief!'

'I was worried that you'd asked your aunt to stay close because you didn't want to talk about it and then we'd have to pretend this was all some kind of ridiculous romance.' He pushed his hands through his hair and smiled, and she found herself grinning happily in return, feeling as if she were seeing him for the first time.

Now that they were in agreement, she liked him a great deal more than she had a minute ago. He even looked more handsome, his thick, raven-black hair standing up in wayward spikes and the sharp planes of his face softening as his lips curved. He looked much better dishevelled. Strangely enough, his eyes even appeared blue again, like the middle of the ocean. Not that she'd ever seen an ocean, but the way she imagined an ocean to look. Deep and fathomless and purely, piercingly, intensely blue . . . And how could her mind be wandering about a man she was determined not to marry?

'I'm desperate to talk about it!' She gave her head a small shake. 'We're not remotely suited. Do you remember that day we met as children? You were so superior and serious and *clean*! You were exceedingly worried about getting your clothes dirty.'

'You were wilful and bossy and determined to cover yourself in mud.'

'You said that boys know best!'

'I did! It was too wet to play in the woods.'

'I detested you.'

'The feeling was mutual.'

'You see?' She laughed with delight. 'We're the last people on earth who ought to get married!'

'At least I recognize you again now.' He chuckled. 'I wasn't convinced that we'd got the right person earlier.'

'I was trying to be nice. I thought it would make you more likely to agree with me.'

'Well, I definitely do.'

'Perfect!' She stretched a hand out, ready to shake his. 'That means we can end our engagement right now.'

'Ah . . .' There was another long pause, the spark in his eyes arrested as he glanced down at her hand and then leaned back in his chair.

Essie drew her brows together, uneasy at yet another change of demeanour. She must have imagined the blue because there was no trace of a spark any more. 'So that's what we should do.' She spoke more forcefully this time. 'I don't want to be a countess and I'm sure that you . . . well, actually, I don't know what you do or don't want in a wife and that's the whole point. We don't know each other and we should be free to make our own choices.'

'True.' He stretched his arms out to the sides before folding them behind his head. 'We should be. The problem is, I don't really know *what* I want in a wife. I confess I've never really thought about it.'

'How can you not have thought about it?'

'We were engaged at such a young age. I can hardly remember a time when we weren't, so there seemed no point in thinking about it when there was no choice. I suppose I thought I'd put up with whatever I got.'

'Well, I'd rather not be the "whatever" you have to put up with.' She bristled. 'Wouldn't you rather fall in love with someone?'

'Again, not something I've ever considered.'

'Maybe you should try.'

'Why don't you want to be a countess?'

'Because I have better things to do.'

'I'll be sure and tell my mother you said so. What better things?'

'I have a few ideas . . .' Essie glanced up at the ceiling evasively. She'd never told anyone about her acting ambitions and she certainly wasn't going to start with him. 'And I'm sure I'll think of some more. Travel, for a start.'

'Anywhere in particular?'

'Italy. Florence. Rome.'

'Are you interested in art?' He looked intrigued.

'I suppose so.' It was on the tip of her tongue to mention Lucrezia Borgia and Catherine de' Medici. 'As well as a few other subjects.'

'I see.' He twisted his face to one side, firelight bouncing off his cheekbones as he stared into the leaping flames. 'Essie, I'm sorry for my behaviour ten years ago. However, I'm afraid that you've misunderstood me. Much as I agree with you about the unfairness of our situation, not to mention our complete incompatibility, it's not in my power to end our engagement. I wasn't the one who arranged it.'

'But that's just it, don't you see?' She leaned forward. 'It was our fathers' scheme, not ours – but these are *our* lives! And there's no legal contract, only a gentleman's agreement.'

'*Only* a gentleman's agreement?' There was a hint of steel in his voice. 'That makes it a matter of honour.'

'Our fathers' honour, not ours!'

'Family honour, then.' He clenched his brows and rubbed a knuckle between them. 'Have you told your father how you feel?'

'Yes. Once. I wrote.'

'And?'

'And . . .' Essie squirmed in her chair. Her father's reply had come in a letter to her aunt. She hadn't been permitted to read the contents herself, but after three full hours of scolding, she'd managed to glean most of the details. All of her correspondence thereafter had been thoroughly scrutinized before sending. 'He wasn't pleased.'

'So he'd be unhappy if you were to break the engagement yourself?'

'You might say that.' Honestly, she preferred not to dwell on what punishments her father might devise if she went against his wishes, but Anne Boleyn sprang to mind again. 'That's why I'm appealing to you. If *you* talk to him then he might pay more attention. You could say that your affections were engaged elsewhere.'

'And go against my dead father's wishes?' He gave her a long look. 'Besides, having met your father, I'm afraid that I'd be wasting my breath. His last correspondence set out arrangements for us to marry this summer.'

'*This* summer? But Caro and I are going to London for the Season!'

'Exactly.'

'You mean . . . ?' She was vaguely aware of her mouth dropping open, but she seemed powerless to close it again. She'd wondered why her father had insisted on her having a Season when she was already engaged, but she'd supposed it had been to keep Caro company. Now the truth was horribly, blindingly obvious. If her father wanted them to marry during the Season then it was because he wanted a spectacle. He wanted the whole *ton* to witness his daughter becoming a countess. Which meant that he'd be there too. It was probably the only reason that he'd deign to see her again.

'Brandy?' Her fiancé stood up and reached for a decanter on a nearby table.

'No.' She looked between him and the bottle, still struggling to come to terms with his announcement. 'I'm only allowed a little wine occasionally.'

'You don't strike me as someone who pays too much attention to rules.' He lifted an eyebrow. 'I won't tell.'

'Just a little then.'

'A little is plenty.' He poured out two glasses, his fingers brushing lightly against hers as he passed one across. 'Look, you've been honest with me so here's my side of things. Even if my dead father's honour wasn't involved, and even if I thought that your father would agree, I still couldn't release you. You're too rich.'

'I beg your pardon?'

'I know. That was a bit blunt.' He dragged his chair forward and sat down in front of her, so close that their knees were almost touching. 'But I want to be honest too and you deserve the whole truth. I need your dowry. My estates are close to ruin.'

'But you're an earl! How is that possible?'

'Earls are only people too, and you know that father I just mentioned? The one with the honour?' He draped his arms over his knees, one lock of dark hair tumbling forward over his forehead. 'Do you know *why* he made that gentleman's agreement with your father?'

'Because they were friends.' She made a face. 'And because my father's a snob who's obsessed with titles and being a baron isn't good enough for him and he wants to be father-in-law to an earl.'

'All right, but there was also the matter of your dowry. Your father promised a considerable sum. And since you're also his heir, my father probably thought it was a good arrangement. Ironically, it might be the one decent financial decision he ever made.'

'What do you mean?'

'My father was extremely bad with money. Actually, that's an understatement. He was spectacularly, phenomenally bad, probably one of the worst people with money who ever lived. He had a genius for picking bad investments and a knack for trusting all the wrong people. Unfortunately, I didn't know any of this at the time, but after he died . . .' He dropped his gaze to his brandy. 'Let's just say, there were a few surprises in store. There's still a little of the family fortune left, but not enough to save the estate in the long run. We have enough to keep going for another two years, if we're lucky.'

'Oh.' Essie bit down hard on her bottom lip, beginning to feel a spiralling sense of panic. Their *nice* conversation wasn't going remotely the way that she'd planned. He was supposed to have released her from their engagement by now. She was supposed to be back in her own room with Caro, celebrating with a plate of millefruit biscuits she'd sneaked out of the kitchen earlier. 'Can't you sell some land or something?'

'I'd love to, but most of it is already mortgaged. And the rest won't make anywhere near enough to save the estate.' He looked up again, his eyes hooded. 'Nearly everything about me is a lie. All the servants and jewels are just a show to keep up appearances for my mother's sake. Our situation isn't widely known and she intends to keep it that way.' He sighed. 'I wish I could just walk away and start again on my own, but I can't. So I'm afraid that I don't have a choice. I can't release you.'

'But there are other heiresses!' Essie protested. 'Richer ones! Marry one of them instead, one who actually *wants* to be a countess!'

'I'm afraid that time is somewhat of the essence. Besides, I was never happy about marrying for money in the first place. I certainly don't want to go out looking for it. I might not have much, but I still have my honour. If I break our engagement, I'll lose that too.'

'But what if —?'

'There are no what ifs. I don't like our situation any more than you do, but there's no other way.' He clinked his glass gently against hers. 'I'd drink that now, if I were you. You look like you need it.'

She responded without thinking, lifting the glass to her lips and taking a large mouthful. The fiery liquid burned her throat, making her eyes water, but she felt too numb even to cough. He was right; from his perspective there was no choice — but what about hers? Why was hers so unimportant?

'So you're saying that because your father ruined your inheritance, we both have to suffer for it?' A surge of anger swept through her.

'That's about the long and short of it, I'm afraid.' He sounded genuinely regretful. 'You know, on the day we buried my father I was grieving, but a part of me felt as though I was being dragged down into the grave alongside him. It was like an abyss.'

'So now you're trying to drag me down too? Can't you hear how selfish that sounds?'

'I suppose so. On the other hand, do you have any idea how many people depend on me? Hundreds. And they have leaky roofs and poor farm equipment and hungry children because I'm not taking care of them properly. So as much as I'd love to do what you ask and free us both from this bloody awful situation, I have to be selfish and put them first.'

'That's emotional blackmail.'

'Welcome to the family. Which reminds me . . .'

She stared after him as he stood and walked across to his bedside cabinet. 'Reminds you of what?'

'This.' He came back almost immediately, holding out a square, red leather box. 'I meant to give it to you this afternoon, but your aunt was watching and I don't appreciate an audience.'

'What is it?'

'A birthday present. Open it and see.'

She got to her feet suspiciously, lifting the lid to find a bright silver chain ornamented with a large, teardrop-shaped diamond.

'My mother thought you ought to have something from the family collection so I chose this,' Aidan explained. 'I suppose it ought to have been a ring, but that struck me as more of an engagement present and I wanted to have this conversation first. Well . . .' He lifted his shoulders. 'Not *this* conversation, but you know what I mean. Essie's short for Celeste, isn't it? A diamond was the closest I could get to a star.'

Essie stared at the pendant, part touched, part horrified. It was exquisite, shimmering in the firelight as if it were trying to hypnotize her, but if she put it on then it would be as good as accepting defeat . . . wouldn't it?

'May I?' He lifted the chain and moved behind her, draping the pendant around her throat and fastening the clasp.

Essie swallowed as his fingers brushed lightly against the nape of her neck. The brandy was obviously taking effect because she was beginning to feel strangely dizzy. There were no mirrors, but she could imagine how the pendant would look, nestled between her breasts. She was on the verge of lifting a hand to touch it when an image of her mother, dressed in finery but wearing an expression of abject misery, flitted into her mind, breaking the spell.

'Thank you, but I can't accept it when I've no intention of marrying you.' She reached behind her, unfastening the clasp and almost throwing the necklace back into its box. 'I'm sorry about your situation, but I have my own life to lead.'

'I think we've just established that neither of us has a choice.' Aidan moved around to face her again. 'Think about it, Essie. Even if I did agree to break our engagement, what's to stop your father from finding you another titled husband? One less tolerant about his future wife visiting men she claims to have no intention of marrying in the middle of the night.'

'Only to *talk*!' She glared at the sarcasm. Unfortunately, her father probably *would* try to find her another titled husband, but it would take time. The London Season wasn't referred to as the Marriage Mart for nothing. It would be bursting with richer, prettier debutantes all vying for the same eligible bachelors, hopefully giving her some breathing space to progress her own plans. 'But don't worry. You won't have to suffer any more of my conversation. I can feel a headache coming on. One that's going to last for the entire length of your visit!'

'I'm sorry to hear that.' He sprawled in his chair, adopting the same position as when she'd entered. Apparently the sardonic earl was back, infuriating her all over again.

'This isn't over!' She clutched at the edges of her stole, summoning as much dignity as she could muster. 'There'll be ice rinks in hell before I marry you!'

'Then the Devil better put his skates on. The date is set for the first of June at St George's in Hanover Square. Your father's already made the arrangements.' He threw her a look that was almost sympathetic. 'But if it helps, I really am sorry about it.'

'It doesn't help. Not one tiny bit!'

She shot him a death glare, flinging the door open wide since she couldn't slam it behind her before fleeing back along the darkened corridors.

'Well?' Caro was waiting, perched on the edge of her bed when she burst back into their chamber, breathless with exertion and anger.

'When are we going to London?'

'About six weeks. The middle of April.'

'Six weeks.' Essie counted the time until June on her fingers. That meant they would have approximately another six weeks in London before the wedding. Three months in total.

Three months. Twelve weeks. She sucked the insides of her cheeks. A lot could happen in that amount of time. Plan

A might have been an utter and dismal failure, but Plan B was just beginning to take shape. If Aidan thought she didn't pay attention to rules now, just wait until he saw her again in London. If she couldn't convince him to end their engagement through fair means, then she had no choice but to use foul. She was going to give the greatest performance of her life – that of a woman no self-respecting earl, or anyone else for that matter, could ever dream of marrying!

B was for Break Every Rule She Could Think Of.

PLAN B: BREAK EVERY RULE

Sister, I was grieved to receive a missive from Celeste this morning, the contents of which offended and alarmed me considerably. Since I can only presume you were ignorant of the sentiments expressed therein, I shall summarize them as follows: adolescent nonsense. I write not in the spirit of accusation, but to impress upon you the importance of curbing her wayward tendencies. I insist that she learn to accept and be grateful for her situation, else I shudder to think what her future husband will think of her . . .

Alfred Craven, Lord Makepeace, to his sister Mrs Emmeline Foyle, 2nd November 1814

Chapter Four

(Six Weeks until the Wedding Day)

The London residence of the Dowager Lady Makepeace, Honoria Craven, was in the fashionable vicinity of Mayfair. Cavendish Square to be exact. Although not as grand as some of the others around it, the five-storey townhouse was as distinctive as its owner, with an incongruously large portico held up by two gargantuan Corinthian columns, all stuccoed in a shade of cream designed to give the impression of marble. An equally oversized, circular-shaped window overlooked said portico, from which, as Essie and Caro descended the steps of the Foyle family carriage, they could see their grandmother gazing down upon them with a lorgnette raised to her gimlet eye.

'Oh no.' Caro gripped Essie's hand. 'She doesn't look very pleased to see us. Do you think she's angry that Mama hasn't come?'

Essie, who was busy admiring both the effect of the lorgnette and her grandmother's ability to intimidate from a distance, shrugged. As far as she could remember, their grandmother rarely looked pleased about anything, preferring to keep whatever emotions she might feel to herself, though it was easy to understand why she might look disgruntled today. Being entrusted with the coming-out of two eighteen-year-old girls wasn't exactly a situation to be relished, especially by a woman halfway through her seventh decade, but it had been the only alternative after Aunt Emmeline had sprained both of her ankles by tripping over a trunk of clothes the day before they were due to set out, leaving Uncle Charles to escort them on the four-day journey to London.

Personally, although sympathetic towards her aunt, Essie had been thrilled by the development. She barely remembered their grandfather, no more than she did her maternal grandparents, but she positively idolized their grandmother, who'd always made a point of visiting Cleveland every summer, bringing gifts and taking her and Caro out on private excursions away from Redcliffe. It hadn't taken long for Essie to realize that her grandmother's bark, though loud and frequently scathing, was a great deal worse than her bite, both of which were preferable to her aunt's constant nattering. Caro, on the other hand, remained only slightly less nervous of their grandmother than of being attacked by highwaymen.

'Come on.' Essie laced her fingers through her cousin's, tugging her towards the portico. 'There's only one way to find out.'

A huge black door swung inwards as they approached, held open by a six-foot copper-haired butler, looking so much like a classical statue that Essie barely restrained herself from checking for a strategically placed fig leaf. His features were so sculpted she might actually have been tempted to swoon if it hadn't seemed like such a ridiculous thing to do.

'Here we are.' Her uncle led them over the threshold, rubbing his hands together with satisfaction. 'Safe delivery of two young ladies for the Season.'

'*That* remains to be seen.' Their grandmother's voice boomed like a cannon from the top of the staircase before she descended regally, accompanied by a particularly rotund and wheezy-sounding pug.

'My lady.' Her son-in-law made a polite if slightly nervous-looking bow. 'You look younger every time I see you.'

'Don't be absurd!' The dowager swatted the air, as if the words were bothersome insects buzzing in front of her face. 'Compliments may work on Emmeline, but you're wasting your charm on me. Now, let me take a look at my granddaughters. How long has it been since I last saw the two of you?'

'Ten months.' Essie smiled enthusiastically.

'Is that *all*? Yet you've both grown an inordinate amount. No doubt your heads are all filled with young lady nonsense too? I don't know what my daughter was thinking, saddling me with your coming-out. I've no idea how I shall cope at my age.'

'Emmeline sends her apologies —' Uncle Charles started.

'Of course she does. She ought to. What kind of careless person injures *both* of their ankles? One is quite sufficient for most people. I thought that I raised her better. Still, I suppose I can hardly refuse to let you in now.' She lifted her eyes to the ceiling. 'You may as well come upstairs.'

'Actually, if it's not too inconvenient, I was going to start back to Cleveland straightaway.' Uncle Charles cringed, as if confessing to some heinous crime.

'Are you *so* desperate to get these two off your hands?' The dowager arched an eyebrow. 'You're fortunate that I know my daughter's temperament so well. She can't manage without you, I suppose? Very well, you can see yourself out.'

'Goodbye, Papa.' Caro dutifully kissed her father's cheek. 'I'll miss you.'

'He'll be back in a few weeks for this one's wedding.' The eyebrow tipped towards Essie. 'You'll barely have time to miss him. Now do come along before Mildred bites someone.'

Essie took Caro's hand in another firm grip as they followed their grandmother and the pug, presumably Mildred, up the main staircase, past another conspicuously handsome footman and into a vast and extravagantly decorated drawing room, in which yellow and rose-striped wallpaper vied for attention with heavy, gold-leaf encrusted tables and garishly pink furniture. Three couches sat in front and on either side of an ornately sculpted fireplace, above which hovered a full-sized family portrait depicting Essie's grandmother, grandfather, aunt, and father as a severe-looking young man. She gazed up at it for a few seconds, wondering if there had ever been a time when he *hadn't* looked severe.

'Well, hello.' She was distracted by a pair of paws tugging at the front of her dress. 'We haven't met before.'

The dowager positioned herself on the centre couch. 'I found her on the street a few months ago. You wouldn't think it now, but she was all skin and bones, the poor darling. We've become quite inseparable, haven't we, my sweet little one-headed Cerberus?' She patted her lap and Mildred scrambled up obediently and flopped down, seemingly worn out by her recent stair-climbing exertions. 'Now let me examine you properly.' She held the lorgnette to her eyes, her gaze moving appraisingly between them. 'Yes, it's as I thought the last time I visited. You both take after your mothers, and since Emmeline takes after her father, that means neither of you look like me. No matter. I shall endeavour to like you anyway.'

'Thank you, Grandmama.' Caro bowed her head.

'Thank you?' One side of the dowager's mouth tilted upwards. 'Don't be ridiculous, child. It's the least I can do. I'm not hypocrite enough to pretend I like every member of my family, but I have a curious fondness for the two of you. Or at least I do at the moment. So, to business.' The lorgnette dropped again. 'As I understand it, my task for the Season is that of a chaperone and sponsor. We have six weeks until Essie's wedding, during which time our principal aim is to find Caro a husband. Will another earl be good enough, do you think? Or do you insist on outshining your cousin? Must we find you a marquess or duke?'

'I don't . . .' Caro looked flustered again.

'I'm being facetious. Both of my children may be obsessed with rank, a vulgar trait they inherited from their father incidentally, but there are other, more important considerations. We'll see who you favour and take it from there. With your looks, you shouldn't be lacking in suitors, and you have a reasonable-sized dowry besides. All in all, I think that this should be quite easy.' Her gaze came to rest upon Essie. 'So long as there's nothing else I ought to know about?'

Essie bit her lip, caught off guard by the question. She'd spent a large part of the journey from Cleveland to

London pondering whether or not to tell her grandmother what she really thought of her engagement, and now she was there she was no closer to reaching a decision. She didn't know how the dowager would react, and after a month and a half of near-constant lectures from her aunt, the last thing she wanted was another scolding.

'I don't think so, Grandmama.'

'Good.' The dowager's eyes narrowed slightly though she refrained from further comment. 'Now, first things first. Wardrobes. You'll be pleased to hear that your fathers have both set aside a frankly ludicrous sum for the purchase of new clothes and I intend to make sure you spend every last shilling. To that end, I've instructed a modiste to attend us tomorrow morning. After that, we may start to attend a few select events. Mildred gets distressed when I leave her for too long so I draw the line at four a week. I've already sent acceptances for five balls, six dinners and four garden parties and we shall choose the rest as we go along. Any questions? No?' She picked up a small silver bell on the coach beside her and gave it a vigorous shake. 'Then I believe that's all for now. I feel excessively worn out by all this already.'

'Caro?' Essie opened her cousin's bedroom door and peered into an airy, lavender-coloured bedchamber. 'Are you in here?'

'Outside.' Caro's head appeared around the edge of a curtain. 'There's a balcony overlooking the garden.'

'Really?' Essie ran across the carpet to join her on a ledge protected by a cast-iron railing. 'Oh, how lovely. My room's at the front.'

'It's beautiful, isn't it?' Caro sighed happily, gazing out over an expanse of flower beds, brimming with peonies and bluebells. 'I can hardly believe that we're finally here. It's like a dream come true.'

Essie wrapped her fingers around the railing, feeling a tremor of excitement despite her own slightly more nightmarish plans for the Season. The city seemed so vast and full of possibilities. Full of theatres too. If she wanted to be an actress then this was surely the place to do it.

She nudged her cousin's arm with her elbow. 'Do you think all the men in London are handsome or does our grandmother only employ the best-looking ones?'

'You noticed that too?' Caro giggled. 'I wonder what Father thought of her butler?'

'I think he was too desperate to escape to notice anything.'

'I'm not surprised. Grandmama's even more terrifying here than when she visits.'

'That's because she's in her own territory, like a queen bee. I think she's wonderful. She just says and does whatever she wants. I'd like a lorgnette some day.'

'I think that would suit you.' Caro nudged her back. 'I don't know why Mama always insists that you get your rebellious streak from your mother's side when it's obviously from Grandmama.'

'She's probably scared to admit it.'

'Although I noticed you didn't tell Grandmama about not wanting to marry the earl. Have you changed your mind then?'

'Not even slightly. I'm just getting my bearings.' She tightened her grip on the railing. 'I'm still going to embarrass and mortify him into ending our engagement. So many of Society's rules are ridiculous, I can probably break most of them without even trying. I've already forgotten half of the etiquette lessons your mother gave us.'

'What if your father finds out and guesses you're behaving badly on purpose?'

'He won't. It's not like I'm going to do anything drastic. I'll be subtle.' She looked out over the rooftops of London and heaved a sigh of anticipation. 'Subtle-*ish*, anyway. And I won't do anything to embarrass *you*, I promise.'

'Thank you.' Caro tipped her head sideways, resting it on Essie's shoulder. 'I know I said I was excited, but I'm a little terrified too. My parents expect me to make a good marriage this year, but I hope it can be a love match as well.'

'Then don't accept anything else. There's no rush.'

'Don't you listen to anything Mama says? A woman's value in the marriage market decreases with every Season she's out.'

'That's ridiculous. A Season is a matter of weeks and they're expecting you to find the right person, conduct a courtship, get engaged and preferably married all in that space of time! It's not long enough to make a good cheese.'

'Don't you believe in love at first sight?'

'No, and I've no intention of falling in love either. Quite the opposite, in fact.'

'So how are you going to start?'

'Like Grandmother said, first things first. Wardrobe.'

Chapter Five

Madame Liliane Charbonnier arrived in Cavendish Square at ten o'clock precisely the next morning, armed with a collection of fashion plates, two cases filled with assorted squares of material, a box of pins and a tape measure that she wielded with the skill, speed and precision of a consummate professional. If she'd been a marksman, she would have been lethal.

She was also, Essie quickly realized, a woman of exquisite taste, natural style and rapid but searingly accurate judgements. Within an hour, both she and Caro had been twisted, turned, measured and then presented with an assortment of designs, fabrics and colour schemes, the overall effect of which was to leave her feeling somewhat dizzy.

For the flaxen-haired, cornflower-eyed Caro, Madame Liliane suggested an assortment of pinks and pastels, even one hard-to-wear, but surprisingly attractive, lemon chiffon. For *her*, meanwhile, she proposed a stronger palette, a collection of purples, blues and greens to complement her brown eyes and accentuate the hitherto undetected auburn sheen of her hair. Every suggestion was so lovely that Essie found herself sorely tempted to drool. Unfortunately, they were much *too* lovely. Which meant that they wouldn't do at all. If she was going to persuade Aidan to break off their engagement then she needed the opposite of lovely. She needed hideous.

'Do you have any orange?' she queried, putting aside a particularly gorgeous aquamarine silk with a pang of regret.

'Orange?' Professional though she was, Madame Liliane couldn't conceal a look of dismay.

'Yes. I like orange. It's so . . .' Essie puckered her lips, searching for an appropriate word. 'Juicy.'

'Is that how you wish to be described?'

'Well, maybe not juicy, but bright. Vibrant.' She smiled sweetly. 'Cheerful.'

'I see.' Madame Liliane threw a look of appeal around the room, though to her evident surprise, no help was forthcoming. Caro was staring hard at the floor while the dowager appeared distracted by her own fingernails. Only Mildred rolled on to her back, covering her eyes with her paws in sympathy. 'As you wish.' The modiste reached into the depths of one of her cases and pulled out a few muslin squares, ranging in shade from muted bronze to blazing amber.

'This one's perfect!' Essie pointed to the most dazzling orange of all.

'A-are you certain?' There was a definite note of panic in Madame Liliane's voice now.

'Absolutely. I'd like a ball gown in this colour, and one in this too.' She tapped a piece of anaemic-looking salmon. 'With lots of braiding. And ruffles. As many as you can fit. I adore ruffles. And maybe a day dress in this colour that Caro has too.' She plucked the lemon from her cousin's fingers, aware of the modiste's face paling. 'And do you have any lime green? It goes so well with pink.'

'Lime *and* pink?' Madame Charbonnier looked as if she might actually be sick.

'Oh yes.' Essie wondered if she ought to call for a bucket. 'I want all my clothes to be as visible as possible. I want to be unforgettable!'

Fortunately for Madame Charbonnier, she was saved from answering by a knock on the door.

'What is it, Quill?' If Essie wasn't mistaken, her grandmother's voice quavered slightly.

'Excuse the intrusion, my lady –' the handsome butler appeared in the doorway – 'but the Earl of Denholm is downstairs in the library. He requests the honour of an audience with Miss Craven.'

'*Now?*' Her grandmother glanced pointedly towards the carriage clock on the mantelpiece. 'Oh, very well, I suppose a little enthusiasm in a fiancé isn't such a terrible thing.' She waved a hand. 'You'd better go and greet him.'

'What about my wardrobe?' Essie protested, alarmed to have felt a small thrill at the butler's announcement and unwilling to be summoned so easily.

'We're almost finished. We still have gloves and bonnets to consider, but perhaps you'd like me to choose those for you?' Her grandmother directed her gaze to the square of lemon-coloured fabric. 'It may be the only way to save you from yourself.'

'If you say so, Grandmama.' Essie smiled innocently and stood up, deciding that four hideously unforgettable gowns ought to be enough to scare off even the most tenacious of fiancés. 'Choose whatever you wish. I'm sure that you know best.'

'Of course I do, although in my experience, nobody who says so is ever up to any good. However, do inform the earl that my preferred hours for calling are between one and three in the afternoon.'

'I'd be delighted, Grandmama.'

Essie followed the footman down the stairs, wondering which version of the earl she was going to find in the library – the haughty one, the sardonic one, or a new man entirely? With any luck, he'd spent the past six weeks realizing the error of his ways and was there to break off their engagement and apologize. Now, an apologetic earl would be *very* interesting.

Unfortunately, her hopes were dashed the moment she stepped into the library. Judging by his sober expression and posture, the haughty earl was in residence. Oddly enough, she was aware of a faint sense of disappointment, which was curious because she hadn't realized that she'd wanted to see *any* version of him. More annoyingly, despite her best efforts to think of him as a villain, he was a great deal more handsome than she'd remembered, dressed in a perfectly fitting, silvery-grey morning coat with black breeches and another pair of impeccably polished hessians, with his dark hair swept back from his face to accentuate the square set of his jaw and those razor-sharp cheekbones. As for his eyes . . . still grey.

'Good morning.' She advanced a few steps into the room, adopting an expression that she hoped passed for aloof poise.

'Miss Craven.' He snapped his feet together and bowed. 'It's good to see you again.'

'Is it?' Her spirits plummeted even further. His greeting sounded altogether too enthusiastic, albeit delivered in a haughty earl voice. It didn't sound like the start of an apology either, unless he was just warming up with pleasantries?

'I thought so.' His gaze moved over her face as if he were trying to read her thoughts. 'Although I suspect you have a somewhat different opinion about seeing me.'

She lifted one shoulder, refusing to contradict the statement. 'How did you know I was in town already?'

'Gossip travels quickly. Your carriage was seen arriving at half past three yesterday afternoon. Therefore, your presence had been announced in every drawing room in the vicinity of Mayfair by dinnertime.'

'Really?' She felt genuinely taken aback. 'I wouldn't have thought my arrival was of such consequence.'

'The *ton* likes to keep itself informed, especially when the lady in question is young, wealthy and already engaged to an earl. The *ton* would also expect me to call this morning, so . . .' He spread his hands out. 'Here I am, doing my duty.'

'Oh.' She drew her brows together, surprised to find herself disappointed again. It wasn't as if she'd wanted him to rush and see her for her own sake, but the word 'duty' felt like a stone in her stomach, making her resent him even more. 'My grandmother says this is the wrong time to call.'

'True, but I thought I should see how you were feeling.' He quirked an eyebrow. 'You were suffering so badly with headaches when I left Redcliffe. You couldn't even bring yourself to say goodbye, as I recall.'

'Mmm.' She lifted her own eyebrow in reply. Apparently, the sardonic earl was in the room too, which shouldn't have pleased her and yet, in a strange and frustrating way, it did. 'They were most trying.'

'I trust that you're fully recovered now?'

'For the time being. Strangely enough, I made the most amazing recovery the moment your carriage left our drive.'

'What a remarkable coincidence.'

'I thought so too.' She moved across to the window, looking out at the small park in the square beyond. She was being abominably rude, she knew, but she had a point to make and the stronger she made it, the better. She only regretted not being able to wear one of the gowns she'd just ordered today. Her white cotton day dress struck her as far too demure for this reunion.

'I take it you haven't changed your mind then?' He moved to stand beside her, his tone lower and more guarded. 'I admit, I was troubled after our last meeting.'

'Troubled enough to change *your* mind?'

'I'm afraid not. As I explained, it's not so simple. Despite my best efforts, I've been unable to find any priceless gems hidden down the back of any furniture. However, I'd hoped that once you'd had some time to consider, you might come to understand the situation a little better.'

'I understand it perfectly. I just have a different opinion as to what the outcome should be.'

'I see.'

Essie clenched her jaw, his intractable behaviour infuriating her as much as it had at Redcliffe. He'd actually admitted that he didn't want to marry her either, and yet he was acting like some kind of docile kitten, as if they ought to have no say in their own future at all!

'How can you be so defeatist?' She swung towards him. 'There has to be another way around this if we just think hard enough.'

'There isn't.'

'You could let me find you a replacement bride. Someone dutiful and dignified, like your mother described.'

'My mother's not the one getting married.'

'Just tell me what kind of wife you'd like. Start with eye colour. Blue, brown, green, grey?'

'I've honestly never thought about it.'

'Then start thinking. What about hair? Blonde, red, brunette?'

'Brunette.' His gaze latched on to hers in a way that caused a sudden, strange fluttering sensation in her abdomen. 'I like brunettes, but Essie, I can't let you find someone else. I told you, it's a matter of honour.'

'Oh, fiddlesticks!' She clamped a hand over her rebellious stomach. 'Why aren't you angry about all of this?'

His eyes flashed with something that looked like temper, although if it was, it vanished again quickly. 'What good would that do?'

'It would make me feel better.'

'Then I'm sorry to disappoint you. Again.' He sighed, a single lock of dark hair tumbling forward over his forehead just as it had that night in his bedchamber. For a brief, startling, quickly suppressed moment she found herself tempted to push it back. 'I gather that you're attending some events in town this Season?'

'Yes. My aunt isn't able to travel so my grandmother is chaperoning Caro and me.'

'Then I hope to have the honour of seeing you again soon.'

'It won't make any difference.' She tilted her chin up. 'I've made up my mind and I *never* change it. You could save yourself a lot of trouble if you just call things off now.'

'Is that a threat?' His gaze clouded.

'No. It's a declaration.' She pushed herself up on her tiptoes until her nose was a scant inch away from his. 'Of war.'

'*Denholm?*'

They both jumped and spun around to find Essie's grandmother standing in the library doorway, lorgnette glittering interrogatively as it caught a ray of light from the window. Even Mildred's small round head was tilted to one side with a quizzical expression.

'A little early to be arguing, isn't it?' Her grandmother's gaze lingered on Essie's face a little too long for her liking. 'You're not married yet.'

'We're practising.' Aidan made a formal bow.

'A lover's quarrel, then? How quaint.' The dowager's lips curved infinitesimally. 'You'll be attending the Cumberworths' ball on Thursday evening, I expect, Denholm?'

'I intend to, yes.'

'Excellent. In that case, Essie will be delighted to reserve the first set for you. Won't you, my dear?'

Essie ground her teeth, biting back an honest answer. 'If that's what you wish, Grandmama.'

'It is. Now if you've quite finished practising for married life, it's time to change into your court dress.'

'My what?' She blinked, taken aback by the abrupt change of subject.

'Your court dress for your presentation this afternoon. I had to order it in advance, of course, based on Emmeline's instructions, so we'll just have to hope that it fits.'

'I don't understand.' Essie shook her head in confusion. 'Who am I being presented to?'

'The Queen, my dear. Not every girl enjoys such a privilege, but I was able to pull a few strings. After that, you'll be officially out in Society.' The dowager waved a hand as if she were talking about a mere stroll in the park. 'Didn't I mention?'

'No, you most definitely did not.'

'How curious. Caro just said the same thing. We should probably go back upstairs before she actually faints.'

'Well . . .' Aidan cleared his throat. 'It appears that you're busy. I'll see you on Thursday evening.'

'Wait! Won't you be at this presentation . . . court . . . thingy?' Essie reached a hand out as he moved past her, though she had absolutely no idea why.

'Unfortunately I have another engagement.' His steps faltered briefly as his hand skimmed against hers. 'Lady Makepeace. Miss Craven. Good luck.'

Performances didn't just happen, Essie thought indignantly, glaring up and down an ante-chamber bursting at the seams with identically dressed young ladies and their attendant sponsors. Actors required time to rehearse and get into character, a process her grandmother obviously had no respect for. She'd come to London prepared to play the role of a rebellious, badly dressed eccentric, not some prim debutante for the Queen. The adjustment was enough to give a girl stage fright, although at that precise moment she had another, far more pressing concern. One that was beginning to ache.

'You would only have panicked sooner.' The dowager was justifying herself to Caro for the umpteenth time since that morning. 'You wouldn't have slept a wink last night if I'd told you yesterday. Although I'm quite certain that I did.'

'If you'd mentioned it, I could have practised walking in this dress. I've never worn a hooped skirt before!' Caro wailed, glancing over her shoulder at her train. 'And now you say we have to walk backwards too?'

'Only away from the Queen. One never turns one's back on royalty.'

'I'm going to trip and fall, I know it, and then the whole Season will be ruined.' Caro dragged her hands over her face before letting out a scandalized gasp. '*Essie!* What are you doing?'

'Bouncing.'

'Why?'

'Because I'm trying to distract myself.' She folded one leg over the other, squeezing tight. 'I need to . . . you know. How much longer can this possibly take?'

'I warned you not to drink so much lemonade, my dear.' Her grandmother waved a fan leisurely in front of her face. 'The Queen's Drawing Rooms are notorious for taking an age.'

'I couldn't help it. It's so hot in here. You'd think that St James' Palace would have a little more room for us all to spread out in.'

'It does, only the King and Queen don't choose to share it.'

'They could at least let us sit down while we wait.'

'I'm not sure I'd be able to in this dress.' Caro's voice was getting higher and higher.

'It's like wearing a plough.' Essie squirmed in agreement. 'I feel like a packhorse. One with an ostrich feather on its head. Why do we have to wear all of this anyway?'

'Good gracious, young ladies really oughtn't to ask so many questions, at least not in public. Suffice to say, the Queen insists upon maintaining tradition. Ah, here we go.' The dowager snapped her fan shut as the line started to move forward. 'Just remember, this is generally considered a great honour. Now, when the Lord Chamberlain calls your name, step forward, make your curtsies, answer any questions the Queen might put to you and then back away slowly.' She glanced at Essie. 'I suppose we ought to have practised a little. Never mind, the whole thing takes less than a minute. After that, we'll find you a closet with a chamber pot.'

'*Please* don't mention chamber pots.'

'Then we shall have to hope the Queen doesn't ask too many questions. And none at all about water. Come along.'

Essie waddled forward, squeezing every muscle in her body as they progressed into a long drawing room, devoid of furniture except for a throne at one end, over which was draped a sumptuous red and gold canopy, and upon which sat Queen Charlotte herself, her dark hair arranged into a gravity-defying style on the crown of her head. Two rows of courtiers stood on either side, all wearing identically superior expressions, like whole lines of detestable earls.

Slowly, she dipped into the lowest curtsey she'd ever performed, willing her body not to betray her as she pushed herself up again. It struck her suddenly that if she wanted to humiliate herself, and Aidan by association, then she could hardly have found a more perfect way to do it, but even *she* drew the line at leaving a puddle in front of the Queen. That kind of notoriety would be impossible to live down. No, if she could just get through this, she'd never drink another glass of lemonade in her life. Water, milk, beer, champagne, punch, *anything*, but never lemonade. And she *really* ought to stop thinking about fluids . . .

'Craven . . .' The Queen sounded thoughtful. 'Engaged to the Earl of Denholm, I believe?'

'Yes, Your Majesty.' Essie risked a peek upwards.

'A most handsome and serious young gentleman. The wedding is soon, is it not?'

'The first of June, Your Majesty.'

'How charming. I shall attend your engagement ball.' The Queen waved a hand, as if to bat away any gratitude.

'My wha . . . ? I mean, thank you, Your Majesty.' Essie gulped, horrified by both the offer and the time it was taking to make it.

Thankfully, her grandmother tapped her on the shoulder at that moment and she was able to back away, aware of Caro beside her doing the same thing. The room seemed to go on forever, but at last she bumped into a door frame.

'Grandmama . . .' she gasped as they escaped into a corridor.

'Yes, I know, this way.' Her grandmother took pity on her, gesturing into a side chamber.

'What does she mean by *engagement ball*?' Essie hurried behind a screen, lifted her skirts and let out a relieved groan.

'I would have thought that was obvious. A ball to celebrate your engagement. I must say that I'm impressed. You've taken the *ton* by storm on your very first appearance.'

Essie didn't answer. As debut performances went, hers appeared to have been both a stunning triumph and an utter disaster. It probably wasn't very ladylike to swear in a palace, especially while hovering over a chamber pot, but she did it anyway.

'Bollocks.'

'What was that, dear?' Her grandmother's muffled voice penetrated the screen. 'I didn't quite catch it. Something about frolics?'

'Nothing, Grandmama.'

'Good. As for your engagement ball, I'm quite sure I mentioned that too.'

Chapter Six

'Why do *ton* events involve so much waiting around, do you think? That receiving line was almost as bad as St James' Palace.'

Essie tucked her arm into Caro's as they finally escaped the cricket pitch-length queue and followed their grandmother into an overcrowded, overheated, over-everything-*ed* ballroom. The whole of London Society seemed to be inside already, literally hundreds of people all crammed into one space, dressed, bedecked and enhanced with sumptuous clothes, glittering jewellery and cloying perfumes. Combined with the light from dozens upon dozens of beeswax candles, it was like walking into the centre of a giant crystal chandelier. The overall impression was spectacular.

'Shhh.' Caro, a vision in pale pink, bit her lip. 'I'm too frightened to laugh. Look, my hands are shaking.'

'It's just a ball.'

'Our *first* ball! Grandmama told me not to look so nervous, but I can't help it.'

'Aside from the possibility of being crushed, I really don't see what there is to be frightened about.'

'I'm frightened because the *ton* is a vicious beast with sharp teeth and pointed talons that will eat you alive if you don't keep up your guard.' Caro quoted verbatim. 'That's why. One mistake and our reputations could be utterly destroyed.'

'So why are we here? Why do men of our age get Grand Tours while we get teeth and talons?'

'Because, contrary to popular opinion, women are the stronger sex, my dear.' Their grandmother, whose ears appeared to be far younger than the rest of her, glanced over her shoulder as she led them around the edge of a parquet dance floor.

'She told me not to smile too much.' Caro lowered her voice to a whisper. 'But it's just what I do when I'm nervous. You're lucky that Grandmama didn't tell you not to do anything. She didn't even mention your dress. Thanks to our presentation, you're a success with the *ton* already.'

'Mmm.' Essie pursed her lips. The Queen's offer to attend her engagement ball was a serious setback, she had to admit, but one that could still surely be overcome with a bit of determination. All she had to do was stick to her plan. First she would shock everyone with her appearance, then she would talk to them about politics, or the theatre, or maybe something about ankles; anything that might embarrass Aidan enough to release her.

The first part appeared to be working already. In the privacy of her own bedroom, she'd been positively thrilled with the effect of her new orange ballgown, with its unfashionably high frilly neckline and several tiers of flounces. It had looked even worse than she'd dared to hope, clashing with her complexion so badly that her skin actually appeared to have developed a sickly green tinge.

In case that wasn't enough, she'd also insisted on having her hair scraped up into a severe-looking knot on top of her head. The weight was uncomfortable, but definitely worth it.

Now that she was out in public, however, she couldn't help but feel like an animal on display in a glass cage. Judging by the looks she was receiving, not a very attractive one either. Some kind of poisonous lizard maybe.

'Essie?' Caro looked at her with concern as her steps faltered. 'Are you all right?'

'Oh . . . yes. Perfectly.' She arranged her features into something resembling a smile and kept moving. It was all for a good cause, after all. Whatever disparaging looks she might be receiving now were simply the price of freedom. And it wasn't as if she'd brought a change of clothes. She had no choice but to keep her chin up and ignore all the stares and whispered comments, not to mention the peals of laughter badly muffled behind fans.

'Girls.' Their grandmother stopped so abruptly that they both almost collided with her back. 'Allow me to make a few introductions.' She accosted a woman with mahogany-tinted hair standing between two younger, similar-looking companions, a lady and a gentleman. 'Lady Talbot, what a pleasure to see you. These are my granddaughters, Miss Essie Craven and Miss Caroline Foyle.'

'How delightful.' Lady Talbot's gaze swept over Essie in a way that suggested the compliment was directed entirely at Caro. 'Do allow me to introduce my son, Mr Aloysius Talbot, and my daughter, Miss Jemima Talbot.'

'Miss Craven, Miss Foyle.' The son bowed, though unlike his mother, he kept his gaze fixed firmly on Caro.

'Perhaps Miss Foyle would grant me the honour of the first dance?'

'I'd be delighted.' Caro started to smile and then recollected herself, wrenching her lips back into a straight line. 'Thank you, sir.'

'Excellent.' Their grandmother waved a hand imperiously. 'And Miss Craven for the second, perhaps?'

'Oh.' The poor man looked as if he wanted to shield his eyes with his sister's fan. 'Of course. I'd be . . . honoured.'

'That's quite all right.' Essie shook her head quickly. 'Please don't feel obliged to –'

'Good evening, Miss Craven.' The Earl of Denholm's voice interrupted over her shoulder at that moment. 'May I say how lovely you look this evening?'

She swung around, prepared to make some sharp retort, only to find herself rendered uncharacteristically speechless. Unlike the hapless Mr Talbot, Aidan seemed undaunted by her appearance. He also looked perfectly at ease in the ballroom, his immaculately tailored, black and white evening clothes presenting a stark contrast with her own colourful garb. He looked serious, austere, and quite devastatingly handsome, so much that the edges of her vision actually seemed to blur around him. Somehow the sight trapped all of the air in her lungs and refused to let it out again.

Damn.

If Aidan noticed her stunned expression, he gave no sign of it, extending a hand instead. 'I believe this is our dance? A quadrille, I think.'

'Yes.' Essie bobbed a curtsey to her companions before placing her fingers in his, alarmed to feel a flicker of heat through her gloves, accompanied by a curious tingling sensation that seemed to spread all the way up her arm to her chest, thwarting her attempts to breathe normally again.

'I understand that your presentation at Court went well,' he commented as they joined a square of dancers.

'So I'm told.' She cleared her throat, ordering her body to behave normally. 'Although I'm not entirely sure how. The whole thing was excruciating. They didn't have enough chamber pots and I bumped into a door wearing that ridiculous dress.'

'It sounds eventful.' His gaze swept over her leisurely, taking in every detail from her frilly collar to her flouncy hem as they waited for the music to start. 'I hope that you're feeling more comfortable in your attire tonight?'

'*Very* comfortable, thank you.' She batted her lashes innocently. 'I've always liked vibrant colours.'

'As do I.' They stepped together as the music started. 'They make such a refreshing change. So many debutantes wear identical dresses, all white and pastels. It makes them look even younger than they are.'

'Well, my wardrobe is filled with yellows and pinks and *salmon*.' She lifted her eyebrows, but his expression didn't alter.

'Indeed? Then I look forward to seeing each and every outfit. You make me feel quite dull by comparison.' There was a brief pause as they moved around each other in a circle. 'I only hope that you haven't gone to so much trouble on my account.'

'And why would I do that?'

'I just mention it because I notice you've changed your hair too. You appeared to favour a looser style back in Cleveland.'

'I decided it was time for a change. Now that I'm officially *out*.'

'Then I admire your courage.' He gave her a smile that on somebody else she might have considered quite charming. 'Do you play chess, Miss Craven?'

'Yes, sometimes. Why?'

'Because it's a game of strategy, all about anticipating and staying one step ahead of your opponent. It just came to mind, that's all.'

'Really?' She narrowed her eyes. 'How interesting.'

'You know, there aren't many advantages to being the son of a man who lost almost the entire of his fortune and left his estate in ruins, but one is that you develop a surprisingly thick skin.'

'Fascinating.' She clenched her teeth, resenting the way he appeared to have seen through her so easily.

'Now I flatter myself that I have the hide of a rhinoceros.'

'What a charming image.' She placed her foot on top of his and pressed all her weight downwards. 'What about your toes?'

The faintest of winces crossed his face. 'Not quite as robust, unfortunately.'

'How clumsy of me.'

'Not at all. I suppose I asked for that.'

She threw him a tight smile as they continued to circle each other like a pair of rhinoceroses. Or possibly a rhinoceros versus a poisonous lizard. She was beginning to lose track of her own similes.

'So, what do you think of your first ball?' he asked as they stepped back into formation.

'It's certainly very impressive. And hot.'

'Be glad you don't have to wear a cravat.'

She bit her tongue, unable to think of a reply when the comment only drew her attention to his throat, which also meant noticing the way his jacket fit so snugly across his shoulders. Mentioning the temperature had been a mistake too. Somehow she could feel his body heat all the way through his shirt, her gown and two feet of air, making her cheeks flush and her corset feel a little too tight all of a sudden. She had a horrible feeling that her blush extended all the way from the roots of her hair to the tips of her toenails, although fortunately most of her skin was covered by flounces. Maybe it was the weight of hair pinned on top of her head making her light-headed, but for the space of a few heartbeats, all of the voices and music around them seemed to fade away, as if they were standing alone inside some kind of bubble. Which was ridiculous when they were literally hemmed in by other couples.

'How's your mother?' She cleared her throat heavily, deliberately popping the bubble.

'My mother?' He repeated the word as if he needed a few seconds to understand it. 'She's well, I believe.'

'Isn't she in town?'

'Not at present. She'll be coming up in a few weeks with my sister.'

'Sister?' She blinked. 'I didn't know you had a sister.'

'You never asked.'

'You could have mentioned.'

'During one of your headaches, perhaps?'

'Mmm. What's she called?'

'Sophia.'

'How old is she?'

'Fifteen this summer.' He tilted his head. 'You look as if I've just told you I have a long-lost evil twin. Is it so strange for me to have a sister?'

'I suppose not.' She wrinkled her nose. 'It's just hard to think of you as a brother.'

'Considering that we're going to be married, that can only be a good thing, don't you think?'

'You know what I mean.' She caught his eye, intending to scorch him with a glare but finding herself captured instead . . . His eyes looked blue this evening, she noticed, but not *just* blue, so much as several different shades of it, silvery pale in the middle, twilight dark at the edges. At least that explained how they seemed able to change colour. She didn't think she'd ever seen eyes like them before. At that moment, they were positively mesmerizing.

'So is there a marriage arranged for her too?' she asked before he noticed her staring.

'No.' The corners of his mouth tightened. 'My father was happy to receive a dowry. Providing one was another matter.'

'Oh. I see.' She felt a twinge of regret for the question. It felt cruel suddenly, as if she'd inadvertently cut him with something sharp.

They didn't speak again until the music ended, Aidan's expression seeming frozen into a veneer of studied politeness. Which wasn't her fault, Essie told herself. Considering their own circumstances, it had been a perfectly reasonable question, although she supposed she might have anticipated the answer.

'Perhaps you might reserve the supper set for me, as well?' he asked as they made their way to the side of the room. 'Unless you're otherwise engaged?'

'I can't,' she answered honestly. 'It's a waltz, and apparently I'm not allowed to dance those until I get permission from some old women at Almack's.'

'I believe they prefer to be called patronesses. In that case, perhaps we might get to the supper tables ahead of everyone else?'

'Mmm . . . perhaps.'

He bowed, holding her gaze a moment longer before surrendering her into the nervous-looking arms of Mr Talbot.

To her amazement, Essie found partners for the third and fourth sets, as well as the second, though she refrained from trampling on any more toes, containing herself to discussions about politics instead. Neither Mr Talbot, nor Mr Watson, nor Viscount Abercromb as it turned out, had any strong opinions about the Prime Minister, Mr Jenkinson, although they all looked suitably horrified at her knowing his name. None of them evinced even the tiniest interest in the theatre either and she couldn't quite bring herself to mention ankles. Aidan himself didn't dance again, she noticed, catching occasional chance glimpses of him over her partners' shoulders. *Only* by chance, she assured herself, certainly not because her eyes kept straying in his direction.

She did, however, look for Caro when the waltz arrived, but her cousin appeared to be deep in conversation with a man on the other side of the ballroom and she didn't have the heart to disturb her. Their grandmother, meanwhile, was holding court amidst the chaperones, their chairs clustered together in a way that suggested it might take a crowbar to reach her.

'Oh, Miss Craven?'

She turned at the sound of her name to find Jemima Talbot flouncing towards her, accompanied by two other young ladies, all of them dressed in the very height of fashion, in white silk and crepe gowns ornamented by lace and pearls. They were also making unmistakable tittering noises. Whatever the joke, it was fairly obvious that she was the punchline.

'How are you enjoying the evening, Miss Craven?' Miss Talbot's titter was definitely the loudest.

'It's most enjoyable, thank you.' Essie forced herself to smile politely.

'Allow me to introduce my friends, Miss Uriana and Miss Florentia Deveraux. We were just commenting upon your gown. So original.'

'And it's made you so popular too.' Florentia, whose short bodice was barely visible beneath the vast expanse of her cleavage, smiled poisonously. 'You've had partners for every dance so far.'

'I suppose so, although dancing has made me a little thirsty. I was just going to find a drink, if you'll excuse me?'

Essie made to move past them, but Jemima put a hand on her arm, her long lashes sweeping downwards and then up again with the speed of an assassin's dagger. 'I wish *I* had a grandmother who was quite so commanding. Then I'd have partners all evening too. No matter what I was wearing.'

'I'll be sure to tell her so. In fact, here she comes now,' Essie lied sweetly. 'I'm sure that she'd be thrilled to help you.'

'What?' Jemima jumped backwards with a squeak of alarm, leaving Essie free to escape. Instantly, she spun on her heel, darting towards the French doors at the end of the ballroom and out on to the terrace beyond.

Safely outside, she tipped her head back, took a deep breath and permitted herself a long shudder, trying to shake off the taint of Jemima Talbot and the Misses Deveraux. The night air was cool and refreshing, a world away from the cloying, catty atmosphere of the ballroom. There was a garden beyond the terrace too, she noticed, its gravelled paths and ivy-clad trellises illuminated by lanterns hung from the trees.

'Don't tell me you're without a partner for the next dance?' a male voice drawled from the shadows behind her. 'What a crime.'

'Isn't it? Perhaps we should send for the Bow Street Runners?' She turned around to find out who was baiting her this time. Whoever it was, she wasn't going to run away again. If they wanted to insult her then she would repay them in kind. Unfortunately, while she was obviously visible in the light cast through the French doors, her companion was barely a grey smudge in the darkness. 'If you want to make some comment about my appearance, sir, then just go ahead and say it.'

There was a red glow, like a cigar being drawn on, followed by a languid-sounding sigh. 'I make a point of never commenting on ladies' appearances. In my experience, it can lead to all manner of misunderstandings.'

'You needn't have any worries about my understanding. Everyone else has made it very clear what they think. You might as well too.'

'A difficult evening, then? Lucky for you, it's about to improve.' There was a laugh in his voice this time. 'Now you've met me, that is, and I think you look rather interesting, as it happens.'

'You have a very high opinion of yourself, sir. We haven't even been introduced.' She peered deeper into the gloom. 'Or at least I think we haven't. I can't see you to be sure.'

'We haven't. So why don't we introduce ourselves?'

'Isn't that against the rules?'

'Oh, definitely. All the fun things are, but why don't we forget the rules for one night?'

Essie bit her lip, aware that she ought to bid him, whoever he was, a very firm goodbye and then walk away as fast as her legs would carry her. Even *she* knew that introductions ought to be made via chaperones, but he could hardly have chosen better words to persuade her. Breaking the rules was what she was there for, wasn't it? And what could be the harm in simply sharing their names?

'Very well, but I need to see your face.'

'My pleasure.' The smudge stood up and took a few steps forward into the light. He looked to be around her own age, with a handsome face, platinum-blond hair and lazy-looking yet alert green eyes that matched the row of emerald rings glittering on his left hand. Like Aidan, he was dressed in plain black and white, but his cravat had been loosened and his waistcoat was askew, giving him a more dishevelled, debonair appearance.

'Mr Sylvester Jagger.' He tossed the stub of his cigar casually into the garden. 'At your service.'

'Essie Craven.' She didn't bother to curtsey. 'Why aren't you dancing?'

'Boredom. I was a dutiful bachelor for the first two sets, but then I decided it would be far more interesting to come out here and see what innocent debutantes might fall into my path.' A wicked-looking smile spread over his face. 'And I was right.'

'You sound like a spider.'

'Ah, but my web is only for those who want to get caught.' He tipped his head closer. '*Do* you want to get caught?'

Essie stared at him incredulously. Like Aidan, Mr Jagger didn't seem remotely bothered by her outlandish attire. On the contrary, it seemed to amuse him. 'Are you flirting with me?'

'It's a definite possibility.'

She laughed in disbelief. 'How bizarre.'

'Is it?' He looked faintly bemused himself. 'Care for a stroll? It's a beautiful evening.'

Essie looked out over the garden again. Several couples were enjoying the moonlight, wandering arm in arm along its paths. A walk was definitely tempting, only something about her new acquaintance warned her that being seen in a garden with him might be a scandal in itself. Which would be quite useful if only the earl were to witness

76

them, but if anyone else did . . . She shook her head. She was trying to break off her engagement, not get herself compromised into a new one. It wasn't as if she would be hard to identify in orange.

'No, thank you. I'm actually feeling quite hungry. I thought I might go in search of some supper.'

'What an excellent notion.' He seemed unperturbed by her refusal. 'I'm feeling somewhat ravenous myself. Shall we?'

He presented an arm and, after a moment's hesitation, she took it. After all, there couldn't be anything so very shocking about walking *inside* with him. Probably. Unless that was one of the etiquette lessons she'd forgotten to pay attention to. As for Aidan . . . well, she hadn't promised to have supper with him. She'd said *perhaps*, that was all, and frankly, if he was annoyed then so much the better. She wanted to annoy him! All things considered, it was a quite perfect situation.

She wrenched her shoulders back, bracing herself for more laughter and stares as they walked back through the French doors and through to the supper room, which turned out to be even more spectacular than the ballroom. Her stomach grumbled loudly at the sight of several long tables positively groaning beneath the volume of dishes. Cold ham and beef, prawns, lobster, aspic jellies, salads, pies, blancmange, syllabubs, a mouth-watering selection of pastries and one gigantic trifle, all laid out on sparkling silverware and crystal.

'So many delicacies, so little time.' Mr Jagger handed her a plate as the music in the ballroom drew to a close. 'I always want to try a little of everything, don't you?'

Essie nodded distractedly. The slyness of his tone suggested some ambiguous meaning, but at that moment she was far more interested in eating than understanding. It was only as she sank her teeth into an almond cheesecake that she felt a sudden urge to look over her shoulder.

Aidan was standing in the doorway of the supper room, his expression impassive, but looking at her in a way that somehow made her lose her appetite.

It was barely a second, hardly long enough for her to swallow a mouthful of cheesecake, before he turned his back and left.

Chapter Seven

'Well, yesterday evening was most satisfying, I must say.' The dowager swept into the breakfast room in a cloud of rosewater perfume, taking a seat at the head of the breakfast table and draining an entire cup of coffee before turning a questioning gaze upon her granddaughters. 'I trust that you both slept well after all your exertions?'

'Very well, thank you.' Caro answered enthusiastically, her cheeks as pink as if she'd only just finished dancing.

'I'm glad to hear it, and what about you?' The dowager turned her attention to Essie, absently piling spoonfuls of sugar into her newly filled cup.

'Quite well, thank you.' Essie reached for some toast to hide her expression. In all honesty, she'd barely slept a wink, unable to get the look Aidan had given her out of her mind. She hadn't even recognized what it was. Not reproach exactly. Or disappointment. Or even hurt. It had been something else, something worse, something that had made her feel guilty enough to prevent her from enjoying either her supper or a restful night afterwards. Which really wasn't fair when all she'd been doing was making the point that she didn't want to marry him. Which he already knew! He had absolutely no right to make her feel guilty.

'I spoke to Mr Talbot after your dance. He said you had a most interesting discussion.' Her grandmother hoisted an eyebrow up to her hairline. 'Regarding the Corn Laws, I believe?'

'Yes.' Essie dipped her spoon into a dish of strawberry jam, pointedly ignoring Caro's splutter. 'I find them fascinating, don't you?'

'Riveting. I rarely get through a day without sparing a thought for corn. Is that what you and the earl were discussing so intently as well? You appeared to be talking more than dancing at one point.'

'Did we?' She shrugged. 'It's curious, but I forget what exactly we talked about.'

'Indeed? Still, I was surprised that he left at the start of supper. I expected the two of you to sit together.'

'There was some vague arrangement, but then I met Mr Jagger and I decided . . .' Essie faltered beneath the full force of her grandmother's withering stare. 'I don't know what happened. Perhaps he fell ill?'

'Perhaps.' Thankfully, the dowager's attention swung, pendulum-like, back to Caro. 'However, it appears that you've made several conquests already, my dear. The flowers are still arriving.'

'Flowers?' Caro's eyes widened like saucers.

'Oh, yes. How many bouquets are there so far, Quill?'

The square-jawed butler beside the door snapped to attention. 'I believe it was nineteen at the last count, my lady.'

'Roses, I suppose?'

'Yes, my lady.'

'Pink, presumably?'

'Indeed, my lady.'

'Oh!' Caro's cheeks turned positively luminous. 'Can I go and see?'

'In due course. Only, for goodness sake, eat something first or you'll have no energy for your callers later.'

'Do you think there'll be callers?'

'A tedious number of them, yes. I shall require several more pots of coffee, especially since we're to attend a musical soiree this evening.' The pendulum swept back to Essie. 'Aren't you curious to know what flowers the earl has sent you?'

Essie paused with a slice of jam-drenched toast halfway to her lips. '*Has* he sent flowers?'

'Has he, Quill?'

'I believe so, my lady.'

'Roses?'

'No, my lady.'

'Really? Do tell.'

'Marigolds, my lady. Orange ones.'

'Well, how original.' The dowager picked up her coffee again, though not quickly enough to hide the fact that her lips were twitching.

'I can't even see the table!' Caro let out an unladylike squeal of excitement. Unlike the drawing room, their grandmother's downstairs parlour was decorated in muted shades of blue and cream, with white-painted furniture, including one round central table that was almost completely concealed beneath a profusion of identical bouquets. The room might easily have been mistaken for a rose garden, bursting with pink petals and foliage, the only exception being a discreetly sized bouquet of orange marigolds set off to one side. Whoever had carried it in obviously hadn't wanted to spoil the colour scheme.

'I'm sure you would have received just as many if you weren't already engaged.' Caro was already riffling through the bouquets, pulling out cards left, right and centre.

'I doubt that, but since I don't want them, it doesn't matter anyway.' Essie picked up her own card. There was no message, just a single looped D.

'Those are very pretty.'

'I suppose so.' She tossed the card aside. 'So, now that we know who your suitors are, do you have any favourites?'

'It's far too early to say.' Caro shook her head modestly. 'They were all such perfect gentlemen.'

'Who would your mother choose?'

'Oh, that's easy!' Caro buried her face in one of the largest bouquets. 'The Marquess of Bazley. She'd have palpitations if she knew he'd sent me these.'

'He's old enough to be our grandfather! *Great*-grandfather possibly.'

'I know, but still a marquess.'

'Yuck. Wait . . .' Essie sprang forward, plucking out a card that Caro had missed. 'This one has a poem!'

'What?'

'*An Ode to Caroline!* From a Mr Nightingale. How appropriate.'

'Give me that!'

'Oh dear.' Essie read it over her cousin's shoulder. 'He's used "thine" three times in one verse. There are so many other options with Caroline. *Rhyme* for a start, as well as porcupine, philistine, Newcastle-upon-Tyne . . . Still, it's the thought that counts. So long as he's not a septuagenarian, he's my favourite. Point him out this afternoon and I'll give him my permission to court you.'

'You'll do no such thing!' Caro grabbed hold of her hands and danced them both around in a circle. 'Oh Essie, I'm so relieved! I was afraid that I was going to be partnerless all evening.'

'And I told you not to be so ridiculous, didn't I?' Essie beamed back, infected with her cousin's happiness. 'Men were practically tripping over each other to ask you to dance. I was the one whose grandmother had to keep finding her partners.'

'Except for that man you had supper with. Who was he, anyway?'

'Mmm?' She felt a fresh twinge of guilt. 'Oh, his name is Sylvester Jagger. I found him on the terrace.'

'You *found* him? Surely you mean you were introduced?'

'No.' The twinge contorted into more of a spasm. 'We introduced ourselves.'

'*Essie!*'

'Telling another person your name ought not to be so shocking.'

'Maybe not, but you don't know anything about him. He could be one of those men Mama warned us about – a rake!'

'Actually, I think he might be. He was very entertaining during supper. He seemed to know all the gossip.'

'Then you shouldn't have listened.' Caro pursed her lips reprovingly. 'What about the earl?'

'What about him?' Essie tore her hands away. 'He knows that I don't want to marry him so why should I act

83

like I do? Besides, he was being deliberately obtuse! He didn't seem bothered by my dress at all, the provoking man!'

'Or when you stood on his foot. I saw that, by the way. You said you were going to be subtle.'

'*Ish.*'

'At least he has a sense of humour.' Caro wandered across to the marigolds.

'If those are a joke then they're not funny. I'm sending them back.'

'You can't!'

'Watch me, and if he thinks that he can charm me into submission then he can think again.' She reached out and plucked the head off one of the flowers. Maybe she'd send a poem back with them too. A short and pithy one. She already knew the exact combination of words she wanted to say.

Musical soirees, as it turned out, began slightly earlier than balls, at only eight o'clock in the evening, immediately after dinner. Essie had selected her lime and pink gown as the most suitable attire for an evening of opera, although she'd decided not to subject herself to another painful coiffure, simply confining her curls into a hairnet at the nape of her neck instead. Once again, her grandmother had made no comment about her appearance, although since she was wearing half a peacock on top of her own head, Essie was starting to doubt the value of her sartorial opinion anyway. She felt genuinely sorry for whoever ended up sitting behind them.

'Lady Makepeace.' A tall woman, practically dripping in jewellery, greeted them as they climbed the front steps of a grey stone townhouse. 'And these must be the charming granddaughters I've heard so much about.'

'Mrs Birtwhistle.' Their grandmother made the introductions, allowing a footman to take her cloak and present her with a glass of champagne at the same time.

'Do go on through and make yourselves comfortable.' Mrs Birtwhistle's eyes lingered briefly on the peacock feathers, as if she wanted – but didn't dare – to suggest a chair at the back. 'Selina's performance will begin shortly.'

'How delightful. There's nothing I enjoy more than an evening of opera.'

'Which opera is it?' Essie asked as they made their way through the house and into a music room turned impromptu concert hall, where a dozen rows of chairs stood facing a small stage. A cramped-looking string quartet sat on top, although it was hard to see how any of them were going to be able to move their bows without bumping elbows.

'No idea.' Their grandmother selected seats on the front row. 'I can't abide opera.'

'But you just said –'

'I was being polite. I do that occasionally.'

'Then why are we here?'

'Because the music isn't the point.'

'It's a *musical* soiree.'

'On the surface, yes. In reality, this is an advertisement. The invitations might as well have said *The Honourable Birtwhistles present their daughter Selina for the viewing pleasure of marriageable gentlemen.* Only it doesn't do to be too obvious about it so ladies are invited as well. It's an unspoken reciprocal arrangement. Selina's the one with the neck, by the way.'

'Neck?' Essie craned her own.

'Over there.' Her grandmother gestured towards a raven-haired girl standing beside the piano. 'You can't miss her.'

'Oh. That *is* quite long.'

'Ridiculous, isn't it? Like a giraffe.'

'More like a swan, but she can't help the length of her neck.'

'She could stop showing it off so often. Just look at the size of that diamond necklace. *That's* an advertisement too. A little less vulgar than mentioning the size of her dowry in the newspaper, I suppose, but not far off.'

'She's very pretty.' Essie frowned as a new thought occurred to her. 'Wait, when you say reciprocal . . . we don't have to advertise too, do we?'

'Not necessarily. Your cousin seems to have secured enough interest already.' The dowager smiled at Caro, seated placidly on her other side. 'And we already have your engagement ball in five weeks, although why your father insists on it being the night before the wedding, I can't understand. Still, perhaps we ought to do something special to make it stand out. I don't suppose you have any particular skills we might showcase?'

'I can eat a piece of pie in under a minute. Sweet *or* savoury.'

'What a diverting entertainment that would be. I'm sure the Queen would be most impressed.' The dowager made a loud whooshing sound as she twisted her head.

'Speaking of your engagement, there appears to be no sign of the earl this evening. Isn't he a music lover?'

'I've no idea what he is.' Essie lifted her shoulders, thankfully saved from making any further comment by the perfectly timed pluck of violin strings.

A few bars were sufficient to demonstrate that the Birtwhistles had chosen their advertisement wisely. Not only did Miss Selina's neck show to full, swan-like advantage, but her voice was rich and melodious, a great deal more impressive than pie-eating. She both looked and sounded quite beautiful, Essie thought, stifling a pang of jealousy. She could probably carry off orange too.

She snuck a peek over her shoulder between arias, checking to see whether Aidan had arrived late. What, after all, was the point of wearing lime green and pink if he wasn't there to witness it? Unfortunately, her gaze fell upon Florentia Deveraux sitting a few rows behind instead, her mouth twisted into what could only be described as a smirk.

'A masquerade.' Her grandmother tipped her head sideways suddenly, tickling her nose with a peacock feather.

'I beg your pardon?'

'For your engagement ball. That's what we should do. Given your talent for dressing up, I think it would be rather fitting, don't you?'

❧

It took almost two hours, but at last Miss Selina brought her operatic rendition to a close on a lingering high note and one final stretch of her giraffe-or-possibly-swan-like neck. Despite the audience's palpable admiration for both, there was still a collective sigh of relief beneath the clamour of applause, after which they were allowed to escape to a separate room for refreshments.

'What did you think, Miss Craven?' A familiar voice accosted Essie as she stood beside Caro at the dessert table. 'You seemed rather distracted at one point.'

'Mr Jagger.' She smiled in greeting. 'I didn't know you were here.'

'I was seated at the back, admiring your grandmother's feathers for most of the performance. Dirgeful, wasn't it? So many arias. I almost wept.'

Essie bit back a smile. Much as she'd enjoyed the music, it had been quite melancholy. 'She's very talented.'

'Oh, quite. What a *range*!' Mr Jagger rolled his eyes dramatically. 'I thought she might conclude the evening with some scales, just to make sure we all got the point.'

'Hush, or somebody will hear you.'

'You worry too much, Miss Craven. The family are on the other side of the room and I've already told them how deeply affected I was.'

'And they believed you?'

'Naturally.' He waggled his eyebrows. 'I can sound very sincere when I put my mind to it.'

'Poor Miss Birtwhistle.' Essie shook her head, still trying not to laugh. 'Now, if you can be polite, there's someone I'd like you to meet. Miss Caroline Foyle, Mr Sylvester Jagger.'

'Miss Foyle, I believe I saw you dancing at the Cumberworths' ball yesterday evening. You quite took my breath away.' He caught hold of Caro's hand, sweeping it courteously to his lips. 'A pleasure to meet any relation of Miss Craven.'

'You haven't met all of my relations.' Essie snorted. 'Caro is by far the nicest.'

'I don't doubt it. Especially since it appears that your grandmother doesn't approve of me.'

'What do you mean?' Essie twisted around to see peacock feathers bobbing their way determinedly through the crowd towards them.

'They say discretion is the better part of valour, don't they?' Mr Jagger made an exaggerated bow. 'Until next time, ladies. I do hope that it won't be too long.'

Essie gasped and then stiffened as he darted away. For a second, she'd had the impression of a hand touching against her lower back, but she must have imagined it, surely? He wouldn't have . . . would he?

Chapter Eight

'I can't believe I'm yawning at only half past five in the evening.' Essie pressed a hand to her mouth as the dowager's open barouche made its stately way into Hyde Park, joining a procession of other vehicles already rolling along the gravelled track of Rotten Row.

'It takes a little time to adjust to *ton* hours.' Her grandmother sniffed loudly. 'As well as its concept of time. This, for example, is considered the fashionable hour, but in reality it's *three* hours. Strictly speaking, to be truly fashionable we shouldn't arrive for another half hour, but I hate rushing to change for dinner. We shall still see and be seen by enough people.'

'It's hard to see anyone at all when it's so crowded.' Essie twisted around in her seat to view the scene. There were so many gigs and curricles and carriages, not to mention riders on horseback, that traffic was reduced to a somnolent snail's pace. 'I wish *I* was on horseback,' she sighed wistfully. 'I haven't ridden in forever.'

'It hasn't even been two weeks,' Caro corrected her.

'This isn't the correct time of day for riding, not for young ladies anyway. If you wish to ride, then you must come early in the actual morning with a groom *and* chaperone.' The dowager tapped her knee. 'Now sit still.

One never knows whom one might meet. Maybe even your earl, seeing as he hasn't called on us again since your arrival.'

'I hadn't noticed.' Essie folded her hands in her lap, affecting an expression of innocence. The house had been practically besieged by callers for Caro over the past three days, but Aidan had been conspicuously absent.

She was taking that as a very good sign.

'He hasn't sent any more flowers either.'

'I wonder why not.' She opened her eyes wide for good measure. 'Statistically, however, we're far more likely to bump into one of Caro's admirers. There are so many of them, after all.'

'There are not.' Caro waved to Jemima and Aloysius Talbot as they passed by on a curricle. 'I'm sure they're all paying court to several young ladies.'

'I think not. There's only one Incomparable each Season, my dear, and I believe that this year, you're it.' Their grandmother smiled. 'One granddaughter approved by the Queen, the other approved by the rest of Society. Poor Emmeline. If her ankles were up to it, she'd kick herself for missing this.'

'Oh!' Caro exclaimed suddenly. 'Grandmama, you were right.'

'Of course I was. What about?'

'The earl. Here he comes.'

'What?' Essie jerked her head around just in time to catch the moment Aidan saw them. To her chagrin, *he* was on horseback, riding alongside a man with hazel-brown hair and a round, amiable-looking countenance. Both of them removed their hats as they rode up beside the barouche, although Aidan's expression was frostier than she'd ever seen it, without even the tiniest glimmer of warmth. The sight bothered her more than she would have expected.

'Lady Makepeace, Miss Craven, Miss Foyle.' He inclined his head, his gaze passing over each of them in turn without stopping. 'It's a fine day for a ride, is it not?'

'Passable.' The dowager's steely gaze sharpened. 'We haven't seen much of you recently, Denholm.'

'Apologies, my lady. I'm afraid that I've had other commitments. Would you allow me to present my friend, Mr Francis Dormer?'

'Of the Nottinghamshire Dormers?'

'I'm only tenuously connected to the family, my lady.' Mr Dormer acknowledged the words with a smile, as if he were used to them. 'My own resides in Kent.'

'Kent? Ghastly place. Flat and full of marshes, but I suppose that's not your fault. Well then, Denholm. My granddaughter was just saying how much she'd like to stretch her legs. Perhaps you'd be so good as to oblige her with a promenade?'

'I'd be honoured.' Aidan turned his eyes towards Essie, his expression studiously blank and his voice tinged with only the faintest hint of reluctance. 'If that's truly what she wishes?'

'Actually, I –' Essie jumped as her grandmother's boot connected sharply with her ankle. On reflection, she didn't care to find out what it was capable of if she refused. 'I'd be delighted.'

'Then perhaps Miss Foyle would care to accompany me?' Mr Dormer offered. 'We could walk beside the Serpentine awhile.'

'She'd be delighted as well.' Their grandmother's foot twitched again, as if she were on the verge of kicking them both out. 'I'll take a turn of the park and return in half an hour.'

'Allow me.' Aidan dismounted quickly, passing his reins to a waiting groom before helping Essie down from the carriage while Mr Dormer did the same for Caro.

'I'm sorry to interrupt your ride.' Essie turned to face him the moment they were safely over a low wooden barrier and on to the pavement alongside the road. 'My grandmother can be a little blunt.'

'I think she might be offended by such a mild statement.' He quirked an eyebrow. 'I don't believe your grandmother has *little* opinions about anything. It's one of the qualities I admire most about her.'

'Really?'

'Yes. I like people who say what they think. It's a rare quality.'

'Not in our family.'

'No, perhaps not.' He extended an arm, waiting until she took it before falling into step behind Caro and Mr Dormer. 'Your cousin appears to be a great success with the *ton*.'

'Yes.' She curved her fingers around a surprisingly muscular bicep. 'I'm very pleased for her.'

'She doesn't share your ideas about matrimony, I take it?'

'Not remotely. We have very different ambitions in life. I've often thought it was a pity you weren't engaged to her.'

'No doubt. However, it seems that she has her pick of eligible bachelors now. Just look at Dormer. He's already smitten.'

'How can you tell?'

'He's cleared his throat three times since we started walking.'

'Maybe he's getting a cold.' She tipped her head to one side. 'Although he *is* fidgeting a lot. He keeps tugging at his earlobe.'

'Exactly. He's feeling self-conscious.'

'Then he has good taste in women.' She glanced sideways. '*You're* not fidgeting.'

'I'm aware. Speaking of taste, that's another lovely gown. So few people suit yellow.'

'Thank you.' Essie gritted her teeth, telling herself that she ought to be pleased by his sarcasm. Her appearance was obviously having the desired effect after all, although a small, vain part of her couldn't help but be offended.

She turned her face to one side, looking out over the turquoise ribbon of the Serpentine. There were a number of couples walking alongside: enough to ensure quite a spectacle, if she were to accidentally take a tumble. Which she might easily do if she were to draw her arm away from Aidan's to adjust the ribbons on her bonnet, for example ... Falling into the water didn't strike her as particularly dangerous. She could swim well enough and the weather, though not overly warm, wasn't cold either. The worst she would probably suffer was a head cold afterwards. One small slip and a cartwheel accompanied by a dramatic scream, and she could make quite a splash.

'It's not deep enough.'

'What?' She gave a start, annoyed to be interrupted just when her imagination was getting to the good part.

'The water. It's shallow at the edges around here. You might injure yourself if you fell in. Not that I object to playing the knight errant, but then we'd both have to go home in soaking wet clothes which, while inconvenient for me, would be rather more of a problem for you.' He gave her an appraising look up and down. 'Given the clingy nature of that pale fabric you're wearing, you might find yourself revealing rather more of your figure than you'd like. Again, not a problem for me.'

'I've no idea what you're talking about.' Essie thrust her chin upwards, willing herself not to blush.

'No? I thought you were plotting, but my mistake. Just in case, however, I believe I mentioned being beyond embarrassment.'

She gave another start, although this time it was one of inspiration. *Beyond embarrassment*. Resigned to it, even. That was what his expression outside the supper room had suggested the other evening. Resignation, as if he'd expected nothing better. As if he were used to disappointment and setbacks. The idea made her feel guilty all over again.

'Why haven't you called on us?' She blurted the question out.

'Ah.' He cleared his throat. 'Your grandmother's right. I ought to have visited again.'

'It doesn't matter. I'm curious, that's all.'

'Honestly, I thought you'd be out exploring London. This is your first time in the city, I believe?'

'Yes, but unfortunately my grandmother doesn't care for sightseeing. I've begged her to take us to the Tower, but all we've done so far is make calls and go shopping.'

'In that case . . .' He hesitated, as if he wasn't sure of the wisdom of what he was about to say. 'Perhaps you'd allow me to escort you?'

'You'd do that?' She jerked her head around, torn between her reluctance to spend any more time with him and her desire to see Traitors' Gate. The gate won. 'Thank you, I'd be incredibly grateful.'

'How would tomorrow suit?'

'That would be perfect.'

'Then I'll arrange it. As for the past few days, the truth is I've been busy with my lawyer. After your father's visit the other day, I needed to –'

'What?' She stopped walking abruptly, feeling as if all the blood had just drained from her face and trickled down to her toes. 'You've seen my father?'

'Yes. He wanted to discuss wedding arrangements and . . .' His voice trailed away as he saw her expression. 'You didn't see him too?'

'I didn't even know he was in London.' She swallowed, wondering if her grandmother had been aware of her son's presence. 'Is he still here?'

'I don't believe so,' Aidan answered haltingly, as if he regretted raising the subject at all. 'He gave the impression of it being a fleeting visit. He may not have had time to call.'

'Yes, it's been a busy ten years for him.' She clenched her fists at her sides. 'Five minutes to visit his daughter would be far too much to expect!'

'Ten years?'

'That was the last time I saw him, ten years ago.' She sniffed, horribly aware of tears welling in her eyes. Oddly enough, they felt cold rather than hot, like icicles crystallizing over her lashes. 'Ignore me, I'm overreacting.'

'If you haven't seen your father in ten years then I'd say it was a reasonable reaction.' His voice softened. 'I had no idea. I'm sorry.'

'It's not your fault.' She blinked the tears away. 'I'm probably better off without his attention. And I shouldn't be surprised he visited you instead of me. A son was all my father ever wanted. No doubt he thinks of you as the heir he never had – an *earl* too. Turning me into a countess is the only way he can make up for the mistake of having a daughter.' She kicked at a stone with the toe of her shoe, sending it flying all the way into the water. 'It's just funny he thinks that I'll be any good at it, given how much of a disappointment I've been to him in every other way.'

'Is that why you wish to end our engagement?' Aidan's tone was thoughtful. 'Because you think you won't be any good as a countess?'

'I definitely won't be, but no, it's not that. It's what I told you at Redcliffe. I have my own ambitions in life and I don't see why I should surrender them just to fulfil my father's. That's what he expects, as if I'm nothing more than a belonging to be disposed of as he sees fit. It's probably never even occurred to him to ask me what *I* want. Well, I'm a person with my own mind and I can be just as stubborn and single-minded as he is. I want to choose my own path. That's not such a bad thing, is it?'

'It's not a bad thing at all.' He held on to her gaze, his own hooded. 'I understand wanting to choose, even if . . .' He paused, his brow furrowing. 'Have you thought any

97

more about your ambitions? Maybe there's some kind of compromise we might come to.'

'There isn't, trust me, and they're private.' She started walking again. 'I've no desire to be laughed at.'

'I won't laugh, I promise.'

'If you do –'

'I won't.'

'All right.' She took a deep breath. 'I want to be on the stage.'

'You want to be an actress? Well, that explains it.'

'Explains what?'

'Nothing. Go on. What is it you enjoy about acting?'

She glanced sideways suspiciously, but he looked genuinely interested. 'Well . . . the first time I performed was only for my uncle and aunt, but it made me feel free. Like I could just forget myself and transform. It felt like a whole fresh start. You know, when I'm playing a character, I work out everything about them. I understand how they feel and what they want and where they belong. And that way, for a while, it's like I understand myself and where I belong too.' She frowned, afraid that she'd just revealed too much. 'Only then the play ends and I have to go back to being myself.'

'Is that so terrible?'

'Not always. But sometimes, playing somebody else seems easier. Haven't you ever wanted to pretend you were someone else?'

'No. I detest artifice.'

'I'm talking about acting, not artifice, and you were the one who said everything about you was a lie.'

'That's why I despise it.'

'Fine, forget pretending.' She rolled her eyes. 'What if you could stop being the earl and be someone else? Who would you be?'

'I don't know.'

'Because you've never thought about it because there was no point in thinking about it, I suppose?'

'Exactly. I've never had a choice about who I am.'

'Are there *any* rebellious bones in your body, do you think?'

His tone hardened. 'If you're asking me whether I've ever seriously considered letting down my family and abandoning all of my responsibilities then no, I haven't.'

'And that's what you think I'm doing? Letting my family down?'

'I didn't say that.'

'It was implied.'

'Actually it wasn't. Considering what you've just told me, I'd be more inclined to say that your father has failed you.'

'You would?' She nearly tripped over her own feet in surprise.

'Yes.' Aidan grasped hold of her elbow, holding her steady, though the look in his eyes was enough to pin her to the spot. Their expression was sympathetic, almost tender. Somehow it chased away any temptation to cry, replacing it with a warm feeling in her chest instead, a glow that seemed to expand outwards through her body, making her skin tingle from the inside out. She swallowed hard, aware of her pulse beating far too fast and too frantically all of a sudden, which was not, emphatically not, the way she wanted to feel when she was looking at him! And he was still holding on to her elbow, she realized, yanking it quickly away from his fingers.

Unfortunately, she yanked a little too hard and too fast, stumbling backwards and losing her balance in the process.

'Help!' She spun her arms wildly in mid-air, struggling to right herself, but it was no use. Her limbs were already out of control, plummeting towards the water. It was exactly the situation she'd been planning a few minutes ago, only now that it was actually happening, she wanted to remain on dry land, warm glow or no warm glow!

She'd finally resigned herself to her watery fate, knowing there was nothing she could do now to prevent an unceremonious dunking, when a pair of hands wrapped themselves around her waist, catching her mid-fall and hauling her upright again. Which would have been an excellent turn of events if a duck hadn't shot up from the water with an ear-splitting squawk at the same moment, causing her to fling the entire front of her body against Aidan's, then realize what she'd done and jump backwards again, inadvertently pulling him past her.

'Oh no!' She stretched her arms out uselessly as he landed in the Serpentine with an enormous splash. 'I'm so sorry. It was an accident!'

On a more positive note, the water was indeed as shallow as he'd said, though sadly still deep enough for him to be completely submerged for a few seconds before he broke the surface again, looking like a large and extremely grumpy toad.

'Don't tell me you're afraid of waterfowl?' He gave his head a vigorous canine shake as he stood up, water streaming from his clothes.

'No, but it just flapped up out of nowhere. I didn't mean to push you in, I swear.'

'How reassuring.' He waded back towards the edge, waving away her offer of assistance as he plucked a few straggly pieces of pondweed from his hair and then hauled himself out. 'That was a lot colder than I expected.'

'Aidan!' Dormer came running towards them, Caro at his heels. 'What happened?'

'A misstep.' Aidan grasped the ends of his tailcoat and squeezed. 'No harm done.'

'It was my fault.' Essie scooped the earl's hat out of the water before it drifted away. It was probably ruined, like the rest of his clothes, but she felt the need to do something, not to mention distract herself from the sight of his broad chest, visible through the now transparent material of his shirt. 'Aidan saved me from falling, but then there was a . . . a duck.'

'A duck?' Mr Dormer and Caro echoed together.

'Yes.' She looked down at the hat and pressed her lips together, feeling a completely inappropriate tickle of laughter at the back of her throat. She coughed, trying to stifle it, but it refused to be stifled. She could feel it bubbling up inside, demanding release.

'We'd better get you home before you catch a chill,' she heard Mr Dormer say. 'You can wear my jacket.'

'Not much point when the rest of me is sodden, but thank you.'

A small burble of laughter broke past Essie's lips.

'Essie!' Caro sounded mortified.

'I'm sorry.' She clapped a hand to her mouth, speaking through her fingers to Aidan. 'I'm not laughing at you, truly. It's just that you look so bedraggled and you're usually so pristine. I just –' Another burble erupted. 'It's not funny. It must be very uncomfortable.'

'*And* cold.'

'Yes.' She gave up attempting to muffle her giggles, spreading her arms out instead. 'Here, you can push me in too. Get your revenge, I deserve it.'

'Tempting though that is . . .' In all honesty, he *did* look sorely tempted. 'I believe it's time that I returned you to your grandmother.'

'But –'

'Another day, perhaps.' He shot her a dark look. 'Personally, I like a little time to plot revenge.'

Chapter Nine

'I resign.'

'What?' Essie looked up from the chessboard indignantly. 'You can't just resign. You have two bishops and five pawns left.'

'You're still going to win and I'd rather not delay the inevitable.' Caro knocked her king over with her little finger. 'Why are we playing chess anyway? We haven't for years.'

'Because it's all about strategy and outwitting your opponent.'

'Oh good. Nothing to do with the earl then?'

'I'm honing my reflexes.'

Caro placed an elbow on to the table and propped her chin in her hand. 'Maybe you should just play with him.'

'I don't want to do anything with him.'

'Except to go to the Tower of London this afternoon?'

'*That's* a matter of convenience. Grandmama won't take us and he offered. It doesn't mean anything.'

'I'm surprised he's still prepared to, honestly, given the risks. You know they have ravens. They're even more terrifying than ducks.'

'Yesterday was an accident. As I've said. Repeatedly.'

'I know and I believe you. Only you can see why he might not.'

'Mmm.'

'Considering the way that you laughed at him.'

'I remember.'

'And since he knows you're trying to embarrass him into ending your engagement,' Caro continued. 'Some men would have been angry.'

'I wish he had been.'

'Yet he was a perfect gentleman about it.'

'Quite.'

'I wouldn't have thought it possible for a person to look so noble and soggy at the same time.'

Essie drummed her fingernails on the top of the chessboard. She couldn't deny that, even with dripping wet hair and transparent, skintight clothing, Aidan *had* looked somewhat noble. He'd attracted a large number of female stares on their way back to her grandmother's barouche too, some of them quite thorough. She'd had the sneaking suspicion that one or two ladies had actually been following him.

'Apparently, he's not so easy to embarrass,' Caro concluded.

'That's what he says, but he must have some weakness.' Essie glowered. 'Maybe he has character traits we don't know about yet, ones I could use against him.'

'Or maybe he's as gentlemanly as he seems?'

'We should still keep our ears open for rumours.'

'You go ahead. Personally, the worst I've heard is that he's overly serious sometimes.' Caro tucked a stray coil of hair behind her ear with a guileless expression. 'Are you *certain* you want me to come to the Tower with you?'

'Positive.'

'Oh, very well, I'll come, but only because I want to see the animals. I hear there are leopards called Peggy and Nancy.'

'Animals, I can cope with.' Essie turned her face towards the window, glaring at a passing pigeon. Just so long as there weren't any ducks.

∽

'The poor creatures.' Essie shook her head as they walked away from the royal menagerie several hours later. 'They shouldn't be in cages.'

'I agree, although better that than running around the streets of London, don't you think?' Aidan arched an eyebrow though the look in his eyes was friendly. If he was harbouring any latent ill will about his drenching in the Serpentine the day before, he wasn't showing it. He was being a perfect gentleman. *Again.* It was becoming more and more annoying.

'I don't know.' She mused aloud. 'They wouldn't be any less objectionable than some of the people I've met. Given the choice between a man-eating lion and Jemima Talbot, for example . . .'

'Essie.' Caro threw her a reproving look.

'You're right, it's not a fair comparison. I'm insulting the lion.'

'So what do you think of the Tower?' Aidan changed the subject tactfully.

'It's even more impressive than I imagined.' She twirled around, taking in the many towers and crenellations and walkways. It was a beautiful day and the glow of sunshine on her skin filled her with a deep-seated sense of contentment. It would probably give her freckles too, or so her aunt would tell her, but she was enjoying herself too much to care. Considering the company she was keeping, the feeling surprised her.

She turned back to face him, supposing she ought to give credit where it was due. 'Thank you for escorting us.'

'You're welcome.' He consulted a small pamphlet. 'So where next? There's still the Horse Armoury and the Jewel Office to visit.'

'The Jewel Office,' she answered emphatically. 'I feel like we've seen enough armour for one day.'

'Didn't you like the Hall of Kings?'

'Yes. I just feel like when you've seen one suit of armour, you've seen them all.'

'This way then.'

'I'm just going to look at that . . . wall.' Caro drifted away to one side.

'Your cousin doesn't share your interest in history, I take it?' Aidan murmured, slowing his steps.

'No. She's never shown much interest in walls before, either.' Essie lowered her voice to match. 'She's leaving us alone in the hope that we might solve our dilemma by falling in love. She's a hopeless romantic.'

'You make that sound like a bad thing.'

'It is. If history teaches us anything it's that romance can't be trusted. If love stories don't end tragically then they inevitably lead to marriage and after that . . . well, think of Anne Boleyn and Katherine Howard. This is where they ended up. All because they married one of the worst husbands in history, a man who probably claimed to *love* them. That's marriage for you. It's not a fair arrangement for women. Men get all the power.'

'Not every wife ends up on the execution block.'

'True. Some of them get abandoned or imprisoned.'

'Again, not a universal experience.'

'It still happens far too often for comfort. Look where we are. Try to name one interesting queen that history doesn't denounce as a villain.' She tapped her foot, waiting. 'You can't, can you?'

'I'm thinking . . .' He clicked his fingers. 'Eleanor of Aquitaine.'

'The same Eleanor of Aquitaine who was imprisoned by her husband for sixteen years?'

'Oh. Right. I forgot about that.'

'Caro says I'm only interested in bad women, but they're only bad in history's opinion. History is written by the victors and the victors were all men, ergo . . .' She spread her hands out. 'Any woman who breaks the rules is called bad.'

'What about Elizabeth I?'

'A woman intelligent enough not to marry.'

'*Touché*.' His gaze clung to hers for a few seconds before he turned around and pointed. 'If I'm not mistaken, that's the Bell Tower where she was imprisoned.'

'For two months. It must have been terrifying, looking down at the place where her own mother was executed.' Essie shuddered. 'You know, my mother was called Anne too.'

'I remember. I only met her that one time when we were children, but she seemed a gentle kind of lady.'

'She was, or at least I think she was. I know what she looked like from portraits, but whenever I try to imagine her, there's never any expression on her face. I was eight when she died, but I can't remember her voice either. Isn't that strange?' She clenched her brows. 'But then my father was always a stronger character. It was like everything she was, her whole identity, was just overwhelmed by him.'

'It wasn't a love match, then?'

'Ha! She was the only daughter of the second son of a marquess. If my father loved anything about her, it was that. Unfortunately, she didn't give him a son, just yours truly.'

'You mean that he blamed her?'

'Oh yes, he called her a failure often enough. I remember that much. He reduced and reduced her until eventually she simply faded away. I woke up one morning and she was just . . . gone.'

'What happened?'

'A chill.' Essie wrapped her arms around her pelisse as a shiver passed through her. 'It was nothing really, just a cold, but she was so unhappy I suppose she didn't even bother to fight. My nurse came and told me that she'd passed away during the night, but my father himself never said a word.' She drew in a breath slowly and then released it in a hurry. 'I don't think Anne Boleyn would have let herself be reduced like that. She would have fought back, but then look what happened to her. Marriage destroyed her just as surely as it did my mother.' She squared her shoulders. 'Perhaps there's no way for a woman to win, except not to marry.'

'You might be right.'

'Really?' She looked up at him in surprise.

'Yes. My parents were happily married, just not particularly communicative. They each had their separate roles and were content with that. My mother never suspected a thing about the mess my father had made of the estate. Even when there was gossip, she never listened, so when he died so suddenly, it came as a double shock.'

'Your poor mother.'

He nodded, his gaze fixed on one of the turrets. 'I was away at school when it happened, but when I came home she seemed broken. Betrayed. She'd devoted nearly the whole of her life to a place he'd almost destroyed. The ironic part is that she has a good head for business. She runs the household like an army. If he'd only confided in her, things might have been different.'

'So neither of our parents' marriages was ideal.' Essie shook her head. 'You'd think they would have learned better than to arrange our match. But if your mother felt betrayed, why did she say all of those things to me at Redcliffe about duty and honour and privilege?'

'Honestly, I've no idea how my mother's mind works. Maybe she finds it hard to accept that my father concealed so much from her for so many years. I know I do.' There was a rough edge to his voice suddenly. 'Maybe being the countess is all that she has left.'

'She still has you and your sister.' Essie stopped outside the door to the Jewel Office. 'What's Sophia like? She didn't come with you that first time we met.'

'She was still in the nursery. That was back when I thought little girls existed only to annoy me.'

'No offence taken.'

'I try to be a better brother these days.' He gave a half-smile. 'Which is another reason I can't break our engagement.'

'What do you mean?'

'I mean that I agree with a lot of what you've just said. Marriage isn't fair on women. However, if I can't find a way to save my estate then Sophia's value as a bride will plummet. There are men who'll take her just for her name, but I want her to have the freedom to choose her future – and for that I need money.' He winced. 'I'm aware of how it sounds. Your freedom in exchange for my sister's. All I can promise is that I would be a good husband. I would never try to reduce you or hide things from you or hold you back from doing anything you wanted.'

Essie felt a flare of heat in her stomach, though it passed so quickly she thought she might have missed it if it hadn't felt so strange and new, like nothing she'd ever experienced. And there was that tingling sensation on her skin again, like she'd felt at the ball, only it seemed to have moved to other parts of her body now as well, to areas where she'd never felt tingles before.

'But we'd still have to marry.' She frowned, unsettled by the sensation.

'And you'd rather be an actress?'

'Yes, and I've never heard of a countess on the stage.'

'There's a first time for everything.' He lifted a shoulder and then dropped it again. 'Although probably not that.'

'Then we're still at an impasse.' She put all thought of tingles aside and tossed her head. 'And just because we have something in common doesn't mean that we're friends. This is still war.'

'Understood.' He quirked an eyebrow. 'Only perhaps we're not quite enemies any more?'

'No.' She met his gaze and swallowed, concentrating hard on keeping her breathing even. 'I suppose not.'

Chapter Ten

I would never try to reduce you . . .

Aidan's words echoed around Essie's head as her grandmother's carriage rolled along the dark London streets en route to yet another ball, until a sudden lurch and loud exhortation about potholes from the driver jolted her back to the present.

Relieved, she stared down at her lap, wondering whether the speed with which Madame Liliane had produced so many hideous dresses was down to talent or simply a desire to get them out of her sight. She and Caro were both wearing pink that evening, but whereas her cousin's gown was a pretty pastel shade, hers was more of a luminous peach, adorned with several rows of coral beads around the neck that rattled when she moved. Personally, she thought it had some nerve calling itself pink at all, but it was the very least attractive of all her gowns, which made it perfect for what she had planned for that evening.

Desperate times, she'd concluded after her trip to the Tower, called for desperate measures. Aidan wasn't going to break their engagement easily. He had too much loyalty to his family and too many stupid ideas about duty and honour, not to mention a thicker skin than she'd anticipated. Meanwhile, *she* was wasting time. She hadn't done the slightest thing to further her ambitions since arriving in London. She hadn't even visited the theatre! And now there was only just over four weeks left until her wedding! All of which left her with no choice but to break her word to Caro and do something decidedly *un*subtle.

Something so shocking that Aidan simply wouldn't be able to countenance her as a bride.

Something vulgar. Something heinous.

Something that would give debutantes nightmares for years to come, and give her near-mythical status as an example of how *not* to behave.

She'd spent most of the day planning. While Caro had been surrounded by her usual crowd of admirers, she'd taken herself off to a window seat and thought. And thought. And then come up with an idea. And then told herself that she couldn't possibly go through with it. And then assured herself that she absolutely could, that needs must and she simply had to be brave. And if she couldn't be brave then she ought to drink several glasses of wine first, going back and forth so many times that she'd given herself a ferocious headache in the process.

Her eventual plan involved their entertainment for that evening, a ball hosted by the Duke and Duchess of Faulconer. Although notorious for his exploits as a young man, according to her grandmother anyway, the duke had become a paragon of virtue in later life, but he still threw some of the most sensational *ton* parties. It was one of *the* social events of the Season. Nobody refused an invitation unless they were literally at death's door, and even then some made the effort. The only condition was that guests needed to be on their best behaviour, the duchess refusing to tolerate even the faintest whiff of scandal in her reformed household. Anyone who violated that rule risked social ruin for as many Seasons as it took her to forget their crime, and she had a notoriously long memory. Just in case, however, Essie intended to be unforgettable.

Slowly, she smoothed her kid gloves over the already smooth, peachy flounces of her gown and went over the plan in her mind. She was going to wait until the room was sufficiently crowded with witnesses before tripping and swooning at a strategic moment, throwing her drink all over the duchess before landing in an inelegant heap at her feet. If she could tear the duchess's dress on the way down, so much the better.

It was going to be awful and mortifying and the most humiliating moment of her entire life, but at least her eyes would be closed. She would channel the great tragic heroines. She would be Ophelia! Jocasta! The Duchess of Malfi! And if destroying the dress of the *ton*'s most terrifying duchess wasn't enough to make her *persona non grata* for the rest of the Season then nothing was. Her grandmother would have no choice but to keep her hidden away in her house afterwards, from where, hopefully, she would be able to sneak out and put her own secret ambitions into action.

The carriage slowed as it joined a queue of others leading up to the Faulconers' elegant Portman Square address, but Essie could already see the front door, like a black portal beckoning her to her doom. Her head was still throbbing, as if an entire sheath of arrows were trying to pierce their way into her skull, but she'd made up her mind. The most important thing was to make whatever happened tonight look like an accident. Even her father couldn't punish her for that . . . probably . . . She sucked her bottom lip into her mouth, considering. Actually, he probably could, but she'd just have to deny everything and hope for the best.

'Here we are.' The dowager got to her feet as the carriage finally shuddered to a halt and a coachman let down the steps. 'About time too. I've never seen such a crush of vehicles. The ballroom's going to be horrific.'

Essie followed her out on to the pavement, gulping several times as they made their way inside. The crush was just as bad as predicted – hot, loud and airless – so that by the time they reached the ballroom, her headache had already quadrupled in strength, as if the cluster of arrows had turned into a whole battalion of cannons.

Her mouth turned dry as she spied the duke and duchess through the crowd, surrounded by a group of fashionable-looking dandies whose bored expressions suggested they were enjoying themselves immensely. She wavered, wondering whether to wait until later in the evening or to get the scene over with. There were certainly enough witnesses already, and even if they couldn't see exactly what happened, the story would spread like wildfire. She didn't want to ruin the evening completely for Caro, but on the other hand, she daren't risk losing her nerve. And if she saw Aidan, she had a horrible feeling that she might. *I would never try to reduce you* . . . The last thing she needed tonight was to start doubting herself.

'Miss Craven.' A man blocked her view suddenly, bowing in front of her. 'If you aren't otherwise engaged, might I request the honour of this dance?'

'Oh, Mr Dormer.' She recognized him through a kind of haze, scrambling for an excuse and coming up with nothing. 'Thank you.'

She took his arm and stepped reluctantly on to the dance floor. As usual, she could see people looking at her gown and making comments, but this time she genuinely didn't care.

'It's excessively crowded tonight,' Mr Dormer commented good-naturedly.

'Yes.' She licked her lips, making a supreme effort to loosen her tongue. 'Although I'm sure that makes it a great success.'

'Oh, undoubtedly. Every hostess wants her event to be called a crush.'

'Shouldn't it matter whether or not the guests actually enjoy themselves?'

'It should.' He chuckled. 'But the *ton* has other priorities.'

'Is Ai – I mean, is the earl here tonight?' She couldn't resist asking. She hadn't seen Aidan since the Tower two days before and she hadn't thought to ask about his social plans then. Part of her hoped that he wasn't in attendance. Making a fool of herself in front of the *ton* she could cope with, but doing so in front of him struck her as ten times worse somehow.

'I believe so.' Mr Dormer nodded. 'I thought I caught sight of him earlier.'

'Ah.' Instinctively, she turned her head, searching the crowd for a glimpse.

'I'm sure he'll make an appearance soon enough.' Mr Dormer obviously misinterpreted her interest.

'Of course.' She turned back around quickly. 'So how do the two of you know each other?'

'We were at school together. A more conscientious student you'll never find.'

'You or him?'

'Him!' He laughed outright. 'I was always more interested in cricket, but Aidan never put a toe out of line.'

'That sounds like him.' Essie twirled away, then froze with a rush of panic. Out of the corner of her eye, she could see the duke and duchess moving in the direction of a large marble staircase. It seemed unlikely that they were leaving their own ball, but what if something had happened to call them away? What if she was about to lose her *only* opportunity to humiliate herself?

'Forgive me, but I'm feeling a little faint.' She stepped backwards, breaking the formation of the dance.

'Here, take my arm.' Mr Dormer sounded concerned. 'Allow me to escort you back to your grandmother.'

'No. Thank you, but I'll be quite well on my own.'

She hurried away before he could insist, pushing her way through the throng towards the refreshment table and seizing two glasses of champagne, gulping one and then accelerating her pace towards the staircase with the other. A swift glance sideways showed that the duke and duchess were almost level with her on the opposite side of the room. If nobody waylaid them, they should meet at the staircase at the exact same moment . . .

She barrelled forward, barely noticing the shoulders she was bumping into or the glares being levelled in her direction, clamping her spare hand over her roiling stomach and willing herself not to be sick. Spilling wine over a duchess was one thing. Vomiting over one would mean leaving the country, possibly the continent, forever. The noise of the ballroom had receded to a dull thrum in her ears, drowned out by the ribcage-bruising thud of her heartbeat and the rattle of coral beads against her chest. This was it. The moment of truth. The act that would take care of everything if she just held her nerve.

She was almost there now, the stem of the champagne flute clasped tight in her fingers. A few more steps and all she had to do was throw the drink, close her eyes and pretend to faint. Which really shouldn't be too hard when her mind was already spinning like the blades of a windmill. A windmill on top of a tall peak in a thunderstorm, with an oncoming hurricane and maybe a few screws loose as well . . .

Just a few more steps. Four at the most.

This. Was. It.

She lifted her arm.

'Miss Craven?' A hand grabbed hold of her wrist, yanking her backwards so abruptly that she spilled half of the champagne on to the floor before the flute was plucked from her fingers and deposited on a passing tray. 'You look like you need some air.'

'What the –?' Essie inhaled sharply, struggling to make sense of what was happening as the noise and bustle of the ballroom whooshed back in on her. All she could see of her assailant was the back of his head and shoulders, but she recognized those perfectly. Only the harsh tone of his voice was new.

'Let go of me!' she protested, trying to draw her arm away as Aidan hauled her to the edge of the hall and behind a tall pot plant.

'Not until I know that you're not going to do something foolish.' For the first time since they'd met, he looked really angry.

'What *I* do is none of your business.'

'It is when you're about to assault a peer of the realm.'

'I wasn't, actually!' She thrust her chin up defiantly. 'I was aiming for his wife. And how did you know?'

'I could tell by your expression.' He peered around the plant as if to make sure that no one was watching, his right hand still clamped firmly around her wrist. 'I don't know what you were hoping to achieve, but it was a bad idea, trust me.'

'That's my business!'

'You're my fiancée!'

'Why the hell else do you think I was doing it?!'

There was a heavy moment of silence before he twisted his face away, a muscle flexing in his jaw. 'Come with me.'

'What? Where?'

'Somewhere private.'

'Why?'

'To talk.'

'We can talk here.' She lifted her chin a notch higher and then regretted it as a fresh wave of nausea washed over her. 'I need to stand still for a few seconds.'

'Are you all right?' His expression softened slightly. *Very* slightly.

'Just a bit queasy. *And* I have a headache.'

'Take some deep breaths. Do you want me to fetch you a chair?'

'No.' She blew air between her teeth. 'I think it's getting better.'

'Good.' He looked around again. 'Essie, we can't talk here.'

'I'm not leaving this spot.' She dug her heels into the floor. 'I know what goes on in private rooms at balls.'

'Is that so? Enlighten me.'

'Well, I don't know *exactly*. I'm not supposed to for some reason, but . . . *debauchery*.'

'Debauchery?' The anger in his eyes faded, replaced by a different kind of gleam. 'I suppose that's one word for it.'

'What's another?'

'Pardon?'

'I don't know any other words and nobody will tell me. I've offered shillings to all of my aunt's maids, but they refuse to talk about it. Even Felix won't tell me.'

'Felix?' His brows snapped together.

'My cousin. He's away at Oxford, but he won't tell me a thing.'

'Ah. I'm not surprised.'

'It's ridiculous!' She finally succeeded in wrenching herself away from him, queasiness replaced by indignation. 'Everyone knows you find out what debauchery is *after* you're married, so why not explain it before? All the secrecy just implies that men are hiding something awful.'

'Quite.' He gave a small cough, his eyes glinting suspiciously. 'Essie, I don't know how we got on to this subject, but it's not my place to tell you either.'

'Why not? You're my fiancé, as you're so keen on pointing out. Who better to tell me?'

'This isn't the time or the place.'

'Then I'm not going to come and talk in private with you.'

'Believe me, I've no intention of compromising you. Or otherwise.'

'You can't just say *otherwise*!' She threw her head back in exasperation. 'You could at least tell me one other word for it.'

'Essie . . .' Aidan's voice had a pleading note to it. Now that he'd said her name, he seemed unable to say anything else either, his lips pressed together as if he were struggling to contain laughter. If she wasn't mistaken, his shoulders were shaking too.

'Don't you *dare* laugh at me!' She swung about, ready to storm away, then stopped as one of his arms coiled around her waist, tugging her back against him. She sucked in a breath, caught by surprise as his lips brushed the shell of her ear, whispering a word she'd never heard before.

'Really?' She half turned her head as a tremor rippled all the way down her spine to her lower back, an area that was now located shockingly close to his front. With his arm around her waist, holding her like an embrace, their respective positions struck her as scandalously intimate. His fingers were only touching fabric, but she felt them as surely as if they were caressing her skin. And just the thought of that caused an ache in her stomach as if there was a whirlpool churning inside of her.

'Really.' He sounded different, less amused and more husky, as if he'd inadvertently swallowed some gravel. 'Only I wouldn't repeat it here.'

'No.' The whirlpool spun outwards and then shrank suddenly to a tight yet surprisingly powerful vortex. 'I don't suppose the duchess would approve.'

'*Now* will you come with me?' His breath skimmed the nape of her neck, making her heart perform an odd kind of stutter. 'It's important, Essie.'

She licked her lips, surprised to find herself prepared to agree to almost anything. 'Yes.'

'This isn't a room.' Essie looked around as they reached the top of a narrow spiral staircase. It led on to a balcony that ran along the whole edge of the ballroom.

'No, it's not.' Aidan rested his forearms on the railing as if he were settling in to watch a play. 'Don't tell me you're disappointed?'

'Of course not.' She felt horribly conscious of the fact that she was, just a teeny bit. 'So what was it you wanted to talk about?'

'*Us.*'

'Oh, good.' She shot him a dirty look though he wasn't looking at her, his eyes fixed on the dancers twirling below. She followed his gaze, surprised to see Caro being twirled around the dance floor by Mr Jagger.

'You might be quite pleased actually. I've changed my mind. You win.'

'What?' She jerked her head sideways, gaping in astonishment.

'You win. I concede.'

'You mean you'll break off our engagement?'

He nodded, still not looking at her. 'On one condition.'

'Anything!'

'It was your own suggestion actually. Find me another heiress.'

She tensed, caught off guard by a spontaneous and confusing mixture of jealousy and triumph. For a second, she hardly knew if she wanted to embrace him or cry on his shoulder. 'What made you change your mind?'

'Because ever since we spoke at Redcliffe, I've felt like I've been trapped between two bad choices. Breaking a gentleman's agreement or forcing an unwilling woman into marriage. At first, I hoped we might find some kind of compromise, but after our talk at the Tower the other day . . .' He sighed, his shoulders slumping forward. 'I suppose now I understand your objections a little better. I'd almost made up my mind to release you, and seeing what you were prepared to do tonight only confirmed my decision. I'm not happy about the situation, but hopefully I'm taking the path of least dishonour. So find me an alternative, a *willing* bride this time, and I'll release you.'

'Do you absolutely mean it?' She forgot about jealousy as excitement took over, a future filled with possibilities seeming to open up before her. 'You won't change your mind?'

'You have my word of honour.' He turned to look at her finally, placing a hand over his heart. 'Mine this time, not my father's.'

'Oh, thank you! I'll find you the best wife you could possibly imagine. She'll be perfect in every single way, I promise!'

'Just one more thing.' He lifted a hand. 'Flattering though your enthusiasm to be rid of me is, I still get to approve of your choice. If that happens then we'll find a way to end our engagement discreetly and without throwing champagne at anyone, Society doyennes in particular. In the meantime, I'd like for us to be civil to each other.'

'Of course!' She beamed. 'I don't enjoy being rude.'

'Yet you're so good at it.'

'But I can be pleasant too. Here, give me your arm.'

'Pardon?'

'We should promenade, don't you think?'

'I don't recall asking for the honour.'

'You just said that we ought to be civil. Promenading together is civil.'

'Incredible.' He shook his head, throwing her a look that she couldn't interpret before crooking his elbow. 'Very well. Miss Craven, would you be so obliging as to take a turn of the balcony with me?'

'I'd be deeelighted, my lord.' She tucked her hand deftly around his arm, feeling her headache lift and drift away as if by magic. 'Now, have you thought any more about what qualities you might want in a wife? Aside from a large fortune, obviously.'

'I'm afraid not.'

'In that case, perhaps you should tell me a little bit more about being a countess? Then I can work out who would suit.'

'Are you asking me for a job description?'

'I suppose so. Presumably somebody who likes socializing, throwing dinner parties, paying calls and arranging galas, that sort of thing?'

'None of which appeals to you, I take it?'

'I could probably manage a picnic, but as for the rest . . .' She shuddered. 'Besides, your mother told me that a countess only has one really important job, and it's not a job so much as an incredibly painful process of self-abnegation.'

'I know I'm probably going to regret this question, but –'

'Having a son.'

'Ah.' He closed his eyes briefly. 'My mother told you that?'

'Yes, during dinner that first night. It put me completely off my mock turtle soup.'

'I'm not surprised. No wonder you came and begged me to release you afterwards. My mother's desire for grandchildren can be somewhat alarming.'

'Don't you want children?' She asked the question before she could think better of it. As from two minutes ago, it was really none of her business.

'In a few years, but not yet. Unfortunately, she's quite determined.'

'It doesn't seem very fair, treating your own son like a stud bull.' Essie scrunched her mouth up. 'Although that would mean she thinks I'm a heifer and I'd be the one carrying the calf, so it's really much worse for me.'

'Do we have to be cows in this analogy?'

'What would you prefer to be? A stallion?'

He made an oddly strangled sound. 'If you insist. Maybe we should just agree that neither of us are thrilled by the prospect of imminent parenthood.' He inclined his head to a passing couple. 'What do you think about ice cream?'

'As an alternative to parenthood? *Much* better.'

'In that case perhaps you'd care to meet me at Gunter's tomorrow so we can discuss our plans in more detail?'

'Gladly! It'll give me time to think up some names of potential brides.' She gave a small skip. 'This is exciting!'

'I'm glad one of us thinks so. Gunter's tomorrow it is, then.'

'I'm already looking forward to it. C is for choice. Or countess. Or conspiracy!'

'What does the letter C have to do with anything?'

'Oh, nothing.' She tightened her grip on his arm. 'Trust me, this is all going to work out perfectly.'

PLAN C: CONSPIRACY

My dear Emmeline,

The Season marches on apace, as Seasons are wont to do. I confess that this one is proving more entertaining than most, largely thanks to the company of my granddaughters. Caro continues to entrance every man in the vicinity, although she seems unable to choose between her many suitors. Perhaps once your ankles are recovered — surely you can't bear to sit still for much longer? — you might come and choose for her. She's so obliging, she'll likely abide by your decision. In truth, she's so sweet-natured I often find it hard to believe that we're related. Essie, on the other hand . . .

Honoria Craven, the Dowager Lady Makepeace, to her daughter Mrs Emmeline Foyle, 1st May 1816

Chapter Eleven

'So I thought about it all night.' Essie waved her spoon in the air enthusiastically. 'And I've made a list.'

Aidan, who'd inexplicably chosen a pistachio rather than chocolate-flavoured ice, paused with his own spoon in mid-air and lifted an eyebrow. 'That was quick.'

'I've met a surprising number of ladies in the past week. Of course most of them consider me a laughing stock, but I won't hold that against them. What do you think of Selina Birtwhistle?'

'I think I'd rather not marry someone who calls another person a laughing stock.'

'Well, so far as I know, she didn't say it out loud. Now, she has black hair, a very long neck and she sings beautifully. Like a swan.'

'Have you ever heard a swan? They make a horrible noise. More like a honk.'

'I meant the neck part. Selina Swan-neck, that's how I think of her, like Edith Swan-neck.'

The other eyebrow joined its companion. 'Are there two ladies with long necks I ought to know about?'

'No. Edith Swan-neck was the first wife of King Harold. You know, Battle of Hastings Harold?'

'I'm aware of who he is. I just didn't know the dimensions of his wife's neck.'

'So that's one option. As for the others, I'll need to do some digging about dowries. Who has the biggest, I wonder?'

'I don't know and I don't want any part in the conversation.'

'Grandmama will *definitely* know, but I'll have to be subtle asking.'

'That ought to be a new experience. Have you ever tried being subtle before?'

'Believe it or not, it's what I *have* been doing.' She gave him an arch look. 'In the meantime, you'll need to accompany me to a few *ton* events.'

'So just to be clear —' Aidan leaned back in his chair — 'after declaring war and doing everything you possibly could to get rid of me, now you want us to spend *more* time together?'

'Precisely.'

'No. I told you, I don't want to go shopping for a fortune.'

'It's not mercenary, it's practical. If I'm going to present you with a list of candidates then you need to know who I'm talking about.' Essie scraped her spoon around the edge of her glass bowl, optimistically searching for any ice she might have missed on a previous sweep. 'Otherwise I might put all my effort into finding a woman *I* think is perfect only for you to find them annoying or objectionable.'

'I can't imagine what that would be like. Just find me someone who doesn't argue every point and I'll be happy.' His gaze dropped to her mouth as she licked the back of her spoon. 'Care for another? You're practically eating the cutlery.'

'Yes please. It's so delicious and clever too. I'd heard that Gunter's was special, but I never expected to eat a chocolate ice shaped like an apple.'

'I'm glad you approve.'

'More than approve. I want to live here, but since that's probably not allowed, I'll settle for trying every flavour. Do you think they could make me a bowl with a sample of each?'

'I'm sure it could be arranged.' He lifted a hand to a passing waitress. 'How many flavours do you have today?'

'Twelve, my lord. Lemon, pineapple, chocolate, violet, maple, jasmine, elderflower, pistachio, coffee, parmesan, cherry and artichoke.'

'Would it be possible to provide us with a bowl of small samples?'

'*Small* samples?' Essie narrowed her eyes as the waitress bobbed a curtsey and moved on.

'I don't want to make you sick like you almost were last night.'

'You woefully underestimate my capacity for dessert. Now, about those engagements I mentioned?'

'Fine, a couple of engagements and you can show me the . . . what did you call them?'

'Candidates.'

'How romantic. You make them sound like politicians.'

'It's a better word than choices. That implies you can just pick one without them having any say in the matter. Candidates suggests that they've *chosen* to compete in the Marriage Mart. In which case, we're simply selecting a winner.'

'I see. Candidates, it is.'

'Good. Now we only have four weeks until the date for our wedding so we need to find someone quickly. That way you can still get married on the same day and –'

'I will *not* use the same day.'

'Why not? St George's is already booked. So if you can make a decision by the start of next week then we can break off our engagement immediately afterwards, meaning that you can propose a week after that –'

'A one-week courtship?'

'You'll have to say it was love at first sight.'

'Absolutely not.' His eyes darkened. 'If I propose then I'll set it out in purely practical terms.'

'No woman wants to hear that! You have to exaggerate a little. *I* might not believe in romance, but I'm not your typical debutante.'

'You astound me.' His jaw tightened. 'I'm not exaggerating anything. How would you have felt if I'd pretended to be in love with you?'

'I wouldn't have believed you.' She snorted. 'All right, no exaggerations, but you could try to be a little more charming.'

'Is that so?'

'There's no need to look so offended. I'm not saying you're completely charmless now, just that you could do with a little practice.'

'Yes, that sounds much better.' He nodded his thanks to the waitress as she set a fresh bowl of ices between them.

'Oh my.' Essie licked her lips enthusiastically.

'There are ungentlemanly comments I could make about charming behaviour right now.'

'I'm sure there are. Fortunately, we're not talking about me.'

'Quite.' He tapped his fingers on the tabletop. 'So what do you suggest?'

'Well, you *can* come across as a little haughty sometimes.' She slid the spoon into her mouth and groaned. 'Oh, the lemon is delicious. Do you want to try some?'

'I'm too busy being haughty.'

'Your loss. So, granted, you're an earl and people expect it of you, but a smile now and then wouldn't go amiss. Even the Queen thinks so.'

His eyes snapped to hers. '*What?*'

'The Queen. She described you as serious. Oh my goodness, the jasmine . . .'

'All right, I'll smile. Now and then.'

'How about now?'

'I prefer then.'

'You're only reinforcing my point.' She shook her head in exasperation. 'Try giving me a compliment.'

'I beg your pardon?'

'Not to criticize, but you haven't given me a single compliment since we met.'

'I've given you plenty.'

'Sarcastic ones about my clothes. I want a real one.'

'I complimented you at Redcliffe.'

133

'No you didn't.'

'Really?' He looked taken aback. 'I must have said something complimentary when I arrived.'

'You said I looked cold.'

'Ah. Well, I hardly got a chance before you asked to break off our engagement.' His expression looked arrested. 'Please tell me that wasn't because I didn't compliment you?'

'Of course not. I'm not quite so shallow, although if I *had* wanted to marry you then I might have felt quite taken for granted.'

'In that case, I'm sorry.'

'Apology accepted . . . *and*?'

'And you're wearing lemon again. You want me to be honest, don't you?'

'Oh, for goodness sake! If I wasn't enjoying these ices so much, I'd throw my spoon at you. Compliments shouldn't be this hard! There must be *something* not entirely objectionable about me.'

'There are several not objectionable things.'

'Such as?'

'You have nice eyes.'

'*These* eyes?' She fluttered her lashes.

'Yes, those ones.'

'Do they remind you of anything? You need to be a little more descriptive. For example, if my eyes were blue you might say they were like bewitching tropical pools you wanted to drown yourself in.'

'A bit morbid, don't you think?'

'It shows depth of feeling.'

'Didn't we just discuss exaggerations?'

'Just –' she clenched her teeth – 'try.'

'All right.' He put his elbows on the table and leaned forward, staring intently at her face for a few seconds, closer than he'd ever been before, so close that she could sense the very warmth of his skin, close enough to make her feel flustered. 'But since your eyes are brown and not blue . . . they're warm like . . . tea. Or coffee. To drink, not drown in, just to clarify.'

'*Tea* or *coffee*? That's the best you can do?'

'I like coffee. Very much. I wish I'd ordered one for this conversation.'

She lifted her eyes to the ceiling. 'Perhaps I ought to write down some compliments for you? Then you can use them whenever you want to say something charming.'

'You being an expert on the subject, I take it?'

'Not remotely, but I've read some of Caro's cards and she seems to like them. At least a dozen men have wanted to drown themselves in her eyes already.'

'Then she'd better hurry up and choose a husband. Write what you want, but no drowning, burning or references to any other elemental disasters. I don't like melodrama and I strongly object to pain. For the record, however, your eyes are your best feature. They crinkle at the corners when you smile and they can light up a whole room when you laugh. The whole effect is enchanting. Not that I get to see it very often.'

'Oh.' Essie swallowed a mouthful of cherry-flavoured ice, causing a sudden searing pain in her temples. 'Well, you will from now on. Now that we're friends or conspirators or . . . something.'

'Mmm. Let's stick with *something*.'

'Anyway . . .' She cleared her throat, trying to focus. 'As I was saying, we have one week to find a candidate, another for you to court her, then a couple more to prepare the wedding.'

'No. Find me an appropriate *candidate* and I'll see to the rest. I won't be kept to a schedule.' He rubbed a hand over his forehead. 'I'm beginning to have second thoughts about this.'

'You can't. You gave me your word.'

'In a moment of weakness, I know. That reminds me, however, I need yours too.'

'Why?'

'Because when we break this engagement, I want it to be entirely my fault.'

'What?' She frowned. 'I don't think –'

'Essie.' He reached across the table, placing one of his hands directly on top of one of hers. 'We've already established that your father won't be pleased, that he might even punish you if he suspects you had anything to do with it. That was another reason I was so hesitant at first, but since you're determined enough to risk drenching a duchess, I presume that you've decided the risk is worth the potential reward?'

'You were trying to protect me?' She opened her eyes wide, aware of her fingers trembling slightly beneath his.

'*Another* reason, I said.' He drew his hand away again. 'But I don't want anything else on my conscience. Your father needs to believe that our break-up is entirely my fault. When the time comes, I'll simply tell him that I've met someone else. Which will also happen to be the truth, sort of.'

'But what about *your* reputation? It's not fair for you to get all the blame.'

'Earls' reputations have a way of recovering. Young ladies', unfortunately, do not.'

'Well, that's true.' She tapped the side of her spoon against her teeth, considering. 'Still, it doesn't feel right.'

'None of this feels right, but it's the best we can do, so no more stunts or salmon-coloured dresses. As far as your father is concerned, your conduct this Season will have been nothing short of exemplary.' Aidan fixed her with a hard stare. 'Now, either give me your word or we forget this whole thing.'

'Do you always resort to blackmail? All right, you have my word. I'll play the perfect model of a fiancée. I'll even fawn over you if you like.'

'Just be yourself. No fawning required.'

'It'll be easier if I think of it as a performance.'

'I'd rather you were yourself. *Please.*'

'Oh, very well, I'll try, but not *too* much myself. I know men don't like that either.'

'What do you mean?' He sounded surprised.

'Well . . .' She felt mildly embarrassed. 'My aunt always warned me not to talk about anything serious with gentlemen, but I thought it wouldn't hurt to get a reputation as a bluestocking. And I really am interested in politics.' She sighed. 'I expected them to be shocked, but I didn't think they'd glaze over or spot acquaintances on the other side of the room every time I tried to start an actual conversation.'

'Cowards.'

'I don't suppose *you* have an opinion on the Corn Laws?'

'Yes.' He plucked her spoon from her fingers and helped himself to a scoop of lemon ice. 'I think the intention was good, but the law itself ill thought-out. The only effect was to raise the price of bread for those who couldn't afford it.'

'Oh.' She opened her lips, closed them again and then nodded. 'I agree.'

'Will wonders never cease?' He suddenly spontaneously grinned. 'We ought to have discussed politics sooner.'

Essie blinked. At that moment, she didn't have a single political opinion in her head. If her smile could light up a room then his could surely melt every ice in the building.

⌘

'I don't think I'm going to need any dinner.' Essie patted her stomach as they stepped out on to the pavement. 'Thank goodness the current fashion is for loose dresses.'

'Again, charming.' Aidan touched the brim of his hat to a passer-by. 'You walked to Gunter's, didn't you?'

'Only from the other side of the square. Grandmama set us down on her way to Hyde Park, but I don't mind walking back. I have my maid to accompany me.' She twisted her head to smile at the girl trailing a few paces behind. 'Did you enjoy your ice, Sarah?'

'Very much, thank you, miss.'

'What flavour did you choose?'

'Chocolate, miss.'

'Definitely the best, although the lemon came a close second.'

'I also recommend the pistachio.' Aidan extended his arm. 'I'd be happy to escort you both home if you'd care for a walk through the park? It's a beautiful afternoon.'

'That would be lovely.' Essie smiled. 'Perhaps we might pass some potential *candidates* on the way.'

'Wouldn't that be exciting? You'd better think up a few compliments for me just in case.'

'Dropping the sarcasm should be sufficient.'

She gave him a pointed look and he responded with a dry smile as they crossed the road to the large oblong-shaped garden in the centre of Berkeley Square. The lawn was dotted with plane and lime trees, all set around a statue of King George III, sitting proudly but precariously on horseback.

'So where do you live in town?' Essie looked up at Aidan inquisitively. 'I noticed that you walked rather than rode too.'

'Yes. Denholm House is only a short distance away, in Grosvenor Square.'

'So we're almost neighbours?'

'Almost.'

'And is Denholm House very vast and imposing?'

'I suppose you might call it that. I much prefer Middlemount.'

'Where's that?'

He gave her an incredulous look. 'You don't know?'

'Should I?'

'It's my principal seat in Hampshire.'

'Oh.' She wrinkled her brow. 'Maybe I did know that. It sounds vaguely familiar now that you mention it.'

'You've really never taken an interest in being a countess, then?'

'None at all.'

'Isn't a tiny part of you even curious?'

'Not compared to playing Desdemona.' She shrugged. 'Now tell me about your interests.'

'Any particular reason?'

'Because I'm trying to find a new mistress for Middlemount, and the more I know about you the more chance I have of finding your perfect match.'

'I see. In that case, I like art. Painting. I'm not particularly talented, but I enjoy it.'

'Portraits?' She remembered the one of her she'd seen by his chair that first night at Redcliffe. Even upside down, it had looked pretty good. 'Wait, did you hear that?' She stopped and clutched at his arm, looking around for the source of a small and tragic-sounding meow. 'Oh no!' She pointed. 'There's a kitten stuck in that tree! A tabby! I don't see anyone who looks like its owner about either.'

'I'm sure they're not far away.'

'We have to rescue it.'

'Actually, we don't. If it got up there, then it can get down.'

'What kind of logic is that?' She drew her arm away from his. 'I could probably climb to the top of a house if I wanted, but that doesn't mean I could slide down just as easily.' She marched towards the tree and started looking for footholds in the trunk. 'I'm going up there.'

'Absolutely not.'

'Absolutely yes. I'm not just abandoning the poor creature.' She braced her hands on her hips. 'Unless you intend on doing something about it?'

'Oh, bloody hell.' He stormed after her, divesting himself of his hat and jacket on the way, before shimmying expertly up the trunk.

'Slow down.' Essie made a face as the kitten let out another wail. 'You're frightening him. Or her.'

'Ungrateful wretch.'

'He's scared.'

'I wasn't talking about him.'

'What we need is a piece of fish.'

'Sadly, I'm not carrying any kippers in my pockets today.' Aidan sat astride one of the boughs. 'I can't go any higher anyway. The branches don't look strong enough.'

'You're right. I'll have to do it.'

'Essie, you can't –' He closed his eyes, adopting a pained expression as she climbed up behind him. 'Apparently you can. Lovely day up here, isn't it? We're giving the *ton* plenty to gossip about.'

'We're doing a good deed.' She stood up in the lee of the tree. 'If the *ton* doesn't appreciate *that*, then their opinion isn't worth having.'

'I never suggested it was.' He cleared his throat. 'Not that I'm complaining, but did your aunt never teach you about not showing your ankles in public?'

'Repeatedly, although I've never understood why it's so shocking. Some ladies wear necklines so low they're practically belts, and yet showing an ankle is supposed to send men into paroxysms of lust.' She frowned. 'What's wrong with my ankles anyway?'

'Nothing. I'm trying to be a gentleman and not look.'

'Because they're not attractive?'

'I didn't say that. They're perfectly nice ankles.'

'*Nice?*'

'Neat. Trim.' He sounded exasperated. 'Whatever ankles are supposed to be.'

'You're not suffering a paroxysm of lust, then?'

'Not at the moment, no, but I'll let you know if I feel one coming on.'

'*Do.*' She hauled herself on to a higher branch and stretched her hands out. 'Here, kitty, kitty.'

'Be careful.'

'Don't worry, I've climbed plenty of trees before. What are you doing with your arms?'

'Bracing myself to catch you in case anything snaps. I don't like the look of that bough you're leaning against.'

'Good idea. Come on, little one. We won't hurt you.'

'*I* might if anyone sees us.' Aidan muttered something that sounded decidedly uncomplimentary under his breath.

'I thought you said you were beyond embarrassment?'

'I stand corrected. And that animal's not moving so much as a whisker.'

'I wonder if an ice would tempt him closer? Maybe I could ask Sarah to run and fetch one?'

'Yes, by all means, let's draw more attention.'

'What flavour do you think cats prefer?'

'Mint.' He turned his head at the sound of a shout. 'Oh good, some people are coming.'

Essie looked down to see a young girl running towards them, accompanied by a maid and a footman carrying a ladder.

'Sir Purrsalot!' the little girl wailed from below.

'Is he yours?' Essie gave a reassuring wave and then stretched up a little higher. 'Just a bit further . . . Aha! Got him! Oh, you poor, adorable little creature. No more climbing trees until you're a lot bigger, Sir Purrsalot, do you hear?' She dropped a kiss on to the kitten's nose before passing him down to Aidan and smiling at the girl. 'He's not injured, but I'm sure he'd appreciate some cuddles after such an ordeal.'

'Thank you, miss.'

'Come on.' Aidan handed the kitten down to the footman and then climbed back up for Essie. 'Why didn't *we* think of a ladder?'

'Because we didn't need one.' She ignored his outstretched hand, clambering on to the bough opposite and preparing to jump.

'Essie, that might not be such a good idea.'

'Don't be silly. It's not that far down.'

'No, but –'

She jumped, landing squarely and safely on her feet. Unfortunately, half of her dress stayed where it was, making a loud ripping sound as the skirt snagged on a branch, tearing the fabric all the way from the hem up to her waist.

'Oh, bollocks.' Essie looked down in horror. Showing an ankle was one thing. Showing an entire leg, hip and waist, even ones clad in lacy unmentionables, was quite another. 'How am I going to get home like this?'

She threw a look of appeal towards Aidan, only to find him staring at her legs with a disconcerting directness.

'Mmm?' It took him a few moments to respond. 'Right. There's only one thing for it.' He unhooked the material from the branch, jumped down, and then wrapped it around her. 'Hold that there.'

She stiffened, acutely aware of his proximity, not to mention the brush of his fingers against her thighs. 'I can't walk like this.'

'I know. Don't wriggle.'

'Why would I –? Oh!' She kicked her feet out as he lifted her into his arms. 'Put me down!'

'Would you rather hop all the way home?' He inclined his head to the growing crowd of onlookers. 'Ladies. Gentlemen. Good afternoon.'

'I'm perfectly capable of walking,' Essie protested as he strode off through the park. 'It's not like I'm injured.'

'True, but you can hardly walk through the streets of Mayfair with your dress gaping open. Anyone might see those ankles.' His eyes looked unnaturally bright all of a sudden. 'You know, I hate saying I told you so.'

'Then don't. This is absurd. You can't carry me all the way to Cavendish Square!'

'We'll have to see about that. Honestly, I'm a little dubious about our chances myself.'

'*Now* do you see why I'm not cut out to be a countess? I'm an embarrassment even when I'm not trying!'

'Caring about defenceless creatures isn't such a terrible quality. Although you have rather an interesting vocabulary too.' He lifted an eyebrow. '*Bollocks?*'

'It was the first word that came to mind. *Drat* didn't seem sufficient.'

'Good point. Still, I doubt you could have done all that deliberately. It was quite dramatic.' He cleared his throat. 'Though of course, not remotely humorous.'

'At least we saved Sir Purrsalot.'

'Yes, think of all the additional seconds he might have spent in that tree waiting for a ladder if we hadn't rushed in.'

'I don't think he would have gone to that footman anyway. He only liked me.'

Aidan glanced down at her in his arms, his gaze filled with a mixture of what looked like surprise and warmth. 'Inexplicable as that sounds, I think you might be right.'

Chapter Twelve

'I can't *possibly* ask Grandmama that!' Caro dropped her embroidery frame into her lap with a scandalized expression.

'Why not?'

'Because other debutantes' dowries are none of my business!'

'People talk about money all the time. The chaperones know exactly how much everyone's worth.'

'Then ask one of them. Or ask Grandmama yourself.'

'I can't or she'll wonder why I'm taking an interest. Whereas if you do it she'll think you're just trying to work out the competition. She'll probably admire you for it.'

'The answer's still no, and I think this whole scheme is a terrible idea, by the way. It's even worse than your last one.'

'Why?' Essie folded her legs up beneath her on the sofa. 'Aidan needs a rich wife and there are plenty of heiresses in London who'd be positively thrilled to replace me. This way everyone can be happy.'

'Not everyone.' Caro pursed her lips. 'I saw the way he was looking at you yesterday. The earl may have a greater regard for you than you think.'

'What?' Essie sat bolt upright in shock. 'Don't be ridiculous!'

'Why is it ridiculous?'

'Because I've been nothing but horrible to him since we met.'

'Maybe he likes mean girls. Or maybe he's a glutton for punishment.'

'Caro!'

'He carried you all the way from Berkeley Square in his arms!'

'He didn't have much of a choice.'

'He didn't look like he minded.'

'He's a gentleman.'

'Or he *really* likes you.'

'If you think that, then you're deluded. We're conspirators, that's all.' Essie lifted her chin, aware of her cheeks flushing an incriminating shade of pink at the memory of Aidan's arms around her. 'Now, how about *I* start off the conversation at luncheon? I'll mention Miss Birtwhistle. We already know she has a large dowry. Then all you have to do is ask who else does.'

'You won't give me any peace until I agree, will you?'

'That makes me sound awful. I'll give you plenty of peace. I'll just simper at you while I do it.' She batted her eyelashes and emitted a high-pitched giggling sound. 'This is how debutantes are supposed to behave, isn't it?'

'Stop it. I don't even know what that sound was.'

'Tittering. Am I doing it wrong? Should I languish too?'

'Don't you dare.' Caro picked up her embroidery and then tossed it aside again. 'All right, I'll ask.'

'Thank you!' Essie jumped up to kiss her cheek. 'But it *has* to be this luncheon.'

'Why?'

'Because it's the Smedley-Bullingdons' annual garden party this afternoon.' She grinned. 'The perfect opportunity for countess-hunting!'

❧

As afternoons went, the Smedley-Bullingdons couldn't have chosen a better one for their garden party, Essie reflected as she climbed the front steps of their riverside townhouse. The sky was a cloudless, lavender-infused blue, the exact same shade as her dress, she noticed with satisfaction, looking between it and her soft muslin pleats with a smile. She'd been dismayed initially to discover that her grandmother had made some last-minute additions to her wardrobe from Madame Liliane, but now it was a pleasure to wear something so gorgeous. With her chestnut hair twisted into ringlets at the back of her neck, she felt almost pretty for once too. At least today she wouldn't be the butt of every joke, not unless people had heard about Sir Purrsalot anyway.

'You look lovely,' Caro whispered as they removed their cloaks in the Smedley-Bullingdons' immense blue and white stuccoed hallway, watched over by a frieze of frolicking sea creatures that included dolphins, seahorses, assorted starfish and one inexplicably grumpy-looking lobster.

'I did look awful before, didn't I?'

'I'm sure the earl will still recognize you. He doesn't seem to mind what you wear.'

'Don't start all that again.' Essie gave her cousin a chiding look as they made their way straight through the house and on to a terrace overlooking a wide lawn that sloped down to the Thames. There was a small jetty and boathouse at the edge, as well as a few boats already out on the water.

'What a beautiful place.' Caro sighed, taking in the view of weeping willows and twirling parasols as the dowager sallied forth to greet some acquaintance. 'It's hard to believe that we're still in a city.'

'I have it on the best authority that Mrs Smedley-Bullingdon pays her head gardener more than her housekeeper,' a male voice drawled behind them.

'Mr Jagger.' Essie turned and smiled at the approaching figure. He was holding a glass of champagne in one hand and a red rose in the other. 'You know, our hostess might not appreciate you stealing her flowers.'

He grinned wolfishly, revealing a row of perfect white teeth. 'I paid a quick visit to the hothouse and I couldn't resist, but you're quite right. I ought to hide the evidence by passing it on. Here.' He held the rose out with a flourish. 'Now you can take the blame.'

'No, thank you.' She laughed and took hold of the stem, snapping it in half and tucking what was left into his buttonhole. 'There. Now it looks like you came with it.'

'You have a devious mind, Miss Craven, a quality I greatly admire in a woman, incidentally. And Miss Foyle.' He turned towards Caro. 'I'm particularly charmed to see you again. Perhaps the pair of you would care to join me on the river?'

'Not me,' Essie answered quickly. She wasn't going to find a replacement countess stuck on a rowing boat. 'I get seasick.'

'On a river?'

'Sometimes on a pond. Do you feel that?' She held a finger up. 'There's a very slight breeze. Almost imperceptible.'

'You obviously have finer sensibilities than I do. What about you, Miss Foyle? Can I tempt you?'

'Oh, I'm not sure –'

'You wouldn't be as cruel as your cousin, surely? One rejection is bad enough. Two would be crushing.' Mr Jagger leaned closer. 'If it makes you feel any safer, I'll find another couple to join us.'

'V-very well.'

'Excellent.' He grabbed Caro's hand, tucking it inside his arm before she had a chance to change her mind. 'Come along, then. Before those waves become too tumultuous.'

Essie waved them off, repressing a pang of guilt at Caro's panicked expression, before turning her attention back to her self-appointed task for the afternoon. There was no sign of Aidan yet, but there was a veritable plethora of potential countesses all around, including the three at the very top of her list: Miss Selina Birtwhistle again, Miss Alicia Culpepper and Lady Phoebe Lestrange. According to her grandmother, each of them had dowries of at least thirty thousand pounds. And they all seemed pleasant and poised and *countessy* enough.

She wandered down the stone steps of the terrace and into the garden, breathing in the heady aromas of jasmine and honeysuckle. The flower beds were magnificent, with bulging early peonies towered over by deep purple lupins and delicate acanthus. Birds and bees and butterflies were all enjoying the scene too, chirping and buzzing and fluttering around the tall stems. Caro was right – it was hard to believe they weren't in the countryside.

Someone called her name and she turned around, heart sinking at the sight of Miss Jemima Talbot. For once, her tormentor appeared to be alone, but her smile still held about as much warmth as a snake trapped in a block of ice. In the North Pole. At night.

'Miss Craven. How different you look this afternoon.'

'Do I?' Essie answered half-heartedly. At least it was some comfort to know that Miss Talbot's behaviour had ruled her out as a candidate.

'Why yes. Usually you're so distinctive.'

'Thank you. Isn't that the same dress you were wearing at the Cumberworths' ball?'

'What? Of course not.' A wash of colour swept over Miss Talbot's cheekbones. 'This one is quite different. Look, it has lace sleeves.'

'Ah, my mistake. They just all look so similar.'

'Miss Craven?' Mr Aloysius Talbot came over to join them at that moment, his expression ten times more enthusiastic than his sister's. 'My word, I didn't recognize you at first. Would you care for some refreshment? Lemonade, perhaps?'

'No, thank you. I've sworn off it.' Out of the corner of her eye, she spotted Aidan standing at the top of the garden steps. 'Now if you'll excuse me, I need to go and greet my fiancé.'

She dropped into a token curtsey before making her way across the lawn, aware of Aidan's eyes first skimming past her before darting back again.

'Essie?' He stared for a few seconds before descending the steps. 'You look –'

'Different? Yes, so people keep telling me.'

'That wasn't what I was going to say.' He reached for her hand, pressing his lips softly against the backs of her knuckles. For a moment, they lingered there, his gaze locked on hers, before his brow creased and he stepped back abruptly. 'So here I am, as instructed. What now?'

'Now . . .' She was faintly alarmed by the squeaky pitch of her voice. 'We take a turn about the garden and discuss your options.'

'*Another* promenade?' He sighed, though his eyes sparked with humour.

'I'm afraid so.'

'Who would have thought that finding a wife involved so much walking? Very well. Lead on, Miss Craven.'

'*And damned be him that first cries, "Hold, enough!"*' she responded with alacrity.

'*Macbeth*. One of my favourites.'

She smiled and started along one of the paths, surprised when Aidan clasped his hands behind his back instead of offering an arm. For some reason, he seemed determined to keep a foot of air between them too. 'How's your back?'

'If you're asking whether I've recovered from carrying you the entire length of Mayfair yesterday, then it appears so. I took a long bath for my aching muscles and vowed never to accompany you anywhere without a spare set of clothes again.' He glanced towards the Thames. 'It might be best to keep away from the water's edge today. I saw a dangerous-looking moorhen a few moments ago.'

'I've had enough bird jokes from Caro, thank you very much.' Essie stuck her nose into the air. 'And if you hadn't carried me yesterday then you'd have an elbow in the ribs at this moment. Now, if you'd be so good as to direct your attention to the left, you'll notice Lady Phoebe Lestrange. She's the one in the white dress.'

'I see five ladies in white dresses.'

'The blonde, but not the blonde with ringlets, the one with a chignon.'

'Understood.'

'Next, on your right, with the black hair, you'll see Miss Selina Birtwhistle. Remember, the swan I told you about? Her dress *looks* white, but it's actually a very pale shade of blue.'

'Duly noted.'

'Then there's Miss Alicia Culpepper, but I can't see her . . .' She rocked back on her heels, twisting her head to search the gardens. 'Oh, there she is in a boat with Mr Jagger and Caro. We'll have to wait for them to come ashore so that you can take a closer look.'

'I'd prefer a conversation.' He frowned. 'Is Mr Jagger paying court to your cousin?'

'If he wasn't before then he probably is now. She seems to have that effect on men.' Essie tugged on his arm. 'So, off the top of your head, who do you favour, Lady Phoebe or Miss Selina? Bearing in mind, you'll have to listen to a vast number of depressing arias with Miss Selina.'

'Off the top of my head, I believe I mentioned preferring brunettes.'

'Miss Selina, then. Although Miss Culpepper's hair is brown too.'

'Since I won't ultimately be basing my choice of wife on hair colour, it hardly matters.'

'But you – oh!' She stopped beside a gap in the hedge. 'Is this what I think it is?'

'Yes, so long as you think it's a maze. Quite a good one, if I recall from my last visit.'

'It could be fun. I'll race you to the middle.'

'Aren't we in the middle of something now?'

'You go right and I'll go left.'

'That's hardly fair when I –'

'*Go!*'

She sprinted off along the left path, glancing over her shoulder at the corner to check that Aidan was heading in the opposite direction. Quickly, she hoisted her skirts up around her knees and ran, first into one dead end, then another, before turning around, retracing her steps and trying another avenue. And then another. And another. Some were narrow and dark, others wide and airy, a few more were occupied by couples she didn't wish to disturb, but at last she made it to the centre, panting, breathless and, evidently, too late. Aidan was already there, stretched out on a stone bench, one of his feet dangling over the edge with the other braced on the floor.

'You made it eventually then?' He turned his head to greet her, smiling lazily. 'I was just taking a nap.'

'You haven't been here *that* long.' She looked around, impressed. The centre of the maze had trellises on each side, ornamented with trailing ivy to form a leafy canopy in the corners. It would be a lovely place to sit and read, if only she'd brought a book.

'I feel quite rested.' He swung his other foot to the floor and sat up, the dappled sunlight adding a bluish sheen to his dark locks. 'You know, you forgot one important strategic point.'

'Which is?'

'I've done this maze before.'

'Oh.' She slid on to the bench beside him, fanning her face. 'You're right, I ought to have thought of that. Now I'm all hot and sweaty.'

'I believe the correct term is "becomingly flushed".'

'Then I'm becomingly flushed and sweaty, although my aunt would say a lady isn't supposed to sweat at all.'

'Or to mention sweat, probably.'

'Are gentlemen allowed to?' She tipped her head sideways and sniffed. 'Sweat, that is.'

'Are you smelling me?' He sounded startled and amused at the same time.

'Only a little.' She pulled her face away in a hurry. The truth was, he smelled good, a combination of bergamot and musk and something else that was just . . . him. As scents went, it was surprisingly potent, making her heart perform a small leap in her chest, like a bird taking flight. Or doing a somersault. Or both.

'And?'

'You smell . . . nice. Not sweaty at all.'

'So do you.' He moved his face closer to hers, causing the bird to perform several more aerobatic contortions, as if it were trying to escape up her throat. Becomingly flushed was one thing, but the touch of his breath on her cheek was making her feel damp all over. 'Like rosewater.'

'That's just my hair. My grandmother's maid suggested rinsing with it.'

His shoulder nudged lightly against hers. 'I like it.'

Essie opened her mouth to respond and found that she couldn't. The air seemed too heavy, too charged with some unspoken feeling, rendering speech impossible. He seemed to feel the same way because they both remained completely motionless, as if time had just stopped and they were the only two people in the maze, or the garden, or the whole world for that matter. She felt far too aware of her own heartbeat, of the scent of bergamot lingering in her nostrils, of the light pressure of his arm against hers. She had a feeling that she was never going to smell bergamot again without also remembering this moment. This intense, heady, pulse-accelerating moment. She fixed her gaze on a wasp climbing the trellis beside them, afraid to turn her head in case she did something foolish. Something that would ruin all of her plans and ambitions for the future, even if part of her was tempted. A bigger part than she would have expected.

'Beautiful.' His voice penetrated her thoughts finally, sounding deeper and huskier than usual. 'That's what I was going to say earlier. Not that you look different. That you look beautiful.'

'Oh.' Her head seemed to turn of its own accord, her eyes holding his for a second before dropping to his mouth. She hadn't noticed before, but his top lip was slightly fuller than his bottom one. It looked temptingly soft too. How would it feel? She could find out if she just leaned over and pressed her own against it . . .

'Found it!' A boy came hurtling around the corner of the hedge at that moment, closely followed by two companions.

'Well done.' Essie leaped to her feet as if they were miniature vagabonds wielding swords.

'Sorry, miss!' The first boy skidded to a halt. 'Sorry, sir.'

'There's a statue somewhere.' The second boy was less apologetic, his red face bursting with enthusiasm. 'We have to find it to prove we reached the centre!'

'It's over here.' A third boy was already burrowing through the ivy. 'It's a Cupid!'

'So it is.' Essie peered closer. The statue was holding a bow and arrow, its pointed tip aiming straight towards the bench where she and Aidan had just been sitting.

'There's an engraving too,' the third boy continued. '"Love looks not with the eyes, but with the mind, and therefore is winged Cupid painted blind." Urgh!'

'Shakespeare,' Essie murmured. '*A Midsummer Night's Dream.*'

'That wasn't worth finding.' All three boys looked deeply unimpressed.

'Don't you think?' Aidan's gaze latched on to hers, filled with a new intensity. 'You might see things differently one day.'

'It's about time you reappeared.' The dowager marched up to her at one of the refreshment tables.

'Sorry, Grandmama.' Essie put on a smile, trying not to look as shaken as she still felt. 'I was exploring the maze.'

'I know exactly where you were *and* who you were with. Who do you think sent those boys in after you?'

'What? We were only talking!' she answered defensively, horribly aware that she couldn't quite look her grandmother in the eye as she said it.

'It doesn't matter what you were or weren't doing. It's what you might have been perceived to be doing that concerns me, especially under the circumstances.'

'What circumstances?' She tensed, alerted by something in her grandmother's tone.

'I may be old, my dear, but I have eyes and ears and I believe that you may be playing a very dangerous game.'

'I don't know what you mean.'

'Of course you don't.' Her grandmother rolled her eyes before turning to survey the garden. 'Fortunately for you, I'm even more displeased with your cousin.'

'Caro? But she never does anything wrong.'

'Except for spending the past hour with *that man*.'

'Mr Jagger?' Essie blinked, surprised but relieved not to be the subject of her grandmother's attention any longer. 'Don't you like him?'

'You're missing the point again. Liking is irrelevant. I don't trust him. The man's a rake, if ever I saw one.'

'Well, she's not with him now. She's talking to Mr Dormer.'

'I know. I dealt with her situation before addressing yours. Now there's a *much* more suitable gentleman. Only the second son of a viscount, but with a reasonable fortune, unlike Mr Jagger. From what I hear, *he* owes money all over London. Altogether, it's been a downright vexing afternoon.'

'Sorry, Grandmama.'

'Meanwhile, it appears your fiancé has found himself another young lady to talk to.'

'Has he?' She followed the direction of her grandmother's gaze to where Aidan was conversing with

Lady Phoebe. And not just conversing, but laughing too. Which was exactly what she'd told him to do, she reminded herself, even if the sight made her reach for a strawberry tart.

'Her dowry is sixty thousand pounds. Substantially bigger than yours, my dear,' her grandmother murmured. 'But then you already knew that, didn't you?'

Chapter Thirteen

'What's the matter?' Caro's voice penetrated the thick layer of bedclothes drawn tight over Essie's head. 'Why didn't you come down for breakfast?'

'I'm not feeling well.' Slowly, Essie poked the top of her head over the edge of her quilt, wincing as daylight bounced off her eyeballs. 'I think I ate too many strawberry tarts yesterday.'

'That's never made you sick before.'

'I had three in a row. Or maybe four. And a piece of caraway cake. And some macaroons.' She rolled on to her side, wrapping her arms around her stomach with a whimper. She had a vague memory of a mille-feuille being involved too. The worst part was that she hadn't tasted a bite.

'Why don't we go for a ride in the park this morning?' Caro rubbed her shoulder sympathetically. 'That always cheers you up.'

'It won't, not today. I just want to lie here and moan.'

'What about the Lockharts' garden party later?'

'No more garden parties. They're bad for my health.'

'Well, I enjoyed yesterday,' said Caro. 'Your Mr Jagger is very entertaining.'

'He's not *my* Mr Jagger, and Grandmother says not to trust him.'

'That's what I thought at first too, but he was actually quite charming.' Caro sucked her bottom lip into her mouth and then released it again with a pop. 'Although he did say some terribly wicked things. Did you know that Lady Phoebe turned down a proposal from Sir Reginald Wolstonescroft last week? Sylvester says it's because she's in love with her father's secretary, although I hope that's not true since she'd never be allowed to marry him.'

'Really?' Essie forgot all about her stomach ache and sat up. Now that *was* interesting. Lady Phoebe hadn't looked particularly like a woman in love with another man while she'd been talking to Aidan, especially considering the number of times she'd twirled her hair during their conversation, an average of three times a minute over the course of a full half hour, but then what *did* a woman in love look like? Perhaps she ought to tell Aidan the rumours just in case?

No sooner had the thought entered her head than she flung herself back down on to her pillow again. What kind of a person would she be if she shared scandalous, probably untrue, rumours about another debutante? And even if they were true, Aidan probably wouldn't care. He'd been very clear that he was only looking for a fortune in a wife. He might not even mind if her heart belonged to someone else. It was a supremely depressing thought.

'Maybe I ought to send for a doctor.' Caro pressed a hand to her forehead. 'You don't seem yourself.'

'I know.'

'Have you considered that this might not be entirely due to strawberry tarts?'

'I've no idea what you mean.'

'Yes, you do.' Caro pursed her lips. 'Maybe you're starting to change your mind about the earl. You were in the maze together for long enough.'

'It was a maze! I got lost. And of course I like him. He's much nicer than I thought at first.'

'Well then?'

'Liking doesn't mean we should get married! You know how I feel about that!'

'Fine, but he was stealing glances at you the whole time he was talking to those other debutantes,' Caro argued. 'I really think he likes you. And I know you're as stubborn as a mule, but perhaps you ought to consider how much you like him back before it's too late and he's married to someone else.'

'I don't need to think about anything.' Essie lifted her head expressly to scowl. The very idea that she might be changing her mind was ludicrous. Laughable. Even if she didn't feel like laughing and the combination of pastry regret and something that she refused to accept was jealousy had kept her awake for most of the night. All of her protests felt a lot less convincing now than they'd been two days ago. And she had only herself to blame. She ought never to have let him take her to Gunter's. Dessert was a bad influence.

Caro leaned closer, lowering her voice to a whisper. 'Maybe you should kiss him.'

'Caro!'

'Just to see how it feels. You might like it.'

Essie stared at her normally modest and mild-mannered cousin in amazement. 'Does this mean that *you've* kissed someone?' The coy look on her cousin's face answered the question for her. 'You have!'

'Only briefly, but it was very educational.'

'Caroline Arabella Foyle, who was it?'

'Get out of bed and I might tell you.'

'I can't. I really do feel unwell.'

'Then *I'm* going for a ride and you'll just have to keep wondering.' Caro skipped towards the door. 'Should I send anything up? Tea?'

'No. I'm just going to lie here with my mind boggling.'

'Suit yourself, but you're going to miss all the fun.'

'It was Mr Dormer, wasn't it? Tell me it was him.'

Caro lifted her shoulders one after the other in a curious squirming motion. 'I'll be back in an hour if you change your mind about the garden party.'

Essie stared hard at the door after her cousin had gone, seized with the troubling impression that somewhere in their conversation she'd just missed something important.

'Get up! You have a visitor.'

'Huh? What?' Essie prised her eyelids open again to find her grandmother looming at the end of her bed, ten times louder than Caro and a thousand times harder to resist. 'Who?'

'Your fiancé.'

'Aidan? Now?' She propped herself up on her elbows, shaking her head to clear the fog of sleep. 'What does he want?'

'Yes, yes, and I have no idea.'

'What time is it? Shouldn't he be at the garden party?'

'It's three o'clock and I don't manage his diary, my dear.'

'But why aren't you there? I thought Caro wanted to go?'

'She did and she has. Lady Talbot offered to chaperone her.'

'Urgh.'

'I agree, the daughter does have rather sharp claws. Nonetheless, there's an earl downstairs waiting for you.'

'I'm indisposed.'

'Married ladies are allowed to be indisposed. Debutantes are not. Now, do I need to drag you out by your feet or will you be able to prise yourself up?' The dowager's eyes flashed threateningly. 'I can't abide moping.'

'I'm not moping.'

'Indisposed is code for moping. I've never moped a day in my life.'

'I'll prise myself up.'

'I'm delighted to hear it, especially since I've arranged a treat for us this evening. I thought that you might like to pay a visit to Drury Lane.'

'The theatre?' Essie jumped out of bed, clasping her hands together. 'Oh, thank you! I'd like that more than anything!'

'Good.' Her grandmother regarded her critically. 'Although I admit you do look a touch peaky. I'll ask Cook to make chicken soup for dinner. *No* dessert. Oh, good gracious, look at your hair. Birds could nest there.'

'Aidan doesn't care about hair,' Essie announced confidently, thrusting her arms into a blue satin gown and then catching sight of her reflection in her wardrobe mirror. 'Well . . . maybe I'll give it a quick tidy.'

'Do. In the meantime, I'll regale him with conversation about the weather. I suggest that you take pity on the poor man and make haste.'

'I'll do my best.' Essie sat in front of her dressing table and dragged a brush painfully through her knotted curls. Not that it really mattered what she looked like for Aidan. Caro's words might have hit somewhat closer to home than they would have a week ago, but they were still wildly off target. How could she possibly want Aidan for herself when she still had every intention of finding him a replacement countess? For all she knew, that was why he was visiting this afternoon, to give her news of an engagement already. That would explain why he hadn't gone to the Lockharts' garden party. And he'd spent all that time with Lady Phoebe yesterday . . .

Before she knew it, she was ramming her feet into a pair of slippers and running down the stairs two at a time, the definitely-not-jealousy feeling flaring up with a vengeance that made her stomach churn even more.

'Ah, here she is.' Her grandmother looked around as Essie hurtled inelegantly into the drawing room. 'We were just discussing the possibility of rain on Thursday. Come and have a cup of tea, my dear, if you think you can manage it?'

'Are you feeling unwell?' Aidan stood up at once, his expression full of concern.

'Better since I've had a nap.' She shot her grandmother a pointed look and picked up the teapot, wincing at the sight of a plate of biscuits beside it. 'I'm sure it's nothing to worry about.'

'I really must speak to Cook about that soup.' The dowager got to her feet at the same moment as Essie sat down. 'Do excuse me, Denholm.'

'Of course, Lady Makepeace.'

'I didn't expect to see you today.' Essie lifted her cup to her lips, immediately scalding her tongue. 'I thought you'd be at the Lockharts'.'

'So did I, but my mother and sister arrived in town unexpectedly this morning. I didn't expect them for another two weeks. That's why I'm here, in fact.'

'Oh?' She was aware of the churning abating slightly. No engagement yet, then . . .

'Actually, I came to warn you. I'm afraid that my mother wishes to throw us a dinner party.' He rubbed a hand around the back of his neck. 'To celebrate our engagement.'

'Ah.'

'And since we're still officially engaged . . .'

'Yes, I see.' She forgot about the tea's temperature and scalded herself again. 'That's very kind of her, especially after the way I behaved at Redcliffe. All my headaches, I mean.'

'I tried my best to deter her, but she's quite determined.'

'Well then . . .' Essie lifted a shoulder. 'Perhaps a dinner party won't be so bad? I like food. Usually.'

'You wouldn't mind?' He gave her a curious look. 'I was thinking of proposing a trip to Vauxhall Gardens as an alternative. You ought to visit at least once while you're in town.'

'Vauxhall?' She opened her eyes wide with excitement. She really did want to see the gardens, even if it meant spending more time with him when something told her that wasn't such a good idea, especially when she was supposed to be finding her own replacement . . . although surely there would be candidates at Vauxhall too? 'Oh, that's a much better idea. I'd like that very much.'

'Good. In that case, how about next Friday? We can take a boat from Westminster. Your cousin and grandmother are invited too, naturally.'

'I'm sure they'll be thrilled.' She smiled warmly. 'What about your sister? Will I make her acquaintance then too?'

'About that . . .' He hesitated, sounding as if he were trying to be tactful. 'Forgive me, but I'd prefer it if you didn't. She's particularly excited about meeting you, but given our plans . . . I shouldn't like her to be disappointed when we end things.'

'Oh. Yes, I see.' She felt oddly deflated. 'Of course. Quite understandable. I'll look forward to it anyway.'

'As will I.'

'So . . .' She cleared her throat after a few moments of awkward silence. 'How did you like Lady Phoebe? You seemed to be enjoying your conversation with her yesterday.'

Aidan's good-humoured expression seemed to freeze and then fade, a frown notching itself between his brows instead. 'Yes, she was very pleasant.'

'Good countess material?'

'Undoubtedly.'

'Did you find much in common?'

'As I recall, we kept our conversation on more general matters.'

'What about Miss Selina?'

'Unfortunately, we didn't have an opportunity to speak.' He put his teacup aside. 'Now if you'll excuse me, I have some business matters to attend to.'

'So soon?'

'I'm afraid so.'

'Wait!' She lifted a hand.

'Yes?'

'I . . .' Essie stared at her fingers, at a loss for what she wanted to say. 'Nothing. I've forgotten.'

He inclined his head, his features softening imperceptibly. 'Until next Friday, then.'

'Won't I see you again beforehand? I mean, that's over a week away and there are other candidates we need to discuss.'

'I believe I have enough to be going on with.' A shutter dropped over his face. 'I hope you feel better soon, Essie.'

She nodded, waiting until his footsteps had receded before putting her own teacup aside, throwing herself on to the sofa and burying her face in the cushions.

Approximately five hours later, Essie dropped an orange into her lap, folded her arms over the top of a leather-rimmed balcony and peered into the crowd below. The Theatre Royal was bigger than any ballroom or assembly room she'd ever visited, painted in rich shades of maroon and gold, with velvet brocade curtains draped across the stage and gilt-encrusted columns on either side. The size of the audience was impressive too, though thankfully her grandmother had reserved a box for the evening, giving them a perfect vantage point for viewing both the stage and the crush below.

'*The Merchant of Bruges* . . .' Caro murmured, studying the programme.

'Mmm.' Their grandmother sounded disappointed. 'I admit I was hoping for something a little more bloodthirsty, but it should suffice. There's a new actress tonight, I believe. Hannah something. Now that Mrs Siddons has retired, the theatres are all looking for the next great tragic heroine.' She looked sternly at Essie. 'Don't get any ideas.'

'Wouldn't it be wonderful, though?' Essie grinned in reply. 'Did you ever see Mrs Siddons?'

'Oh yes, and I have to say she was quite wonderful. People actually fainted during her performances. I almost cried once myself during her *Hamlet*. It's hard to imagine another like her.'

'Maybe because you haven't seen me act yet.'

'Haven't I? Besides, life in the theatre isn't all acclaim. Take Dorothea Jordan. Such comic timing! An excellent actress until she became –' the dowager directed her gaze upwards as if she were searching for a *mot juste* in the rafters – '*friendly* with the Duke of Clarence.'

'Friendly?'

'Enough to have a house full of children together. Then five years ago he abandoned her for a wealthy bride and forbade her from ever acting again. They say she lives in a boarding house in Paris now, poor woman.'

'Well . . .' Essie removed her elbows from the balustrade and began peeling her orange. 'I suppose the moral of that story is not to get *friendly* with men. Dukes, especially.'

'Famous last words, my dear.'

'Do you think we could go backstage and talk to the actors afterwards?'

'Absolutely not.'

'But –'

'*Absolutely* not. Only gentlemen go backstage and it's generally not just to give compliments on the performance. Some things are beyond the pale, my dear.'

'Oh, very well.' Essie twisted towards her cousin. 'You're being very quiet tonight. Are you still thinking about the Lockharts' party?'

'Mmm?' Caro gave a small start. 'No, of course not.'

'It wouldn't be a crime if you were. Was Mr Dormer there?'

'Yes.'

'And?'

'And nothing. He was there, that's all.'

'But did you –' She caught her breath, abandoning her question as the curtain lifted suddenly and the play began. It was, to Essie's awe-inspired mind, absolutely mesmerizing. The dialogue was witty. The scenery inventive. The actors sublime. Annoyingly, the rest of the audience appeared less enamoured, barely half of them paying any attention to the play. It wasn't so much of a performance as background entertainment.

'Why are people talking?' she hissed to Caro towards the end of the second act. 'I could hardly hear that last speech.'

'Grandmama says a lot of people come to the theatre just to mingle.'

'But the play is so good! They're insulting the performers.'

'Maybe they're accustomed to it.'

'And *he's* the worst!' She narrowed her eyes at a man in the pit below. She couldn't see his face, only the top of his head, but he was making absolutely no attempt to keep his voice down. He'd even laughed during one particularly affecting soliloquy when the Beggar King had dropped to his knees, lamenting his lost kingdom . . .

'Someone ought to teach him a lesson.' She picked up a piece of discarded orange peel and took aim.

'Essie, don't!' Caro made a grab for her wrist, but it was too late. The peel was already sailing through the air, straight on target, hitting the man squarely on the back of his neck.

'How could you!' Caro dropped from her seat on to the floor.

'Because he deserved it, whoever he is. Oh . . . oh dear.'

'What?'

'It's Mr Jagger.'

'Mr Jagger?' Caro's head popped up again. 'Is he angry?'

'Actually, he appears to be laughing.'

'You know, for someone who doesn't like people disturbing the play, you're doing a fairly good job of it yourself.'

Essie blinked at her cousin's uncharacteristically snappy tone. Caro even looked different, her lips pursing in a way that reminded her alarmingly of Aunt Emmeline. 'I'm sorry. I won't say another word until the end of the act, I promise.'

'Dare I enter?' Mr Jagger's smiling face appeared around the curtain at the back of the box during the interval. 'Or am I likely to be pelted with rotten eggs?'

'It was only orange peel and you're perfectly safe so long as you don't talk during any more of the performance.'

Essie thrust her chin up defiantly. 'Otherwise, it'll be a shoe.'

'Mercy forfend.' He held his hands up. 'You're absolutely right, of course. I've been appallingly rude and I've come to offer my sincerest apologies. In my defence, however, I heard the most salacious piece of gossip earlier and I couldn't resist passing it on.' His eyes glinted. 'Which brings me to why I'm here.'

'We're not interested in gossip.'

'How very dull of you.' He turned his gaze towards Caro. 'I'm sure Miss Foyle here is interested, aren't you, Miss Foyle?'

'Mr Jagger.' Their grandmother interrupted him. 'If you have scandal to impart then I suggest you come and sit here with me. My granddaughters are young ladies.'

'I'd be honoured, my lady, but perhaps I might fetch us all some champagne first? To make amends for my dreadful behaviour.'

'How big a bottle would that require, I wonder? But you're too late.' The dowager gestured to several glasses on the table beside her. 'When it comes to champagne, you'll find I'm generally prepared.'

'Lady Makepeace?' Another face appeared around the curtain. 'I wonder if I might come in and pay my respects?'

The dowager inclined her head. '*You* may.'

'Mr Dormer.' Essie greeted him when Caro seemed utterly tongue-tied. 'How good to see you again. Are you enjoying the performance?'

'Very much. The actors are on particularly good form tonight. And don't look now, but have you seen who's in the box opposite?' He laughed as she immediately turned her head. 'Maria Kemble herself. She and her husband usually perform at Covent Garden, but they must be inspecting the competition tonight.'

'Oh, how wonderful! My cousin Felix told me about her. She looks so elegant and distinguished.' Essie sighed happily, thrilled to find a fellow enthusiast. 'Do you come to the theatre often?'

'As often as I can.'

'What about the earl?' She glanced past him towards the curtain. 'Is he here too?'

'Sadly not. He seems to be avoiding the theatre this Season for some reason.'

'Oh.' She stifled a pang of disappointment. 'So tell me, what are your favourite plays?'

'Shakespeare's histories, without a doubt. *Henry V*, in particular.'

'Who cares about history?' Having imparted his gossip to her grandmother, Mr Jagger drew a chair up behind Essie's shoulder. 'Personally, I favour a love story. *Romeo and Juliet. Troilus and Cressida. Anthony and Cleopatra.* So much more passionate.'

'I'm surprised you're ever able to hear them.' Essie arched her eyebrows.

'*Touché.*' He leaned forward, drawling in her ear as Mr Dormer took the seat next to Caro, 'In that case, perhaps I ought to remain here for the second half where you can keep an eye on me?'

Essie tensed, fighting the urge to recoil. The feeling of Mr Jagger's breath on her neck was nothing remotely like the feeling of Aidan's. The shiver it sent down her spine was entirely different. Mr Dormer was looking in their direction too, she noticed, a troubled expression on his usually cheerful face. She felt a sudden impulse to defend herself, to ask him not to tell Aidan about this either, not that there was anything so shocking to impart. She was conversing with an acquaintance about the play, that was all. Unfortunately, she had a horrible feeling that she wasn't going to enjoy the second half nearly as much as the first.

Chapter Fourteen

'*Where* have you been?' Caro stormed out of the morning parlour, accompanied by an eager-looking Mildred, the moment Essie stepped through their grandmother's front door.

'Hatchards bookshop.' Essie deposited a pile of leather-bound tomes on to the hallway table and then stepped back to let her maid do the same. 'Thank you, Sarah. Now go and rest your arms. I won't bother you for the rest of the afternoon, I promise.' She smiled gratefully before turning back to Caro. 'I told you at breakfast.'

'I didn't think you'd be there all morning!'

'I got carried away. Oh dear, you thought I was someone else, didn't you?' Essie crouched down to ruffle Mildred's ears. 'Isn't Grandmama back yet either?'

'No! And she promised to be back by twelve.'

'She said she was going to visit an old friend. They've probably lost track of time.'

'It's almost visiting hours!'

'And?'

'And we can't receive callers on our own.'

'Then we'll just have to say we're not at home.' Essie grinned. 'I've always wanted to say that.'

'But I don't *want* to not be at home!' Caro stamped her foot in frustration. 'This is so unfair!'

'Why are you so concerned?' Essie cocked her head to one side, wondering who this highly strung stranger in front of her was and what she'd done with her cousin. 'Is something the matter? Or are you expecting someone in particular?'

'No.' Two spots of colour blazed across Caro's cheekbones. 'I just think it's insensitive of you both to be late. I had to eat luncheon all on my own.'

'Then I'm sorry. I wasn't hungry, but I should have thought about you.' Essie spread her hands out apologetically. 'Anyway, I'm here now, and you look very pretty, by the way. I've never seen you with curls before.'

'Thank you.' Caro spun on her heel and went back into the morning parlour, seating herself at the piano and starting to play, her long fingers flying across the keys so fast they barely seemed to stop.

'So . . . what have you been up to?' Essie followed her, leaning over the back of the instrument.

'What do you mean?'

'Today. It can't have taken since breakfast to curl your hair.'

'Of course not. I went for a walk.' Caro's gaze shot back to hers. 'I took a maid.'

'Well, obviously.' Essie rolled her eyes. 'Even *I* know that rule by now. So where did you walk?'

'Just around the square and into the park. I wanted some fresh air.'

'Did you meet anyone?'

'A few of our acquaintances, yes.'

'Mr Dormer perhaps?'

'Why am I being interrogated?' Caro swung around on her stool. 'Especially when you ought to be getting changed.'

'I thought I'd stay like this.' Essie moved away from the piano and lay down on a sofa, making an *oof* sound as Mildred immediately jumped on top of her.

'But you're wearing an outdoor gown,' Caro persisted.

'What does it matter? Nobody's coming to visit me.'

'The earl might.'

'I doubt it. The last time we spoke, he said he'd see me next week.' She sighed and smoothed a hand over Mildred's head. 'I've never seen a dog look depressed before. Grandmama will be back soon, don't worry.'

'That animal's been under my feet all day.'

'It can't be helped. Grandmama says she doesn't like carriages.'

'I wish that she'd try. I've hardly been able to move without her pestering me for attention.'

Essie wrapped a protective arm around Mildred. That settled it. Something was definitely wrong. Caro was usually the softest-hearted person she knew. 'Those are nice.' She gestured towards a vase of red roses on the mantelpiece. 'Is one of your suitors finally branching out from pink?'

'Yes.' Caro's voice was almost drowned out as she started playing again.

'Dare I ask who?'

'I don't know. I got the cards muddled up.'

'What a shame.'

'Yes.'

'Caro . . .' Essie exchanged a profound look with Mildred. 'Are you all right?'

'Perfectly.'

'Because if you weren't, or if you were upset about something, I'm here if you want to talk. Or rant. I know I've been monopolizing the conversation a lot recently.' She paused expectantly. 'I mean, it must feel like a lot of pressure.'

'What must?'

'All of this. The Season. Being expected to find a husband.'

Caro's playing slowed. 'It's not what I envisaged. I didn't think it would be so confusing.'

'What do you mean?'

There was a long pause before Caro's fingers stilled. 'It's just that I know my parents want me to marry well and I know that I have a duty to them. But what if my heart tells me to do something else?'

'If your heart is warning you against the Marquess of Bazley then listen to it. I forbid you from marrying him. I'll object during the ceremony if I have to.'

'Thank you, but it's not just him.' Caro smiled, looking almost like her old self again. 'I must have lived with you for too long because now I think, what about what *I* want? What about –' She stopped talking and sprang to her feet at the sound of the front door opening.

'*Ow!*' Essie yelped as Mildred used her stomach as a springboard to launch herself across the floor. 'I think Grandmama's home.'

'Of course I am!' The dowager appeared in the doorway, Mildred already cradled in her arms like a newborn. 'I said one o'clock and here I am.'

'You said twelve.' Caro's petulant tone was back.

'Did I? Well, never mind, I'm here now, aren't I, my sweetest girly-whirly-twirly-birly?' She tickled the pug's furry belly. 'Mummy missed you so much.'

'Why aren't we your sweetest girly-whirly-twirly-birlies?' Essie lifted her eyebrows.

'Certain positions need to be earned, my dear. *Quill*?' The dowager tipped her head back, booming over her shoulder. 'Tea!'

'Did you have a nice meeting with your friend?'

'Very pleasant, thank you.' The dowager turned briskly to Caro. 'You're looking particularly fetching, my dear. Quite pulchritudinous in fact. No doubt your legions of admirers will be arriving at any moment.'

'Just hopefully not the Marquess of Bazley,' Essie interjected. 'You won't make Caro marry him, will you, Grandmama?'

'Absolutely not. The man was a disgusting young lech in my day and he's a disgusting old lech now. If he lays so much as a finger on you, I'll cut his hand off. And other appendages besides. Now before I forget, we're dining at the house of Sir William Keaton and his wife tonight. He's a dreadful bore, but she was a good friend of Emmeline's in their youth. Take note, they have two sons of marriageable age. One of them is quite tolerable, although I can never remember which.'

'Do we have to go out tonight?' Essie groaned.

'Yes. Incidentally, Lady Keaton mentioned that Mr Jagger will also be attending. I strongly suggest you don't let him monopolize your attention again like at the theatre.'

'That wasn't my fault.'

'No, but it won't do to start any rumours. It would be best for you to avoid him altogether.'

'In that case, maybe I ought to stay here to be safe? I have a pile of new books and you know how lonely Mildred gets. We could eat cheese and play fetch and be sweetest girly-whirly-twirly-birlies together.'

'Most considerate of you, my dear. However, I've already accepted the invitation. Ah.' The dowager tilted her head at the sound of a knock. 'Here come Caro's suitors, beginning with . . .' She paused, waiting for the drawing-room door to open. 'Mr Dormer. How delightful.'

'Do you like snuff, Miss Craven?'

'I beg your pardon?' Essie paused in the act of spearing a stalk of asparagus with her fork, wishing that she'd pressed harder to stay at home with Mildred. The Keatons' dinner party was beginning to feel interminable. She'd been seated between an elderly soldier who hadn't said a single word to anyone all evening and Mr Jonathan Keaton, the elder of the two Keaton brothers, a man with a handsome face and limited conversation. They'd spent twenty minutes discussing the table decorations and soup and then lapsed into complete silence. And there were still ten courses to go.

'Snuff.' Mr Keaton repeated, brown eyes twinkling with a sudden burst of enthusiasm. 'Do you like it? I collect snuff boxes, you know. Twenty-four at the last count.'

'How interesting.' She lifted the asparagus to her mouth, glancing wistfully across the table to where Caro was sitting between Mr Samuel Keaton and Mr Jagger. Whatever they were talking about, it surely *had* to be more interesting than snuff. In fact, it definitely was if Caro's face was any indication. All of her earlier moodiness seemed to have completely evaporated.

'A lot of people think snuff boxes are merely practical containers, but there's a lot more to them, let me tell you. They come in all shapes and sizes. Most are rectangular or oval-shaped, I confess, but I have one in the shape of a shoe.' Mr Keaton laughed. 'A shoe! Can you imagine?'

'Not easily.'

He nudged his chair closer, lowering his voice confidentially. 'One of mine is pure gold, although of course most are lacquer or bone or mother-of-pearl. My personal favourite is silver inlaid with emeralds. It has *four* compartments.'

'Fancy that.'

'Perhaps you'd care to take a look at my collection later? I'd be honoured to show you.'

'Oh.' Essie reached for another stalk of asparagus. Apparently, when Mr Keaton liked a subject, he *really* liked it. 'Perhaps after coffee.'

'Coffee?' Mr Keaton chuckled. 'I never touch the stuff. Doesn't go with snuff, you know.'

Essie smiled politely, actively pining for her lost evening with Mildred. They could have been curled up together beside the fireplace by now, enjoying a cup of hot chocolate and a dish of water respectively.

'Do you collect anything, Miss Craven?'

'Mmm? Oh, no.' She shook her head. 'I'm afraid not, unless you count books. Anything by or about Shakespeare. I find his work endlessly fascinating.'

'Indeed?' Her companion regarded her quizzically. 'A lady who likes reading. How singular.'

'Plenty of ladies enjoy reading, believe me. Do you have any favourite authors?'

'I read an excellent pamphlet about the health benefits of snuff recently. It's excellent for the digestion, you know.'

'I think we may have to agree to disagree. I once knew a man who took so much that his nose turned purple and one side of his jaw —'

'Headaches too.' Mr Keaton spoke over her.

'Indeed?' She gritted her teeth at the interruption. 'Perhaps I ought to take some right now.'

'My dear Miss Craven.' Mr Keaton looked positively overjoyed. 'Nothing would give me greater pleasure, but it's not the done thing during dinner. An insult to the cook, you know. Wait until we retire to the drawing room.'

'What a treat.' Essie moved a little away discreetly, wondering what Aidan was doing at that precise moment. Dining with his mother and sister probably. *Not* talking about snuff certainly. She'd never seen him take so much as a pinch ... Maybe he was busy thinking about the candidates. Maybe he'd already chosen. Maybe he was talking to her, whoever she was, at this very minute. In which case, surely their trip to Vauxhall would be cancelled ... ? She blinked as something bright flashed in front of her eyes suddenly, looking up to find Mr Jagger tilting his fork so that it reflected light from one of the candles into her face. As she caught his eye he gave her a swift grin, followed by an eye-roll, before turning his attention back to her cousin.

She frowned and cast a sideways look at her companion, dismayed to find that he'd obviously witnessed the eye-roll too.

'Ah, I see that my snuff boxes don't really interest you.' Mr Keaton looked crestfallen.

'On the contrary.' Essie felt a pang of guilt. 'I'd love to hear more.'

'There's no need to be polite. Most young ladies aren't interested.'

'But I am. Truly. I like to learn new things. And now that I think of it, the Queen enjoys snuff, doesn't she?'

'Oh yes indeed, she's a greater connoisseur than myself.'

'Then you're in excellent company. Now tell me, how many snuff jars do you have?'

'You know about snuff jars?' He gave a small jolt.

'Oh yes, my uncle keeps one in his study.'

'Capital fellow! I say, Miss Craven.' Mr Keaton smiled shyly. 'I'm jolly glad that I was seated next to you tonight. I do find these events rather trying. Conversation seems to come easily to some people, but I always feel like I'm saying the wrong thing.'

'I know exactly what you mean.' Essie glanced surreptitiously up and down the table. 'Actually, I tried to persuade my grandmother to let me stay at home and eat cheese.'

'Cheese?' Mr Keaton's breath actually seemed to catch. 'Now that's another subject I could talk about for hours.'

'Then you're definitely sitting next to the right person.' She put her knife and fork down with an enthusiastic clatter. 'Now, if you had to choose only one, which would it be? A Somerset Cheddar, a Derbyshire Stilton or a Yorkshire Wensleydale?'

Chapter Fifteen

'I've been hearing great things about you,' Aidan murmured in Essie's ear as they climbed out of the wherry and on to dry land.

'And this surprises you?' She smiled and took his arm as they started up the stone steps leading from the south side of the Thames towards Vauxhall Gardens. It felt easy. Natural. It made her realize that she'd missed him over the past week too. 'What have you heard?'

'It was a bit bizarre, to be honest. I was sitting in my club the other morning minding my own business when one of the Keaton brothers came over and told me how lucky I was. It's not every day a man meets a fellow cheese enthusiast, apparently.'

'Oh.' Essie laughed. 'We were seated together at a dinner party the other evening. There was a small difference of opinion regarding snuff, but in our love of cheese we were united. I ended up enjoying myself immensely.'

'Well, you're a splendid young filly and I'm a damned fortunate buck, he tells me.'

'Of course we are. Did you know that he has twenty-four snuff boxes?'

'I do now, including one –'

'Shaped like a shoe!' she interrupted. 'Actually, he showed it to me afterwards and it was quite pretty.'

'Well, now I know what to get you if I ever need a gift.' Aidan chuckled. 'By the way, I'm sorry that Miss Foyle couldn't join us tonight. Your grandmother said she has a headache?'

'Ye-es. That's what Caro told us, but there was something odd about her, as if there was more she wanted to say.' Essie knitted her brows. Her cousin hadn't looked particularly sick when she'd said that she wouldn't be joining them, although her eyes had been a little over-bright, as if she were agitated about something. 'But I'm probably imagining things. It's such a shame that she's missing tonight. I know she's been longing to visit.'

'We could always come back another time, if you'd rather go home and take care of her?'

'And tell my grandmother she just spent half an hour in a boat for no reason? She'd skin us both alive.' Essie snorted. 'But I appreciate the offer.'

He squeezed her arm. 'I'm sure your grandmother wouldn't have come if she was really concerned about Miss Foyle's condition.'

'I suppose not. Oh!' Essie stopped walking abruptly, her jaw dropping at the vista before them. The great, wrought-iron gates of Vauxhall stood open to reveal a long, open-air walkway lined with private boxes, pavilions and hundreds of trees, all decorated with glowing, multi-coloured lanterns. It looked like a fairyland come to life. 'It's beautiful!' It took her several seconds to find her voice again.

'It's crowded,' her grandmother harrumphed.

'It always is,' the Countess of Denholm agreed. 'Apparently they once had twenty thousand people in one evening.' She placed a hand on Aidan's other arm. 'I never told you this, but your father proposed to me here. He'd already asked my father for permission to pay his addresses so I knew it was coming, but it was still very romantic.'

'I shouldn't ask any questions about it, if I were you.' Her grandmother winked. 'The grottos here are infamous. *His* father might have intended to be leg-shackled, but plenty of men have found themselves trapped into unexpected proposals along these avenues. Speaking of which, the countess and I have no intention of following the two of you around all evening like a pair of guard dogs. My lord –' she addressed Aidan – 'I hope that you can be trusted to behave with honour. I don't care for scandal, not involving my own family anyway.'

'Then I promise to cause none.' He bowed. 'I'll return Miss Craven with her reputation untarnished.'

'Good. In that case, we'll meet you in our box in an hour. If you're late, we'll start supper without you.' She gave her head a small shake. 'Although I must say, gentlemen were far more adventurous in my day . . .'

Essie watched as the pair of older women walked away, waiting until they were out of earshot before bursting into a fit of giggles.

'Did your grandmother just imply that I was *timid*?' Aidan sounded aggrieved. 'Now I don't know if she wants me to keep that promise or debauch you behind a tree.'

'*Aidan!*'

'That was your word, wasn't it?' He grinned. 'And I was only speaking theoretically. We're still looking for your replacement, I believe.'

'Yes.' Essie kept her smile fixed in place although her stomach sank at the thought – which caused a curious juxtaposition of sensations, since the mere mention of debauchery had just caused it to start tingling again. 'If you don't favour any of my previous suggestions, that is?' She paused, but no answer seemed forthcoming. '*Do* you favour any of them?'

'I haven't decided.'

'I only ask because we're running out of time. According to my schedule, you should be almost at the proposal stage by now.'

'And I said I wouldn't be rushed. I'll still break off our engagement in time, don't worry.'

'Well, Caro says Miss Merriwell ought to be here tonight.'

'Merriwell.' He nodded slowly as if he were filing the information away. 'So what should I know about her?'

'Her first name is Dorothea and she has auburn hair, green eyes and a dowry of fifty thousand pounds in addition to a hunting lodge in Scotland. Caro says she's very nice, but then she thinks everybody is.'

'What do *you* think?'

'Me?' Essie bit down on her bottom lip. She'd been introduced to Miss Merriwell at the Cumberworths' ball and she'd seemed pleasant enough. As far as she could remember, she hadn't made any snide comments about her dress either. Still, the thought of her marrying Aidan made her feel slightly queasy. 'I'm not sure.'

'Any particular reason?'

'Just a feeling.' She felt a prickle of guilt at the words. 'But you should probably talk to her yourself and see what you think.'

'I think it might be impossible to find anyone in a crowd like this. What do you say to another walk?'

'*Another?*' She pretended to roll her eyes.

'I know. If nothing else, we're getting plenty of exercise this Season.'

They strolled arm in arm for a while, pausing outside a pavilion where a full orchestra was arranged in a semi-circle behind a stunningly beautiful, red-haired soprano singer. A number of gentlemen were lounging around the walls, their tongues practically hanging out as they admired both the view and the singing. Further on, a tightrope walker in a bright red and blue-chequered costume was making his way along a rope strung between two trees while a pair of similarly clad jugglers performed tricks underneath. Beyond them was a fire-eater, followed by a troupe of acrobats, all perched precariously on each other's shoulders. The atmosphere was like that of a fair, vibrant and lively and exciting.

'It feels so free-spirited!' Essie sighed happily. 'I've changed my mind about living at Gunter's. I want a cottage here instead.'

'I'll see what I can arrange.'

'But why are so many people looking at us?' She tipped her head closer to his. She'd been so engrossed in their surroundings that it had taken her a while to notice, but they were definitely attracting stares.

'Mmm? Oh . . .' Aidan looked mildly embarrassed. 'It seems that we've become quite fashionable.'

'Us? Really?' She gaped at him in amazement. 'I mean, I can see why you would be, what with you being a handsome earl and everybody thinking you're rich, but as for me . . .'

'You're a beauty engaged to an earl and you actually *are* rich.'

'Two out of three. I'm not beautiful.'

'I beg to disagree. You're very beautiful. You just didn't let anyone else see it at first.'

'I'm really not –'

'Essie.' He sounded exasperated. 'Take the damn compliment.'

'Oh . . . All right . . . Thank you.'

She turned her head to hide the embarrassed flush burning spots on her cheeks, unable to stop herself from smiling as they turned off the main avenue and wended their way along a series of meandering paths lined with neatly trimmed topiary, classical sculptures and narrow, tinkling streams. It was like walking through a fairy tale. She was even wearing the perfect gown for the occasion, her favourite of all the ones her grandmother had chosen, a pale apple-green silk with short, puffed sleeves and a scalloped neckline, overlaid with a silvery net like a diaphanous spider's web. It made her feel like some kind of woodland nymph. Although that would make Aidan a satyr . . .

'So how big is this place?' She pushed the image of him as a horned beast out of her mind.

'Several acres, I believe.'

'Oh dear. There's no way we're going to find Miss Merriwell.'

'Never mind.' He shrugged, looking decidedly unperturbed. 'She giggles too much anyway.'

'You mean you've already met her?'

'We've been introduced.'

'Well, why didn't you say so before I started telling you about hunting lodges?'

'I didn't want you to feel like it was wasted research.' He flexed his arm slightly against hers. 'We can still enjoy the evening together, can't we?'

She gulped nervously. Enjoying herself was what she was afraid of. She'd enjoyed her last two outings with him far too much as it was. Although *enjoyment* wasn't quite the right word for what she was experiencing at that moment. She felt tense and jittery all of a sudden, as if she'd drunk several cups of strong coffee and all of her senses were on high alert, waiting for something to happen. She felt aware of every twitch and tingle in her body, of which there were a considerable number. Just the brush of his arm against hers was doing curious things to her insides, as if all of her internal organs were dancing in time to the sound of flutes and violins and the beautiful soprano in the distance.

'Essie?' Aidan came to a sudden halt as they entered a small grove, catching hold of her hand as it slipped through his arm. 'Would it be so terrible, being married to me? I admit that we had a bad start, but I like you. More than I expected to. More than any other candidate. I know it's not what we agreed and there are other things you want to do, but . . . would it be *so* bad?'

'I . . .' She seemed unable to lift her voice above a whisper. 'I like you too. In fact, I think, if I *wanted* to marry then you would be the person I would choose, but –'

'Don't say but.' He moved a step closer. 'Just dance with me.'

'What?' She looked around. 'Nobody else is dancing.'

'I don't care what anybody else is doing.'

'But it's a waltz. I still don't have permission from Almack's.'

'Fuck Almack's.' His blue gaze didn't falter. 'Dance with me, Essie.'

She sucked in a breath, feeling the hairs on her arms and neck stand to attention in shock, both at the word and his close proximity. She felt as if there were goosebumps all over her body, although if anything she was in danger of overheating. She didn't want to feel this way. She wanted to be able to look at him and feel nothing, only she couldn't seem to help herself. He seemed different this evening, less civilized somehow. It would be sheer bliss to dance with him there, beneath the lanterns, if she dared.

She dared.

Tentatively, she placed one hand inside his, threading their fingers together while she put the other on his shoulder, swallowing tightly as his came around her waist, resting just above the curve of her hip. And then his feet moved and so did hers and she had the bizarre impression that her toes had just curled. Her whole body felt as taut as one of the bowstrings belonging to the violins in the background, as if all her muscles were clenching and unclenching spasmodically. As for her heart, it seemed to have skipped so many beats she was amazed she could still stand upright.

She risked a quick look around, vaguely aware that all the other couples had abandoned them. They were alone together. Completely alone. Waltzing. At twilight. In a tree-lined grove illuminated by pink and purple glowing lanterns. Strains of an orchestra permeated the air and there was hardly a hair's breadth between their bodies. If she'd wanted a romantic scene then she could hardly have asked for a better one. She couldn't even feel her feet, as if she were floating a little way off the floor.

'Maybe I should kiss you?' The words were out before she could think better of them.

He stiffened, looking as surprised as she felt. 'What did you just say?'

'Maybe I should kiss you,' she repeated, lifting her chin to hold her nerve. 'To find out how terrible it would be. As a kind of experiment.'

His gaze dropped to her mouth and she wondered how she could ever have thought that his eyes were blue. They looked as dark as midnight, the pupils swollen to black orbs. 'Something tells me your grandmother wouldn't approve.'

'I wasn't planning on telling her.' She felt a momentary misgiving. 'You don't have to if you don't want to.'

'I didn't say that.' He tightened his hold on her waist. 'As an experiment, then?'

'Yes. Just stand there and don't move.'

'Like this?'

'Exactly. Only we need to hurry before anyone else comes along.'

'Agreed.'

'So just a peck, then?'

'If that's what you want.'

'It is.' She pushed herself up on her tiptoes. 'Should I close my eyes?'

'It's up to you.'

'Are you going to?'

'Probably.'

'Just bear in mind that I've never kissed anyone before.'

'I hope not.'

'Have you?'

'Did you say something about being in a hurry?'

'Right.' She swayed forward, skimming her lips briefly against his before setting her feet down again. 'You know, it's really not fair to expect me to do it. Isn't the gentleman supposed to –'

The rest of her argument melted away as Aidan lowered his head and pressed his mouth against hers, kissing her softly and tenderly at first, barely grazing her in fact, before touching her lips with his tongue and then . . . She closed her eyes as his hands pressed against the small of her back. Everything about the kiss was gentle and yet it caused a hot, aching sensation in the very pit of her stomach. Lower even. Which was . . . new. She felt seized with a powerful urge to weave her arms around his neck, to move as close as she could without actually knocking him over, to press the entire length of her body against the entire length of his, as if something inside of him were tugging urgently at something inside of her.

'How was that?' He lifted his head again after an indeterminate amount of time, his hands trailing a path up her spine towards her shoulders.

She blinked several times in rapid succession, her senses reeling. 'It was . . .' She panted, trying to think of an appropriate description. Unexpectedly blissful? Heart-stoppingly intense? Better than cake? 'Satisfactory.'

'That good?' A black eyebrow quirked upwards. 'A successful experiment, then?'

'Ye-es.' She licked her lips, alarmed to find herself swaying, as if she might actually swoon if she wasn't careful. She didn't know which was more alarming, the fact that she might be the kind of woman who swooned or that she wanted to kiss him again. And again. And maybe several more times because experiments needed to be repeated to get accurate results, didn't they? She needed time to analyse her reactions. As well as a sheet of paper and quill to make notes.

'We could try again?' Apparently his thoughts were moving in a similar direction.

'That might be useful.'

She started the kiss this time, emitting a low moan as she leaned back into him, tangling her hands in his hair as his arms tightened around her like steel bands, holding her up, or possibly lifting her up – she couldn't feel her feet again – until she became aware of an insistent pressure against her hip. And then he shifted slightly and it wasn't against her hip any longer. It was –

She gasped, suddenly unable to draw enough air into her lungs as the aching sensation in her stomach intensified, as if there were red-hot sparks of excitement shooting along every nerve, all of them meeting and coalescing in the same spot in the very centre of her body. She even found herself starting to move in response, wriggling and squirming against him until she could feel her pulse there too.

Never in her life had she been remotely tempted to squirm before.

'Aidan . . .' She moaned his name fervently. She could hear her own heartbeat now, like a drum in her ears. It sounded uneven, as if it were overlapping itself, as if she had several heartbeats, in fact . . .

'Oh!' she exclaimed as she realized that it wasn't her heartbeat at all, but approaching footsteps, wrenching herself out of his arms so violently that she bumped into a tree in the process.

'Essie?' His voice was rougher than she'd ever heard it.

'We should get back, don't you think?' She jerked her head pointedly sideways, forcing him to notice the new arrivals. 'Personally, I'm feeling rather peckish.' She made herself sound light-hearted, stumbling towards the widest and best-lit path out of the grove, aware of his gaze boring into the space between her shoulder blades. 'If we don't hurry, then Grandmama will have eaten everything.'

'We were starting to think the two of you had got lost.' The grandmother in question was sitting in the centre of their supper box like a queen, Aidan's mother looking somewhat less elegant than usual beside her. 'We've just been toasting your nuptials.'

'Arrack punch.' The countess lifted a glass, her cheeks suspiciously flushed.

'Not lost.' Essie took a seat, making an unnecessary fuss about arranging her skirts, although it was impossible to completely evade the interrogative glint of her grandmother's eye. 'There was just so much to see.'

'And *do*, I expect.'

'Such a shame that Sophia couldn't join us.' The countess smiled serenely and then hiccupped. 'I do think you were cruel to refuse her, Aidan.'

'Next time perhaps.'

'She's simply longing to meet you, Miss Craven. *Essie*. May I call you Essie?'

'Um, yes, of course.' She exchanged a startled look with her grandmother.

'What a merry party we are.' That lady's lips twitched. 'Now, as you can see, we've ordered a feast. I suggest that we start eating before it starts to congeal.'

Essie reached for a plate, though for the second time in recent memory her appetite seemed to have deserted her. Her pulse was still racing at a dizzying pace, and as for her stomach . . . The ache had been replaced by a dull and disgruntled thrumming, like the embers of a fire that might burst back into life at any moment.

She accepted a glass of punch and risked a peek over the rim at Aidan. He seemed subdued, though he was conversing with her grandmother politely enough. She wondered whether he felt any embers too. He didn't appear to, but she felt as though she knew him better now. She could see past his appearance. Somehow she'd got past the haughty and sardonic versions of him to the real, softer, earthier Aidan beneath.

He looked up at that moment and her throat turned dry. In the light of the lanterns, his eyes were blue again. Clearly, blazingly, dazzlingly blue. *Like pools of tropical water she was tempted to drown herself in . . .* The thought seared across her brain like lightning, making the space between them seem to crackle with tiny sparks.

A burst of noise made her jump out of her seat in alarm as the sparks seemed to ignite suddenly and a succession of fireworks shot up into the sky from somewhere else in the park, exploding in bursts of golden light before trailing downwards like cascades of falling stars around them.

Essie felt her breath hitch in wonder. It had been an evening of firsts – first kisses, first squirms, first fireworks, not to mention the first time she'd ever been called beautiful *or* fashionable – and the world seemed to be spinning around her, knocking her off balance. Another swift glance at Aidan only reinforced the feeling. His expression actually seemed to be smouldering. *Would it be so terrible?* The words seemed to hover like motes of light in the air.

As conspiracies went, this wasn't remotely what she'd planned.

PLAN C, AMENDED: CARO

Dearest, if you're reading this then it means that my plan has worked . . .

Miss Caroline Foyle to her cousin, Miss Essie Craven, 14th May 1816

Chapter Sixteen

(Two Weeks and Three Days before Wedding Day)

Essie tapped lightly on the door to Caro's bedchamber. There was no answer, but she opened it anyway, turning the handle quietly and poking her head inside, disappointed to find the room shrouded in darkness. Briefly, she considered waking her cousin up for an emergency talk and then chided herself for selfishness. If Caro was unwell then she needed her sleep. Whatever emotional turmoil *she* might be feeling could wait until morning.

She was just about to close the door again when she spotted an envelope propped up on the dresser, faintly illuminated by the light from the fire. Now that *was* odd.

Throwing a swift glance at the bed, she hurried across the room, nerves tightening at the sight of her name on the envelope. Quickly, she tore it open, read the contents and then flung herself on top of the sleeping shape on the bed, hoping against hope that it was some kind of bad joke.

Pillows.

'Grandmama!' she shrieked, pelting out of the room and down the corridor, bursting into her grandmother's bedchamber without knocking, only to find that room dark and empty too. Curiously, the fire wasn't even lit, as if her grandmother had no intention of sleeping there.

'Quill!' she shrieked again, hurtling back the way that she'd come and on down the stairs, the contents of the letter buzzing around her head like a swarm of furious bees. She could feel her panic increasing with every step, her breath coming too hard and too fast, scorching her lungs.

'Miss Craven?' Her grandmother's butler emerged from beneath the staircase, looking as perfectly groomed as ever. 'Is there something I might help you with?'

'My grandmother.' Essie clutched at the front of his shirt. 'Where is she?'

Quill's expression turned studiously blank. 'Her ladyship has gone out again.'

'*Now?*' The last time she'd checked it had been two o'clock in the morning. 'At this hour? Where?'

'I'm afraid I'm not at liberty to say.'

'But it's an emergency!' She took note of his clenched jaw and changed tack. 'Just give me a hint.'

Quill glanced around, making sure they were alone before lowering his voice. 'Her ladyship visits a certain house on occasion.'

'What kind of a house?'

'As to that, I *really* couldn't say.'

'Then where is it? I'll go and find her.'

'I'm afraid that won't be possible.'

'Why not?'

'It would be most indiscreet.'

'I don't care about indiscreet!'

'It's also quite a distance. Richmond, I believe.'

'Richmond! But that means she won't be back for hours!' Essie finally released him in order to rake her hands through her hair. 'What time did my cousin go to bed?'

Quill smoothed a hand over his now rumpled shirt. 'I believe that Miss Foyle retired just after you left.'

'Did she come downstairs again afterwards?'

'Not that I'm aware of.'

'But could she have left the house without you noticing? Down the back stairs perhaps?'

For the first time, Quill's expression looked faintly perturbed. 'I suppose it's possible.'

Essie let out a long, cat-like wail. If it was possible then it was surely what had happened. Caro had snuck out when nobody was watching, probably just after they'd departed for Vauxhall, which gave her a more than six-hour head start! But running away was such an *un*-Caro-like thing to do! She was the good one; everyone knew that. The obedient one, the modest one, the girl *least* likely to elope! And without her grandmother there to help, what could *she* do? She could hardly go after Caro on her own or waste time by going to Richmond in search of some house Quill clearly didn't want to tell her about. But what else could she do? Who else could she trust?

'I need to go to Grosvenor Square.' The answer was so blindingly obvious she was amazed it had taken her so long to think of it. 'And if Grandmama's taken the carriage then I'll have to walk. Will you come with me? Please?'

Quill looked startled. 'I really don't think her ladyship would approve.'

'She will when she knows why. I take complete responsibility.' Essie scuttled into the library, writing a hasty note of explanation before rushing back again.

'I took the liberty of fetching your cloak.' Quill already looked resigned to his fate. 'Although I still advise against this course of action.'

'And you're probably quite right, but I've no choice.' She handed him the note. 'When my grandmother returns, give her this and tell her to start a rumour that Caro and I are both sick.'

'Perhaps you ought to consider taking a maid?'

Essie hesitated. He was right – she really ought to take some kind of chaperone, but there was no time and, honestly, if anyone ever found out what she was doing, the presence of a maid was hardly likely to save her reputation.

'No.' She drew her hood over her head and made for the door. 'Now, let's go.'

Essie stayed close to Quill's side on the walk from Cavendish Square to Denholm House, jumping at every shadow and sound. It was only a few streets away, but she felt as though she'd run a marathon by the time they reached the front steps, rapping insistently on the door until a yawning butler appeared.

'I need to speak with the earl.' She didn't wait for him to ask their business, putting on her most authoritative and *countessy* expression instead.

'His lordship is in bed.' The butler's tone implied that he thought she ought to be too. Apparently her authoritative expression was lacking since his positively radiated disapproval. 'Perhaps you might return tomorrow? During *proper* visiting hours.'

'I can't.' She shook her head adamantly. 'Please just tell him I'm here. He'll want to see me, I promise.'

'I'm sure that you think so, miss.'

'Wait!' She rammed her foot into the gap as the door started to close. 'If you don't let me in right now then you'll have to explain to your employer why his fiancée is making a scene on his doorstep in the middle of the night. One scream and I'll wake up the whole square.'

'Fiancée?' The man's expression wavered.

'Yes! Miss Essie Craven. Now. Let. Me. In.'

The butler gave her one last suspicious look before stepping aside, gesturing for Quill to stay in the hall while he led her into a side room. 'Wait here.'

'Thank you.' Essie heaved a deep sigh of relief. The room appeared to be Aidan's office, all deep-red flock paper and walnut wood, dominated by a large, leather-topped desk and floor-to-ceiling bookshelves on two of the walls. The third wall had a large window overlooking the street and the fourth . . . the fourth was decorated with a collection of landscape paintings, watercolours in sombre shades of green, blue and grey, featuring the same scene of rolling hills and woodland, in particular one large oak from different angles, as if the artist had wanted to capture every facet of the tree. Whoever he or she was, Essie didn't envy their state of mind. As beautiful as the paintings were, there was something haunting about them, making her wonder . . .

She wrenched her gaze away quickly. She didn't have time for wondering. She had a cousin to find. And where the hell was Aidan? Every second that passed took Caro further and further away . . .

She was on the verge of running upstairs and forcing her way into his bedroom when he finally appeared in the doorway, barefoot in a navy-blue dressing gown. His eyes looked heavy, as if he were fighting to keep them open, and he was wearing a dazed expression as if he thought that he might be dreaming. One look at her face, however, and he was beside her in three strides. 'Essie? What's happened?'

'It's Caro. She's run away!'

'What?'

'Here.' She thrust her cousin's note at him, fingers trembling. 'I went to see if she was still awake when we got home and I found this. She's *eloped*! It's the only explanation.'

'Who with?'

'That's the worst part. She says that I ought to be able to guess, but I can't! She has so many suitors, but I didn't think there was anyone she particularly liked.' Essie winced at the admission. Maybe if she hadn't been so wrapped up in her own problems then she *would* have known. She only hoped that her worst suspicions were unfounded. 'Whoever it is, they must be heading for Gretna Green.'

'What does your grandmother say?'

'Nothing yet. She's gone to Richmond for some secret reason and won't be back for hours. That's why I came here. I didn't know who else to turn to. Please, Aidan.' She laid a hand on his arm. 'I need your help.'

'To stop the wedding?'

She opened her mouth and then closed it again. In all honesty, she hadn't got that far in her planning. 'Not necessarily, if it's what Caro truly wants, but what if –' She bit her lip, half afraid to put *what if* into words. 'What if some man's taken advantage of her good nature? What if he's not quite respectable? Why elope otherwise? I need to go after her and make sure she hasn't been taken in by some fortune-hunter or rake. I need to be sure she knows what she's doing.'

'It won't be easy to catch up with them.'

'I don't care.'

'All right.' He nodded. 'I'll call for the post-chaise. It's not very comfortable, but it's faster than a carriage.'

'So you'll come with me?' She felt her whole body sag with relief.

'I'll go alone. You go back to your grandmother's.'

'I will not.' She wrenched her shoulders back, outraged by the very suggestion. 'She's my cousin.'

'I know, but Essie . . .' He took hold of her wrists, clasping them tight. 'It's bad enough that you came here tonight, but if the two of us travel together in a closed vehicle and word gets out . . .'

'Then my reputation will be ruined and we'll have to get married. I know, but this is my choice.' She twisted her hands around until she was holding his wrists too. 'And if you refuse to take me then I'll simply hire a carriage myself. I'm going to find Caro even if we have to go all the way to Gretna Green.'

'Gretna Green?' a female voice gasped from the doorway. 'You're going to Gretna Green?'

Essie jumped, looking past Aidan's shoulder to see a

dark-haired girl gazing at them with an expression of dreamy excitement. Judging by the way that her hands were clasped together, she'd just caught the tail end of their conversation and jumped to the obvious, but entirely wrong, conclusion.

'Sophia.' Aidan turned around, frowning. 'What are you doing out of bed?'

'I heard voices. You must be Essie!' The girl rushed forward excitedly. She had a quiet, breathy voice, brimming with nervous energy. 'I'm so pleased to finally meet you. Aidan has told me so much.'

'He has?'

'No. Sophia, go back to bed.'

'I've *always* wanted a sister.' The girl's blue eyes widened. They were a slightly more turquoise shade than Aidan's, Essie noticed, and just as guileless as Caro's. 'I know that we're going to be close.'

'I know it too,' Essie agreed, the girl's obvious sincerity making her feel like an utter fraud.

'That's enough.' Aidan gave her a strange look before catching hold of his sister's shoulders. 'We need to hurry.'

'To Gretna Green? Truly? Oh, I'm in raptures!'

'It's not for the reason you think.' He led her firmly towards the door. 'Don't say anything to anyone – just tell Mother that I've gone away for a few days on business.'

'But you're going together?' Sophia looked over her shoulder, beaming at Essie.

'Yes.'

'Ohhhh!' She gave a small bounce and then clamped a hand over her mouth, speaking through her fingers. 'I won't say a word, I promise. You can trust me.'

'It's really not –' Aidan started to protest again and then shook his head. 'I'll explain later. Right now, I need to get dressed.'

'Here. Tuck this beneath your feet.'

Aidan bent down and pushed a small cloth-wrapped bundle beneath the hem of Essie's gown. They'd stopped at a small coaching inn just outside of London to ask whether anyone had seen a young couple acting suspiciously, but unfortunately the answer had been a resounding no. It had been a long shot so close to the city, but they'd decided to ask at every inn they passed. Caro and her mysterious companion would have had to stop somewhere to rest and change their horses on the journey north, which meant that somebody was bound to have noticed them eventually.

'Ooh, a hot brick.' Essie snuggled deeper inside her cloak as a rush of heat flared up her legs, thawing her insides. 'Don't you have one too?'

'There was only one available. They were surprised to see any vehicle at this time of night.'

'In that case, we ought to share.' She nudged the brick sideways as the post-chaise lurched forward again. 'Here.'

'All right.' He gave her a quick, sideways look and then propped one of his feet beside hers. 'Thank goodness it's May or we'd be frozen already.'

'I can't believe we were watching fireworks at Vauxhall just a few hours ago.' She stifled a yawn. 'How long does it take to reach Gretna Green?'

'Four days in a hurry. Although I warn you, if we're stopping at every inn then it's going to take longer.'

'Are you certain they'd have taken this route?'

'It's not called the Great North Road for nothing. If they want to travel quickly, this is the best way.'

'Can't we go any faster, just in case?'

'Tomorrow, yes. In the middle of the night, no. We need to be careful.'

'In case of ruts?'

'And highwaymen.'

'Oh.' She swallowed. She hadn't considered highwaymen.

'Don't worry, my men are armed. I expect that most robbers will have gone to bed by now too.'

'But what if they were still awake when Caro passed by?' She could feel panic rising again. 'What if her carriage has been set upon by ruffians? Or what if she's so far ahead of us that –'

'Essie.' He reached for her hand, threading his gloved fingers through hers and squeezing reassuringly. 'Worrying isn't going to help. Try getting some sleep instead. You look exhausted.'

'So do you.' She tipped her head sideways without thinking. It was a position she often adopted when travelling with Caro, resting her head on her cousin's shoulder, but she hadn't consciously intended to do it with him. Given the circumstances, it was wildly inappropriate, scandalous even, and yet incredibly comfortable . . .

The post-chaise gave a jolt while she was still trying to decide what to do and her head slid farther downwards, on to his chest. Oops . . . She froze, wondering how to extricate herself while looking as if she'd just inadvertently fallen asleep, but then one of his arms came around her, and she couldn't bring herself to twitch so much as a muscle. This position felt even better, as if she were wrapped in a cocoon of deliciously blissful warmth.

Surreptitiously, she burrowed closer, committed to the pretence of sleep now, relishing the feel of crisp white linen and soft wool against her cheek and forehead. The next time she decided to charge around the English countryside in the early hours then she would change out of her flimsy evening gown and put on a woollen dress first, but for now she was happy to share Aidan's body heat, even if it meant that their thighs bumped together with every roll and sway of the carriage. It was a matter of survival, after all.

She must have actually fallen asleep because it seemed like only minutes later when she was awoken by another violent lurch.

'What is it?' She sat bolt upright, so disorientated that for a moment she couldn't remember where they were or what they were doing.

'It must be another coaching inn.' Aidan was looking somewhat rumpled himself. 'Come on, we'll go inside and freshen up.'

'Is there time?'

'We'll have to make time or my men will be handing in their notice.'

'Fair enough.' She climbed down from the vehicle, yawning, automatically taking Aidan's hand as they headed for the door.

'Do you know what time it is?' A grumpy-looking face appeared at a window after twenty seconds of determined knocking.

'My apologies.' Aidan reached into his pocket and pulled out a few coins. 'But we're looking for someone. A young lady. Blonde hair, very pretty. She would have passed this way earlier tonight.'

'She's not staying here.' The man's expression relented. 'Although it was busy last evening. Hard to say if she passed through.'

'In that case, perhaps we might see to our horses and get some refreshments? I'll recompense you for the trouble, naturally.'

'Aye, I suppose I can fetch you something to eat.' The window closed and the door opened. 'Nothing fancy, mind. There's a room at the top of those stairs where you can see to your needs.'

'Thank you. We're most obliged.'

Essie gave Aidan a wan smile before climbing the stairs and opening the door to a small empty bedchamber. Slowly, she reached her hands down to the floor and then up to the ceiling, relieved to be able to stretch her limbs for a few minutes, before availing herself of the chamber pot and then splashing herself with some cold water left in a bowl on the side. Just those few actions lifted her spirits, making her feel almost optimistic. After all, just because Caro and her mysterious companion weren't in this particular inn didn't mean that they wouldn't find them. And at least she wasn't searching alone. Aidan was with her.

Aidan, who hadn't even hesitated before offering to help.

Aidan, who'd wrapped his arm around her during the journey and let her sleep on his shoulder.

Aidan, who'd kissed her so passionately just a few hours ago . . .

She paused on her way back down the stairs as the memory of their moonlit tryst at Vauxhall washed over her. All the panic about Caro had pushed it to the back of her mind and Aidan hadn't mentioned it either, even when she'd turned up on his doorstep in the middle of the night. If he'd wanted to repeat their Vauxhall experiment, however, he'd had ample opportunity in the post-chaise, although he was undoubtedly far too much of a gentleman to take advantage of the situation. He might have put his arm around her, but that had probably just been for comfort and warmth. Which was definitely for the best, although if he *had* tried to kiss her again . . . She felt the telltale flicker of heat in her stomach, and had a feeling that she would have found it very hard to refuse.

They shared a plate of bread and cheese and two mugs of ale before climbing back into the post-chaise and starting off again. To Essie's relief, a pale band of yellow was already creeping up over the horizon, gradually chasing away the darkness.

'Damn it,' Aidan muttered under his breath suddenly.

'What is it?' She twisted around in his arm. They'd silently adopted the same positions as before, although she wasn't feigning sleep this time.

'I should have given a more convincing reason for leaving. Sophia's a terrible liar. My mother will be interrogating the staff before breakfast.' He grimaced. 'Hopefully Fothergill will be tactful.'

'Fothergill's your butler?' She made a face. 'I don't think he liked me. Actually, I think he thought I was mad, although I can see how he got that impression. What did you tell him?'

'The same as I told Sophia. Business. I doubt he believed it either.'

'I'm sorry about meeting your sister. I know you didn't want me to.'

'It wasn't your fault.'

'I made quite a lot of noise on your doorstep.'

'All right, it was a bit your fault.'

'I hope she won't be too disappointed when we come back unmarried.'

'So do I, but it can't be helped.'

'I'd like to get to know her better whatever happens between us. She seems very sweet. I can see why you feel protective.'

'I'm her big brother.' He sighed. 'This past year hasn't been easy on her either, but she's a romantic. And you've seen how cruel the *ton* can be.'

'First-hand.' She blew her cheeks out. 'So once your mother's interrogated your sister and butler, do you think she'll assume . . . ?'

'The same as Sophia? Unquestionably.'

'Oh dear. I wonder how she'll react. She was nice to me at Vauxhall thanks to the punch, but she'd much rather you married somebody else, wouldn't she?'

'I feel like this is a trick question.'

'Tell me honestly.'

'Honestly?' He shifted in his seat. 'Yes, she would.'

'She'd probably like Lady Phoebe.'

'True, but I'm not going to marry Lady Phoebe.'

'Why not?'

'Because I don't necessarily want to marry someone my mother approves of.'

'Oh.' She tried not to feel too pleased by the sentiment. 'I remember her telling my aunt about the plans for her dower house. Will she really be moving there after you marry?'

'Yes.' He paused. 'That would probably be for the best, don't you think?'

'Mmm. I'm sure any bride would agree.' Essie nestled her head against his shoulder again, almost purring when he smoothed a hand across her hair. Theoretically speaking, if she *did* find herself compromised into marrying him, things were looking a great deal better already.

Chapter Seventeen

'Six inns and no sightings. Not even a hint of a glimpse.' Essie put her head in her hands with a groan. Her optimism had gradually drained away as the morning had worn on, like a cup with a hole in the bottom. Now she felt as if she were down to the dregs. It was almost noon and they were no closer to finding Caro than when they'd set off.

'Unfortunately, a girl with blonde hair travelling with a man we can't describe isn't a lot to go on, but don't worry.' Aidan's shoulder gave hers a reassuring nudge. 'If they came this way then we'll find them eventually.'

'What do you mean, *if*?' She spun towards him. 'I thought you said this was the fastest road north?'

'It is.'

'So why *if*?'

'No reason.'

'Aidan?'

He swore softly. 'Because there's always the risk they weren't heading to Scotland.'

'What?' It took her a few seconds to grasp the implication. 'Of course they were! Caro would never have agreed to anything else!'

'Maybe not intentionally, but she wouldn't be the first girl to be seduced by a false promise of marriage.'

'You mean . . .' She shivered as if there were a block of ice at the back of her neck, melting slowly but inexorably down her spine. 'Oh, Caro.'

'I'm probably just being alarmist.' Aidan started to backtrack. 'Just because nobody remembers seeing them doesn't mean they didn't come this way. We won't give up.'

'This is all my fault!' She wrapped her hands around herself, running her fingers up and down her arms as a cold chill seeped all the way to her core. 'I knew she was preoccupied about something, but I was so busy thinking about *us* that I didn't pay enough attention. I should have demanded to know what was going on!'

'You weren't to know she would do something like this. You can't blame yourself.'

'Yes, I can! She's always been there for me, from the very first night I arrived at Redcliffe when I was eight years old and she took my hand and showed me to the room we were going to share and said that we were going to be the best of friends. And she was right. We were – *are*! But I've been a terrible friend. Selfish and self-centred and–'

'Stop it.' Aidan turned in his seat, lifting his hands to her shoulders. 'Self-pity isn't going to help anyone. Now, think back to the last time you spoke to her. Did she give any hints at all?'

Essie knitted her brows. He was right; there would be time for recriminations and regrets later. Right now, she had to think and the truth was that Caro had been acting strangely for the past two weeks. She'd been particularly grumpy on the day of the Keatons' dinner party, but she hadn't mentioned any names. She hadn't really talked about anyone except . . .

She gasped. 'Oh no.'

'What?'

'The other day, after the Smedley-Bullingdons' garden party when I was feeling ill, she came to my room and we talked and I had this feeling that I'd missed something important, but I couldn't work out what it was.' She dropped her voice to a guilty whisper. 'It was a name. She used his first name. She said Sylvester.'

'You think she's with Jagger?'

'It has to be. Either him or Mr Dormer.'

'Dormer wouldn't do this.' Aidan's hands fell away, his voice hardening.

'That's what I'm afraid of. And *I* introduced them.' She shook her head despairingly. 'If only I hadn't gone out on to the terrace at that first ball. If I'd never met Jagger then none of this would be happening.'

He gave her a long look and then wrapped his arm around her again. 'There's no point in looking back. If you were distracted then that's understandable. As for being selfish, right now you're risking your own reputation to go in search of her. Not many people are that loyal. We'll find her, I promise, and then we'll find a way to fix this.'

'Thank you.' She smiled tremulously. 'Not just for saying that, but for coming with me. I know it was unfair of me to involve you, but I didn't know what else to do.'

'I'm glad that you came to me. We're friends, aren't we?'

'Yes, I suppose we are.' She felt a warm glow in her chest. At that moment, friendship seemed more important than anything.

Essie waited for Aidan in the narrow oak-panelled hallway of the next tavern, waving her arms around in circles and bouncing up and down on her tiptoes. It wasn't particularly ladylike behaviour, but then cramp wasn't a very ladylike ailment either. She never wanted to set foot in another post-chaise in her life.

As far as she could guess, it was the middle of the afternoon and only a handful of the tables in the taproom next door were occupied, all of them by men. Another disappointment, as no doubt Aidan was confirming with the innkeeper right now.

Bounced out and sufficiently stretched, she wandered along the hallway towards a door that had been left slightly ajar and took a quick peek inside. It appeared to be a separate dining room, empty of customers now, although the aromas of pie and pudding still clung to the air, making her stomach rumble. She supposed that she must be hungry, although she also knew there was no point in trying to keep anything more than a mouthful down until they found Caro.

She was just turning away when she heard a small sniff and realized the room wasn't completely deserted after all. There was a lone figure in one corner, covered from head to toe in a grey travelling cloak, sitting as still as a statue. She couldn't see the statue's face, but if it wasn't wishful thinking, there was a single blonde curl poking out from the edge of the hood . . .

'Caro?' She didn't even realize she'd moved until she was standing beside the table, whispering her cousin's name.

The statue's head spun around, although for a few seconds Essie thought she'd made a mistake. The face didn't look remotely like Caro's. It was deathly pale except for a few fierce red splotches, with eyes that looked shrivelled and rimmed with purple shadows.

'Essie?' The voice that emerged sounded disbelieving.

'Caro, are you –?' Essie sank on to a stool, then almost toppled off it again as her cousin leaped forward, throwing her arms about her like a drowning woman.

'I'm sorry, I'm so sorry.' Just that action seemed to unleash a torrent of tears.

'It's all right.' Essie held her cousin close, rubbing her back until the crying eased. 'I'm here now. You're safe.'

'I've been so stupid.'

'Don't say that. Whatever's happened, I know it's not your fault.'

'It is!' A second torrent quickly followed the first. 'I should never have agreed to his scheme.'

'Whose scheme? Caro, who are you here with?'

'No one.'

'What?' Essie pulled her head back just as the dining-room door opened and Aidan stepped inside, took one look at them, then turned around and stepped out again.

'But Caro . . .' She tried again, taking her cousin's stricken face in her hands. 'You must have run away with someone.'

'Yes, but he's gone. He left a few hours ago.'

'Who?' She mentally braced herself for the worst. 'Sylvester Jagger?'

'Yes.' Caro's voice was so quiet that Essie saw her mouth the word rather than heard it.

'But why? How? When did the two of you even plan this?'

'I don't know. It was all such a whirlwind.' Caro dragged in a breath as if she were collecting her thoughts. 'At first I thought he liked you, but then he asked me to dance at the Faulconers' ball and said he'd been captivated from the first moment he saw me. I didn't believe him at first, but he was so convincing. He sent me red roses every day. There were letters hidden in the bouquets and then, that day by the river, he kissed me in the herb garden and it was wonderful. I'd never imagined it was possible to feel so . . . transported. It was like I'd been asleep for my whole life and my body woke up all of a sudden. It's hard to explain.'

'I know.'

'You do?'

'I mean, I've read romances.' Essie cleared her throat awkwardly.

'So have I, but it was more than that. It was overwhelming. He made sure to attend all the same events I did and we even met in the park a couple of times. It was dangerous, but I didn't care. His kisses must have done something to my brain because I couldn't think straight. I just knew I'd do anything to be with him. That's how I ended up here.' She cast her eyes downward. 'He said he loved me, but that with his reputation and lack of fortune my parents would never approve of a match and the only way we could be together was to elope. He made it sound so romantic. Everything he said made sense at the time, but he didn't mean a word.'

'How did you find out?' Essie leaned closer, wrapping an arm around her cousin's shoulders.

Caro closed her eyes as if she were steeling herself to go on. 'We stopped here early this morning. It seemed far enough from London and we needed some rest so we took a room. Together. Sylvester said that we were as good as married already so we might as well share a bed.' She lifted her hands to cover her face, muffling the words. 'But once we were laid down, it wasn't sleep that he wanted.'

'Oh no . . .'

'I felt so scared.' She dragged her palms sideways, scraping them over her cheeks. 'When I pushed him away, he got angry. Eventually, he said I wasn't worth the trouble and stormed out. I waited and waited, but he never came back.' Her voice broke. 'Finally, I asked the innkeeper where he was and he said that he'd left in his carriage.'

'You mean he abandoned you for refusing him?' Essie shot to her feet furiously, then sat down again as Caro's face crumpled. 'I'm sorry.'

'I loved him.' A single tear trickled down the side of Caro's cheek. 'I still can't believe that he went so far just to seduce me.'

'I can. He's a selfish, cold-hearted, immoral rake and when I get my hands on him, I'm going to make him wish he'd never been born.' Essie clenched her fists. 'And then I'll set Grandmama on him.'

'I just want to go home.' Caro's expression was distraught. 'But how can I face Mama and Papa after this? I'm ruined.'

'Not if I have anything to say about it, you're not.'

'Or me.' Aidan's voice spoke up from the doorway. 'Forgive me for disturbing you, but I've taken a suite upstairs. You'll have more privacy there.'

'Thank you.' Essie threw him a grateful look as he crossed the room and helped Caro to her feet. She seemed as fragile as a china doll, walking limply between them as they led her up a staircase and along a narrow wooden gallery to a room containing a dining table, four chairs and a sofa by the fireplace.

'There's a bedroom through here.' Aidan opened a connecting door. 'When you've finished talking, sleep for as long as you need. There's no rush. Can I order you anything in the meantime? Tea?' He grimaced. 'That sounds like something my mother would suggest.'

'It still sounds lovely.' Essie smiled before sitting Caro down on the bed and crouching in front of her. 'Now don't worry about anything. We're going to make this all right.'

'How?'

She opened her mouth and then closed it again. She didn't have the faintest idea how, not yet, but she wasn't going to rest until she found it.

❧

It was another hour before Caro finally fell asleep and Essie was able to creep out of the bedchamber.

'Aidan?' She called his name softly.

'Over here.' He stood up from the sofa and rubbed his hands over his face, looking as messy as she'd ever seen him. His clothes were hopelessly creased and crumpled, his hair suggested he'd been dragged through a hedge backwards and his eyes had a glazed sheen as if he'd just been dozing, and yet her heart flipped over several times at the sight.

'Sorry. I didn't mean to wake you.'

'It doesn't matter. How is she?'

'Broken-hearted. It's as we suspected.'

'Jagger.' His expression turned thunderous before he turned away, muttering in a low voice.

'If you're swearing then don't be a gentleman on my account. You can't be saying anything worse than what I'm thinking.'

'You might be surprised. Where is he now?'

'Long gone.'

'The bastard.' He gave her a sharp look. 'I hate to ask, but did they –?'

'She says he touched her and she pushed him away.' She frowned. 'Although, to be honest, I'm still not entirely sure what we're talking about. Debauchery again, I suppose?'

'In this case, yes.' He rubbed a hand over his chin. There was a layer of stubble across it, giving him a slightly roguish appearance. 'Although in general it's not the best word. It makes it sound as if there's something wrong with the act itself. There isn't, not if you care for each other.'

'Really? So, if we were married, you'd want to –?' She left the question unfinished, still not quite understanding, but knowing it involved bed somehow. And stomach tingles. And possibly fireworks.

'Yes, but only if you wanted to as well.' He held on to her gaze for a long moment before clearing his throat. 'So . . . did your cousin write to anyone besides you before she left?'

'I don't know. I doubt it.'

'Well, that's something. With any luck, the only people who know about all this are me, you, your grandmother and our households. My staff are loyal and I'm willing to bet that your grandmother's are too. Which means, if we can just get your cousin back to London without anyone else finding out, maybe there's a chance to save both of your reputations.'

'Unless Jagger's told anyone? You know how much he likes to gossip.'

'Probably not about this. He'd find himself banished from every drawing room in London if it became common knowledge.' He moved a few steps towards her, his gaze softening. 'How are you feeling?'

'Like I want to disembowel him.'

'Understandable, but there may be a queue.' He lifted a hand to the side of her face, rubbing his thumb gently across her cheek, from the corner of her eye down to her jaw. 'Hungry?'

'Ravenous.'

'Then I won't be long.'

She blinked as he turned and made for the door, her cheek feeling bereft suddenly. 'Where are you going?'

'To order us some dinner. I think we've both earned it.'

'I thought earls could just snap their fingers and people would fall over themselves to help?'

'I have perfectly good legs and we're travelling incognito, remember? I'm plain Mr Ravell today.' He threw her a quick, boyish grin. 'I quite like it.'

'So do I.' She couldn't resist smiling back. 'Does Mr Ravell have an occupation? Or is he a gentleman of leisure?'

'Actually he's a gentleman farmer. He has crops mostly, but he also keeps a herd of cattle and has many strong opinions about the Corn Laws. You're Mrs Ravell, by the way. Under the circumstances, I thought it best to say we were married.'

'Good idea. Practical.' She nodded her approval before lying down on the newly vacated sofa. Now that the hunt for Caro was over, she felt exhausted, although she didn't want to sleep yet. She'd just lie here for a few minutes until Aidan returned and then they would have dinner. Together. That sounded nice. As for being Mrs Ravell . . . She sighed and closed her eyes, revelling in the warmth left by his body. That sounded surprisingly nice too.

'Caro?' Essie awoke with a gasp, sitting bolt upright on the sofa.

'Sorry.' Aidan threw her an apologetic look from the table where he was busy emptying a tray laden with cups, bowls and cutlery. 'I was trying to be quiet.'

'If that's dinner then there's no need to apologize.' She sniffed the air. 'It smells delicious.'

'Beef stew with dumplings and a bottle of red wine. I thought it would do nicely.' He tipped his head towards the bedroom. 'Should we wake up your cousin?'

Essie considered for a moment and then shook her head. 'No. Sleep is probably more important right now.' She walked across to the table and picked up a bowl. 'Brr, it's cold over here. Shall we eat by the fire?'

'Why not?' Aidan poured out some wine before following her back to the sofa.

'I think this might be the tastiest meal I've ever eaten,' Essie declared after a couple of large mouthfuls. 'I didn't realize how hungry I was.'

'Me neither.'

They ate the rest in silence, each making appreciative noises before depositing their bowls on the floor and sitting back with contented sighs.

'I'm not sure I'll be able to move again tonight.' Essie placed a hand over her full stomach.

'Then don't.' Aidan finished the last of his wine. 'I assumed that you'd share the bed with your cousin and I'd sleep here, but I could order a truckle bed instead, if you like?'

'No, it's all right. I'll drag myself up soon.' She tilted her head sideways and closed her eyes. 'I just need to digest for a few minutes.'

'Agreed. It's been a long day.'

'Extremely . . .'

She awoke some time later to find them in the exact same positions, only the sky outside the window was black and the fire was reduced to a dull, red glow. It was a strange feeling to wake up beside Aidan. Strange, but not uncomfortable. Slowly, she let her gaze roam over his face. For once he looked relaxed, the slight furrow between his brows smoothed out in sleep and the customary lock of black hair dangling over his forehead.

She slid closer, lifting her hand and smoothing the hair away before touching her fingers lightly against his lips. They felt warmer and softer than she remembered, reawakening that strange, steady thrumming sensation low in her abdomen. It made her want to kiss him again. For hours. For the whole night even, until her lips were completely numb. Just the thought made her smile, but he was asleep and it would be wrong and she really ought to move away and she was *definitely* about to, right up until the moment he opened his eyes too.

'Essie?' He murmured her name softly.

'Yes?'

'Are you awake?'

'Yes.' She caught her breath, considering. 'At least, I think so.'

'Am I?'

'Unless you're dreaming.'

'Ah. That explains it.'

'Explains wh–? She didn't finish the question as his mouth found hers and her mind emptied of words, all words, a phenomenon which had never happened in her life before, but felt surprisingly liberating. It was a gentle kiss, sleepy and soft, as if he were trying to lull her back to sleep, but passionate too, as if he couldn't *not* kiss her. She closed her eyes again as he curved an arm around her waist, pulling her across the sofa and into his lap.

'Did I ever tell you how much I like you?' He murmured the words quietly against her lips.

'Yes.' She smiled as she snuggled against him. 'I told you I liked you too.'

'I know.' She felt him grin. 'I just wanted to hear it again.'

❧

'Good morning, sleepy-head.' Aidan's voice broke through the haze of sleep, accompanied by his hand touching gently against her shoulder. 'Time to get up.'

'Is it morning?' She stretched her arms out to the sides, wincing as her neck and shoulder muscles protested. 'Ouch, I must have slept in a funny position.'

The words made her cheeks flame as memories from the night before came surging back into her consciousness. Although . . . *were* they memories? Aidan was standing up and she was alone on the sofa. Had they kissed during the night or had she dreamed it? If she *had*, then her imagination had excelled itself.

'Sorry about that.' Aidan cleared his throat. 'I thought about carrying you through to the bedroom, but under the circumstances . . . and with your cousin . . .'

'Yes. This was probably best.' Apparently her throat needed clearing too. 'I really only meant to close my eyes for a few minutes. I hope I didn't make it too uncomfortable for you?'

'Uncomfortable?' He looked mildly incredulous. 'Not at all. It was . . . I mean . . . I was just going to fetch us some breakfast. Coffee, in particular.'

'That sounds good.' She clambered to her feet to face him. He was looking even more dishevelled this morning, with twice as many bristles.

'I need a shave.' He obviously noticed her looking.

'Not necessarily. I think a beard might suit you.'

'Really?'

'Yes. You look . . .' She couldn't think of a good word, settling for a bad one instead. 'Hairy.'

'Thank you. I think.' His lips quirked as his gaze moved to her own hair. Judging by the weight of it around her shoulders, the last of her pins had fallen out during the night, leaving it completely loose and falling halfway to her waist. 'You look curly.'

'Urgh. I know.' She touched a hand to her head self-consciously. 'It never behaves for long.'

'It's like a waterfall.' He lifted a hand, the backs of his fingers skimming lightly against one of her breasts as he lifted a ringlet. 'Beautiful.'

'Knotted.'

'Tousled.'

She gulped as the air tensed between them. One tug on the ringlet and he could draw her back into his arms again, back down on to the sofa, back to what they were doing last night. She really couldn't have imagined *all* of it . . .

A small thud from the bedroom shattered the moment.

'Coffee then.' Aidan dropped her hair at once.

'Yes, and I'll –' Essie glanced around the room, looking for something, anything, she might do or comment on. 'I'll go and see how Caro is.'

'Good. Excellent.'

He bowed formally and she found herself dipping into a small, instantly regretted curtsey before he left and she headed for the bedchamber, repressing the urge to let out a howl of frustration.

'How are you feeling this morning?' She sat down on the edge of the bed where her cousin was just stirring.

'Ashamed.' Caro looked up, though she didn't lift her head from the pillow. The red splotches and purple shadows on her face were gone, but her complexion was still pasty and her eyes had lost all of their usual brightness. 'But better now you're here. Thank you for coming after me. I don't know what I would have done if you hadn't.'

'You would have thought of something.'

'Would I?' Caro's voice sounded hopeless. 'Why is the earl with you?'

'He's helping.' Essie was faintly alarmed by her cousin's listless demeanour. 'He won't tell anyone about this either. We're both here to look after you and get you safely back to London.'

'To Grandmama?'

'Of course.'

'What if she doesn't want me back? What did she say when she read my note?'

'Nothing. That is, I didn't get a chance to show her. By the time I found it, she'd gone out again. It was all very mysterious. Do you think she gambles?'

'Probably.' Caro stared blankly up at the canopy. 'Mama will be devastated. She had such high hopes for me and now I've brought shame on the whole family.'

'*I'm* your family and I don't think anything of the kind.' Essie turned her head at the sound of a light tap on the door. 'Aidan?'

'Coffee and hot rolls?'

'Ooh, yes please!' She leaped across the room, flinging the door wide.

'Good morning.' He smiled at Caro as he placed a plate and steaming cup on her bedside table. 'You're looking better already, Miss Foyle.'

'Thank you.' She turned her face away, as if she didn't want to look him in the eye.

'I've told my men to be ready to leave in an hour.' He turned his attention back to Essie. 'It'll be a bit of a squeeze in the post-chaise, but if we aim to arrive in London around dinnertime, we might be able to get through Mayfair unnoticed.'

'Good idea. Did you hear that, Caro?'

'Yes.' Her cousin reached a hand out, catching at her fingers. 'Essie, you won't disown me if everyone else does, will you?'

'How can you even ask me such a thing? I'm here for you and I always will be. If it comes to it, we'll *both* take to the stage. You're very good at playing princesses. It'll be like we dreamed when we were younger. We'll be free spirits, liberated from society's rules and expectations and judgements. We'll travel the world and become famous actresses and when we retire, we'll buy a cottage in the countryside with roses around the front door and be a pair of eccentric old spinsters. We'll even get our own Mildred.'

'Could we have honeysuckle instead? I've gone off roses.'

'Whatever flowers you want.'

'And maybe a cat?'

'A whole clowder of cats!' Essie grinned. 'Then we'll look back and say this was the best thing that ever happened to us.'

'Except that I can't play princesses any more.' Caro sniffed. 'They're always virtuous and I'm one of your bad women now.'

'You're not exactly Lady Macbeth either. You made a mistake, but Jagger was the one in the wrong, not you. We're certainly not going to let it ruin the rest of your life.'

Essie reached for a hot roll and took a defiant bite, glancing up to find Aidan staring at her with an oddly intense, tight-lipped expression. She swallowed, struck with the uneasy impression that she'd just said both the right and wrong thing at the same time.

Chapter Eighteen

The return journey was long, cramped and uncomfortable in more ways than one. They had no idea what rumours might already be swirling around London and the uncertainty made the atmosphere in the cab thick enough to cut with a knife. They spoke little and stopped only when absolutely necessary. The post-chaise had a single bench so Essie sat in the middle, Caro on one side and Aidan on the other, his profile tight and drawn, as if all the muscles in his face were clenched. It was only as they approached the outskirts to the city that he finally spoke, though he directed his attention towards Caro.

'Miss Foyle?' He leaned forward, his tone sympathetic. 'I hesitate to ask, but do you happen to know where Mr Jagger currently lives?'

'Close to Piccadilly.' Caro nodded wearily. 'He told me he has rooms in Albany.'

'I see. Thank you.'

Essie threw him an inquisitive look, but he only went back to staring straight ahead, his brow creased in thought.

Thankfully, as he'd predicted, the roads were comparatively quiet around seven o'clock when they finally arrived in Cavendish Square and made their way straight to the mews.

'Come on.' Essie touched a hand to Caro's shoulder as they rolled to a halt, only to find it shaking with nerves. 'It'll be all right, I promise. Grandmama's not going to refuse to see you.'

'Allow me, Miss Foyle.' Aidan stepped down and offered a hand. 'We'll go inside together.'

Essie took Caro's other arm and led them through the trade entrance and up a back staircase. Now the moment of truth was upon them, she couldn't deny that she was feeling more than a little nervous too. She didn't *think* their grandmother would do anything so cruel as to throw Caro out on to the street, but what if she was mistaken?

Thankfully, they didn't have to wait long to find out, the thud of footsteps descending the staircase at a frankly dangerous pace greeting them the moment they entered the hall.

'Oh, thank goodness!' Their grandmother flew across the floor with Mildred hard on her heels, somehow managing to fling her arms around both of them at the same time. 'I've lost years of my life worrying about the two of you.'

'I'm so sorry, Grandmama.' Caro burst into a fresh bout of tears. 'Please forgive me.'

'Oh, piffle. Whatever it is, I'm sure I've done worse. You're back now and that's all that matters.' The dowager took one look at her face and waved imperiously towards Quill, who was looking almost as relieved to see Essie again. 'Tell the maids we need a hot bath and some supper. And maybe some whisky. Goodness knows I need some. Denholm!' She looked as if she might hug Aidan too. 'I don't know how I shall ever repay you.'

'You don't have to. I was glad to be of service, but now if you'll excuse me? I have another matter to attend to.'

'Of course.' The dowager hooked an arm around Caro's waist. 'Come along, my dear.'

'Wait!' Essie made a grab for Aidan's arm as he turned away. 'Are you going after Jagger?'

He nodded, his voice and expression both grim. 'I'll try his rooms first.'

'Not without me, you won't.' She wrenched her shoulders back. 'If anyone gets to castrate him, it ought to be me.'

'Entertaining as that sounds, your cousin needs you.'

'She has Grandmama now.' She pushed past him, striding back the way that they'd come. 'Besides, you might need me for support and if you don't take me, then –'

'Then you'll hire a carriage and go anyway. Yes, I remember. Fine. I'm too tired to argue.'

'Thank you.' Essie watched him draw a hand over his face as they climbed back inside the post-chaise. 'And thank you for everything else too.'

He made a sound like a grunt and she clamped her brows together in dismay. The Aidan she'd come to know over the past week seemed to have drawn further and further away from her on the journey back to London. Now he was no longer the man she'd gone to for help in the middle of the night *or* kissed in the middle of another night. He was the haughty earl again, although she was too tired at that moment to try to work out why. Instead, she closed her eyes, listening to the sounds of hooves and rolling wheels on the cobbles outside.

'Wait here.' Before she knew it, Aidan was getting out again. 'I mean it this time.'

'What are you going to do if you find him?'

'First, I want to hear the whole story. Second, I'm going to make sure he keeps his mouth shut.'

'How?'

'Just leave it to me.'

'What if you need my help?'

'Then I'll come and ask for it.' He started away and then looked back over his shoulder. 'Don't move a muscle.'

Essie leaned back against the headrest obediently, waiting for what seemed like an age before sliding across to his side of the bench and peering outside. The building where Mr Jagger had rooms looked far too respectable for a villain: tall, grey and elegant, with white columns on either side of a normal-looking front door. There were no sounds of violence that she could hear either. No banging or crashing or even shouting. Which was undoubtedly a good thing. Even if the bloodthirsty part of her found it a little disappointing.

She jumped as the door opposite flew open and Aidan climbed back inside, his tone accusing. 'You moved.'

'Only across the seat. I didn't see you come out of the building.'

'I used a different door.'

'So?' She looked him over critically as the post-chaise lurched forward again. He didn't seem injured. In fact, there didn't appear to be a single scratch on him. 'Did you find him?'

'No. I spoke to his manservant. He hasn't seen him for two days.'

'How do you know he wasn't lying?'

'I don't, but if Jagger knows that we're looking for him then he'll probably lie low for a while.'

'So that's it?'

'No. I'll make further enquiries tomorrow.' His jaw tightened. 'I'll send a message to your father first thing in the morning too.'

'About Caro?' She blinked in surprise. 'Why?'

'About us. To inform him that our engagement is over.' He gave her a swift sideways look, though his expression was unreadable. 'I won't announce it publicly until I'm certain there are no rumours about any of this, but so long as there aren't, you can consider yourself free.'

'Free?' She felt as stunned as if he'd just pulled off a mask and revealed himself to be the nefarious Mr Jagger underneath. 'What about finding my replacement?'

'I don't give a damn about any replacement.'

'Then what about saving your estate?'

'I'll think of something.' His voice hardened, as if there were actual granite in it. 'That's none of your concern any longer.'

But what about us? She bit her tongue to stop herself from saying the words aloud. There *was* no *us*. She didn't want there to be an *us*! She might have kissed him – repeatedly – but only out of curiosity. It hadn't meant anything. Even if it had felt like something. *Still* felt like something.

'It's over, Essie.' A muscle twitched in his jaw. 'This, whatever this is, or was, is over.'

'Aidan . . .' She sucked the insides of her cheeks, her thoughts spinning so fast it was impossible to make sense of them, let alone string a coherent sentence together. She was only aware that she'd got what she wanted. She didn't know how she'd done it, but she'd persuaded him to release her and she hadn't even needed three months. Ten weeks had been long enough.

She started as a carriage whisked past them, making the cab rattle. She ought to be feeling elated. She ought to be positively giddy at her triumph, patting herself on the back for a job well done, but instead she felt like a glass of champagne left out for too long. All of the bubbles had already popped, leaving her completely flat.

Twenty minutes later, she was back in Cavendish Square, her engagement was over and Aidan was gone.

She was absolutely *not* going to cry.

Chapter Nineteen

'How is she?' The dowager came striding along the third-floor corridor, Mildred wheezing at her heels, when Essie emerged from her cousin's bedchamber late the next morning.

'She's staring at the ceiling again.' Essie closed the door softly behind her. 'I think perhaps we ought to leave her in peace for a while. She needs time to think.'

'Think? The last thing she ought to do is *think*!' Her grandmother sounded aggrieved. 'But I suppose you might be right about giving her some peace. She's had quite an ordeal. As have you.' The look in her eyes softened. 'Come along. If there's one thing I've learned over my three score and something years it's that nothing soothes a weary spirit like a cup of hot chocolate. Quill!' she shouted, taking for granted that the butler would be somewhere within earshot. 'Bring two hot chocolates! Cream and sugar too!'

Essie smiled half-heartedly, allowing herself to be ushered into her grandmother's private sitting room and on to an opulent, pink sofa.

'Now.' The dowager took the space beside her. 'I got the story from Caro during her bath. The abridged version, I imagine, but I have all the essentials. Did you have any luck finding Mr Jagger last night?'

'No. Aidan said he wasn't in his rooms.'

'Good. With any luck, he's gone abroad and won't return for a couple of decades. Naturally, I'd like to send Wellington after him, but I suppose that might draw undue attention.'

'Are you going to tell Aunt Emmeline?'

Her grandmother paused before shaking her head. 'Not unless it becomes necessary. I believe it's Caro's story to tell, not mine.'

'I feel so guilty for introducing her to Mr Jagger.'

'Monkey feathers! If it was anyone's fault then it's mine for not seeing the signs. I was too complacent, but then I didn't think she was the one I needed to keep my eye on.' Her grandmother fixed her with a keen stare. 'I think it's about time we were honest with each other, don't you? Emmeline wrote and told me you weren't particularly excited about your upcoming nuptials, but even if she hadn't, I wasn't born yesterday. When a young lady is engaged to an earl, one with good looks and a reasonable degree of intelligence, she generally evinces a little more enthusiasm about the prospect of seeing him. She doesn't wear orange and tread on his toes.'

'No, I suppose not.' Essie hung her head. 'I was trying to convince him to end our engagement.'

'So I assumed. The question is, *why*.'

'Because I'm not cut out to be a countess. It's not who I am.'

'Don't be ridiculous.'

'I'm not! I'm not beautiful or elegant or refined. And even if I were, I still wouldn't want to give up my freedom. A countess is supposed to behave in a certain way.'

'According to whom, may I ask? For pity's sake, if you're swayed by other people's opinions then you'll never do anything in this life. Do you think *I've* always followed the rules?' Her grandmother lifted her chin, seemingly with the express purpose of peering down her nose. 'But you're an intelligent girl. You know all of this. So, excuses aside, what's the real reason?'

'That *is* the real reason. That, and I have my own ambitions. Why should marriage be the only option? I want to be an actress.'

'Indeed? Well, given your most recent performance, I suspect you'd be very good at it.' Her grandmother inclined her head sympathetically, 'I hate to say I told you so, but I told my son something similar when he arranged your match with the earl all those years ago. You had an independent streak even then.'

'But you've been pushing Aidan and me together!'

'Only because I wanted you to give him a chance. I thought you might learn to like him.'

'I *do* like him, but I can't marry him.' Essie stared hard at the floor. 'You know, I remember the exact moment Father told me about our engagement. He looked so proud of himself, like he expected me to be grateful, while Mother just stood there in the background doing nothing. She always did nothing. And then she died a week later and left me.' She scrunched her mouth up. 'Why didn't she ever stand up to him? Why didn't she fight for me?'

'I've no idea.' The dowager sighed heavily. 'Things aren't always as simple as they appear, especially to a child, but your mother was a timid, unhappy soul from the first day I met her. Your parents' match was a good one on paper, but in reality it saddened me to see how unsuited they were. Unfortunately, my son was too much like my husband, too lacking in imagination and too full of his own importance. He never tried to understand her, and in return she wilted away like a plucked flower. You were the only one who ever made her smile.'

'My mother smiled?'

'Occasionally. She loved you, even though she couldn't stand up for you.'

'Father never tried to understand me either. He abandoned me with Aunt Emmeline and now that I'm grown up he just expects me to fulfil *his* ambitions. Why should I? Why should I do anything to make him happy? I don't *want* to make him happy!'

'I don't blame you for that.'

'Marriage destroyed my mother.' Essie clenched her fists. 'I don't want to end up like her.'

'Oh, I doubt that's possible. You're a very different character altogether, my dear. You're quite as single-minded and stubborn as I am, not to mention your father. Why do you think he was so obsessed with having a son? Because the fool was too blind to see what a jewel he already had.' She placed her hands over Essie's, gently unfurling her fingers. 'However, those qualities can be both a strength and a weakness. They helped you to survive a terrible start in life, but perhaps they also made you a little *too* stubborn? A change of mind, or heart, can be a good thing, especially if it means letting go of the past.' She held a palm up as Essie opened her mouth to interrupt. 'I understand you being afraid and wanting revenge and I wholeheartedly agree that marriage is a dangerous business for a woman. We're expected to subjugate ourselves to our husbands, to trust them as if they're the fount of all wisdom, which is very rarely the case, and if we choose the wrong man, there's no easy escape. But you're not your mother and not all husbands are like your father. Some marriages are very happy.'

'None that I've seen.'

'Perhaps because you've decided not to. Emmeline, for all her faults, is very happy with your Uncle Charles, and I'm perfectly content in mine.'

'What? I thought that you and Grandfather —'

'Oh, we couldn't stand the sight of each other. My second husband, however, is a very different kettle of fish.'

'Your —' Essie was vaguely aware of her jaw dropping open. 'Who?'

'My second husband, Seamus.'

'But I've never heard of him.'

'I should think not. Nobody has.'

'So . . . Wait, is *that* who you were visiting the other night?'

The dowager chuckled. 'I thought about saying it was a gaming den, but now I think the truth might serve you better.'

'But if you're married, why don't you live together? Why all the secrecy?'

'It's rather fun, I think. And your father and aunt would never approve. Seamus runs a delightful little hostelry called The Snoring Leopard. As for not living together, we don't want to. I value my independence and so does he.' She patted Essie's knee. 'My point is, there's no one way to be married, but if you truly wish for an alternative then I'll provide you with one.'

'What do you mean?'

'My friend Mrs Willoughby intends on making a Tour of the Continent later this summer and requires a companion. She's a widow and quite eccentric, what some people would call a bluestocking. I believe the two of you would get along very well.'

'Really?' Essie sat up excitedly. 'Do you mean it?'

'I do. As for being an actress, I wish I could tell you the world is ready for young ladies to forge their own paths in life, but sadly it's not. It wouldn't be an easy existence. Your father, as I think you suspect, would never forgive you, and there would be other sacrifices. You wouldn't be permitted to see Caro again, not officially anyway.'

'But I can't just give up on my dreams.'

'No, never give up, Essie. Just think very hard about what it is that you really want, deep down. To act or to escape. I don't want you turning your back for the wrong reasons on something that might make you happy.'

'It doesn't matter anyway.' Essie dropped her gaze again. 'Aidan broke off our engagement last night.'

'Indeed? Because of Caro?'

'I don't think so. He just announced it on our way back from Jagger's rooms. He said I was free.'

'And how do you feel?'

'Honestly? I don't know whether I'm tired or in shock, but . . . underwhelmed. It's like I don't know what to feel.'

'The two of you have spent quite a bit of time together recently.'

'Yes.' She felt her cheeks darken. 'He also said that he'd wait a few days to make an announcement in case there were any rumours spreading about us.' She didn't know how to feel about that either . . . 'Do you think it'll be possible to keep Caro's elopement a secret?'

'Yes. Surprisingly enough, I do. We're not out of the woods yet, but your cousin was relatively discreet.' Her grandmother looked up as the butler entered, bearing a tray. 'Fortunately, my staff are very good at sniffing out any hints of scandal, isn't that right, Quill?'

'We do our best, my lady.'

'And your best is greatly appreciated. As are these chocolates.' The dowager licked her lips enthusiastically. 'No, from what I can tell, both of your reputations appear to be safe.'

'Well, that's something, I suppose.' Essie lifted her own cup, though for once the prospect of chocolate didn't excite her. 'Except that Caro's heart is broken.'

'Hearts mend.'

'Always?'

'I should imagine that depends on the quality of the love. Something tells me your cousin was just swept up in the romance of the thing.'

'She's not so shallow.'

'Oh, I'm not insulting her. She's a sweet, trusting girl with a kind heart. The thought of redeeming a rake like Jagger probably appeals to that sort of temperament. Unfortunately, it's also the easiest to take advantage of.' Her grandmother shook her head. 'I've often thought we do young ladies a disservice by not teaching them more about the world before they leave the school-room. Caro's learned her lesson the hard way.'

'I doubt she'll be ready to face Society again for a while.'

'Probably not. And I suppose we'll be cancelling your engagement ball next week too. Pity. I was rather looking forward to a masquerade.'

'I'm sorry, Grandmama.'

'Yes, the two of you have proved rather a challenge.'

'There's one more thing I need to tell you.' Essie took a deep breath. 'Aidan said that he'd write to Father first thing this morning. How long will it take for a letter to reach him, do you think?'

'About six hours, I expect. Then six hours to ride back . . .'

'So he'll be here before nightfall?'

'Or early tomorrow morning.' Her grandmother lifted her eyes to the ceiling. 'In that case, drink up. We need to fortify ourselves.'

Chapter Twenty

Essie laced her fingers over her stomach, abandoning any hope of sleep as she stared at the red velvet canopy above her head. She'd dozed for the first few hours after retiring to bed, but with the dawn chorus now tentatively warming its collective throat outside her window, she supposed it was time to stop delaying the inevitable. She wasn't going to get another wink of sleep until she answered the question her grandmother had asked her.

What did she really want, deep down?

In theory, she already *had* what she wanted. Her ambitions were on the verge of being fulfilled. Aidan and her grandmother between them had given her an opportunity to travel, to go to Paris, to Vienna, to Rome even! And when she returned, the stage would be waiting. Ten weeks ago the prospect would have thrilled her, but instead she felt as low as she had when Aidan had deposited her on her grandmother's doorstep and driven away, presumably on his way to marry somebody else. She'd expected the feeling to pass, but instead it had become steadily worse. She felt as flat as she'd ever been in her life. As flat as . . . She turned her head, looking for inspiration and spying a book on her nightstand. As flat as a piece of paper. One that had been ruthlessly scribbled over, scrunched into a ball, thrown across the room and then crushed beneath some weighty tome to flatten it again. So flat with creases, ones she had no idea how to smooth out.

That, in short, was the problem. She felt as if there was a battle raging inside her brain, as if the past few days she'd spent with Aidan had somehow jumbled her thoughts and there was no way to restore her old ideas or to regain her peace of mind, not without throwing the old creased and crumpled page away and beginning a new one.

If only she knew what she wanted it to say.

At last, with an exasperated sigh, she threw her quilt back and went to perch on the cushioned window seat overlooking the street, curling her legs up beneath her as she peered out at the semi-darkness and her own reflection. If she was really going to start soul-searching at four o'clock in the morning then she supposed she might as well look herself in the eye while she did it.

What did she really want?

Her childhood dream had been the stage, but perhaps there were other possibilities that she'd never really given a chance. Like being a countess. Maybe, just maybe, it was time to take a second look, if only to reassure herself that she'd done the right thing and it definitely *wasn't* what she wanted. Perhaps it would have been possible, for example, to have regarded it as a performance. It would have been a permanent role, a lifelong commitment, but maybe it was better to have one definitive part and do it brilliantly rather than several minor ones. And who was to say that a countess *couldn't* act anyway? Up until a century and a half ago, women hadn't been allowed to be actresses at all. Who was to say how things might change in the future?

Somebody had to be the first to do new things. And Aidan had promised that he wouldn't hold her back. And she trusted Aidan. So, all in all, maybe being a countess wouldn't have been *so* bad?

She frowned at her reflection, watching as the world outside turned from indigo to sapphire blue until gradually all the stars faded and a rosy-pink glow suffused the sky over the rooftops. At which point she slid off the window seat and on to the floor, wondering why she was feeling the need to torture herself quite so intensely. There was no point in thinking about being a countess. She wasn't going to be one, not any more. The decision had already been made; a decision that she'd *wanted* and done everything in her power to bring about. The best thing she could do now was get up, stop wallowing in introspection and move on. Except . . . She squeezed her brows together as a thought danced around the edge of her consciousness, darting away every time she tried to reach for it . . .

Bang!

She uttered a small yelp as a door slammed violently downstairs.

Oh . . . bollocks.

There was a moment of absolute silence, like the calm before a storm, followed by a man's voice raging in the hallway below. One she recognized instantly.

She threw a swift glance at her bed, briefly tempted to crawl beneath it, then pulled on some clothes and crept out of her room towards the staircase.

'It's an outrage! He won't get away with this!' Her father's voice echoed around every corner of the house, practically rattling the chandeliers.

'For pity's sake, stop shouting.' Her grandmother's voice was somewhat lower in volume, but just as authoritative. 'You'll wake up the whole square.'

'Damn the square! I'm going to make sure the whole of London knows what he's done!'

'No doubt they've already heard you from here.'

Essie tiptoed closer and peered around the edge of the drawing-room door. Her grandmother was sitting on her customary sofa, dressed in a purple satin robe, while her father stood by the fireplace, hands on hips. Physically, he was just as lean and sharp as she remembered, as if his body refused to tolerate even the faintest hint of softness, but his face displayed the passage of time, his brow so deeply furrowed there appeared to be an actual trench running down the centre. It was also an alarming shade of puce. Age definitely hadn't mellowed him.

'Ah.' Her grandmother caught sight of her, beckoning her in before she could succumb to the powerful temptation to run away. 'Essie, look who's here.'

'Father.' She straightened her shoulders as she entered.

'Celeste.' His dark gaze narrowed as it swept over her. 'What have you done?'

She froze halfway across the room. Apparently that was all the greeting she was going to get. No smile, no compliments, not even a comment about how much she'd grown. Just a hard stare and an accusation. Which really oughtn't to have surprised her, but after ten years she'd forgotten quite how penetrating that stare could be. It seemed to burrow into her skull, making her want to confess.

'I don't know what you're suggesting.' Fortunately, her grandmother came to her rescue. 'Essie has been the perfect model of a debutante. Exemplary in every way.'

'Then what's the matter with her?' Her father swung about, narrowly missing the dowager's wink. 'What's made him change his mind now? I spoke to him only a few weeks ago!'

'Yes, I heard you'd been in town. How nice of you *not* to visit. Whatever the earl's reason, however, my granddaughter is the victim here. I won't have her accused in my own drawing room.'

'Then he'll pay. I'll take him to court for this.'

'No!' Essie found her voice at last, taking an instinctive step backwards as her father threw an acid glare in her direction. 'I mean, you can't. It was only a gentleman's agreement.'

'Who told you that?' Her father's lip curled contemptuously. 'I paid good money for your engagement and I have a contract to prove it.'

'What?' She swayed to one side as the floor trembled beneath her feet. 'But I thought that you and the old earl were friends?'

'Don't be absurd.' Judging by her father's expression, he didn't recognize the concept of friendship. 'We belonged to the same club, that's all. I paid half of your dowry, twenty-five thousand pounds, to save him from some financial mess he'd got himself in, not that it lasted the old fool very long. If his son wants to break the engagement now, he'll have to pay back every penny. With interest!'

'Twenty-five thousand pounds?' She gasped at the enormity of the amount. 'He'll never be able to afford so much.'

'He should have thought about that before he wrote to me.'

'But he must not know about the contract!'

'He will soon.' The lip curl twisted into a full-on sneer. 'I'll ruin him. I'll destroy his name, his home, everything!'

'You can't!' Essie rushed forward, undeterred by his glare this time. 'If you only knew what he'd done!'

'Why? What has he done?'

'I . . . that is, he –' She bit her tongue. If she told her father about Caro then a messenger would be on their way to Aunt Emmeline within the hour. 'Nothing, but he's a good man.'

'Pah!'

'Think how it will look for me if you take him to court!' She tried another tack. 'I'll be a laughing stock.'

'You expect me to just forget twenty-five thousand pounds?' Her father looked incredulous. 'I'm going to my lawyers.'

'Wait!' She leaped sideways, blocking his route to the door. 'Let me speak to the earl first. Maybe I can get him to change his mind.'

'What makes you think you can do that?'

'Because I think . . . perhaps . . . we had a small misunderstanding.' She lifted her chin as her father's gaze turned accusing again. 'But I can fix it, I know I can. Just give me one day.'

'Absolutely not. Nobody makes a fool of me.'

'Please!' She held her hands up, palms outward. 'Father, I'm begging you. I've never asked you for anything before, but just give me one day. One single day.'

'Perhaps you ought to change out of your travelling clothes and into something more respectable before you go anywhere?' The dowager spoke before he could answer. 'You may not care how you appear walking around London, Alfred, but I have certain standards.'

'Quill?' Her father's glare deepened as he waited for the butler to arrive. 'Have my bags been taken upstairs?'

'Yes, sir.'

'All right, I'll change, but *then* I'm going to my lawyers.'

'If that's what you think is best.' The dowager nodded placidly. 'Personally, I intend to have breakfast.'

'Grandmama!' Essie spun around as her father stormed away without a single additional look in her direction. 'How do I stop him?'

'Just a moment. Quill?'

'Yes, my lady?'

'I expect you heard most of that?'

'I did, my lady.'

'Marvellous. In that case, I'd be most grateful if you could deal with the situation.'

'With pleasure, my lady.'

'*Deal* with the situation?' Essie stared at her grandmother in consternation as the butler turned away. 'What does that mean?'

'Nothing to concern yourself with, dear. Suffice to say that, contrary to what *some* people believe, I don't choose my staff simply for their bone structure. Physical prowess has a little something to do with it as well. Your father won't be going anywhere for a while.'

'You mean . . . ?'

'Best not to ask questions. I can give you this morning, if you're certain this is what you want? From what you told me yesterday, your misunderstanding sounded rather final.'

'I know, but I can't let Father do this, not after what Aidan did for Caro.'

'And what about you? Gratitude is all very well, but you've gone to a great deal of trouble to be free.'

Essie glanced at the door and then back again. If she went to Aidan now, there would be no changing her mind a second time. She would become the countess for better or worse, for the rest of her life. But her grandmother was right – she wasn't her mother, she didn't have to do exactly what was expected of her and now that she had the freedom to choose, she knew what she needed to do.

'I don't want my freedom at the expense of his.' She nodded her head adamantly. 'Aidan was forced into this engagement like I was. We're in it together. We've been in it together for the past ten years and I'm not abandoning him now.' She winced. 'Even if it means pleasing Father. The engagement's back on!'

'Well then, it seems Mrs Willoughby is going to be disappointed, after all.'

'Thank you, Grandmama.' Essie dropped a kiss on to the dowager's cheek and charged headlong out of the room. What she needed was a new plan, one that involved undoing everything she'd achieved so far and getting her fiancé back.

D was for Denholm.

PLAN D: DENHOLM

Dear Father,
It's too late for us to talk, but there are things I find I need to say.
I love you, I miss you, but how could you have lied to us for so long?
How could you be so cowardly? I don't know how to forgive you.

Aidan Ravell, 13th Earl of Denholm, to his father (deceased),
12th January 1815

Chapter Twenty-one

(Two Weeks until Wedding Day)

'I need to speak with the earl!'

'Again?' Fothergill sighed, eloquently conveying his lack of enthusiasm about seeing her again. 'I'm afraid that his lordship is indisposed.'

'It's urgent.'

'I repeat, *again*?'

'Yes, again.' Essie gritted her teeth, resisting the urge to say something unladylike. 'I was telling the truth before, wasn't I? I'm his fiancée.'

'*Was* his fiancée, as I understand it.'

'All right, *was* his fiancée, but surely that means something?'

'Sadly not. I'm afraid that I shall have to ask you to leave.'

'Then I'm afraid I shall have to do this. *Aidan!*' she bellowed at the top of her lungs. '*Aidaaan!*'

'Stop that!' A butlery hand shot out to restrain her, but she was ready for him, ducking under his arm and through the door into the hall and towards the staircase, only to find herself confronted by a pair of stern-faced footmen.

'*Aidaaan!*' she shouted again as they closed in around her.

'Good gracious.' Her former future mother-in-law appeared on a balcony. 'You have a curious manner of announcing yourself, Miss Craven.'

'I know.' Essie grappled in the grip of one particularly burly footman. 'But I need to speak with Aidan!'

'He's not here, and even if he was, you no longer have the right to visit him, especially at this hour of the morning. As for myself, I'm not at home.'

'Wait!' Essie applied the tip of her leather boot to the footman's ankles as the countess turned away. 'My father's in town. He says there's a contract!'

The other woman stopped abruptly, turning her head to look back over her shoulder like an elegantly dressed owl. 'What did you say?'

'My father says he paid for our engagement!'

'My husband signed a contract?'

'Yes and –' Essie stiffened, exchanging a startled glance with her captor as the countess let loose a volley of increasingly foul-mouthed expletives. 'Um . . . my lady?'

'I suppose I ought to have expected something like this.' The countess finally came back to herself, smoothing a hand over her bodice before giving a sharp nod to the footman. 'You'd better release her.'

'Where has Aidan gone?' Essie immediately charged up the staircase. 'I need to speak with him urgently.'

'First you can speak to me.' The countess led her into a fashionably primrose-coloured, albeit somewhat sparsely furnished, drawing room and positioned herself beside one of the large bay windows. 'How much?'

'You mean for the contract?'

'Yes.'

'I'm afraid it's quite a bit.'

'How much?'

'You might want to sit down.'

'*Miss* Craven!'

'Twenty-five thousand pounds. Half of my dowry.'

The countess's left eye twitched. 'The fool. The stupid, reckless old fool. If he were still alive I'd throttle him.'

'I thought you were happily married?'

'I was. I'd throttle him, kiss him and *then* throttle him again! And now I suppose your father wants it all back?'

'Yes, with interest, unless Aidan goes through with the wedding.'

'I see.' The countess pursed her lips so tightly they almost disappeared into her face. 'Very well, you've delivered your message and *I* shall pass it along. Now, you may leave.'

'No.' Essie deposited herself into a chair and gripped the arms. They were slightly threadbare, she noticed, but she was prepared to fight an army of footmen before surrendering her position. 'I didn't just come to warn him. I've come to say that I'll marry him, after all.'

'You will?' The countess pressed a hand to her chest, her lips reappearing and looking almost in danger of smiling. 'Oh, thank goodness.'

'Yes, but we need to find him before my father does anything drastic. He'll be ... *restrained* for a couple of hours, but after that he'll go straight to his lawyers.'

The countess rang a small bell, tapping her foot until the butler arrived. 'Ah, Fothergill, I need to know where his lordship has gone this morning.'

'I'm afraid that I'm not at liberty to say, my lady.' Fothergill threw an aggrieved look towards Essie. 'His lordship was most particular in his instructions.'

'Are you saying that you won't tell me?' The countess bore down on him, dropping her shoulders and stretching her neck in a manner that put Essie in mind of an enraged dragon slowly unfurling its coils.

'I . . . I cannot, my lady.' The butler looked as if those same basilisk coils were now wrapping themselves inexorably around his throat and squeezing tight, his expression so desperate that he actually looked towards Essie for help. She shrugged, surprised to feel sorry for a man who'd tried to slam a door in her face – *twice* – but she did. Unfortunately for him, she wanted to know where Aidan was too.

'Let me be perfectly clear.' The countess's voice dropped several octaves. 'You will tell me where my son is or you will leave my employment at once.'

'But his lordship –'

'*At once!*'

'Hampstead Heath, my lady.'

'What?' The countess's hand shot to her throat.

'What's so terrible about Hampstead Heath?' Essie piped up behind her.

'It's not the place itself. It's what happens there . . . Duels.'

'What?' Essie jumped to her feet, all sympathy for the hapless butler evaporating. 'Who with? Sylvester Jagger?'

'I don't know, miss. He didn't say.'

'What time did he leave?'

'Just after dawn.'

'That was hours ago!' She sprang towards the door. 'I have to go after him!'

'It's too late!' The countess's voice quavered. 'Whatever's happened is over.'

'Well, I can't just sit here and wait!' She was already halfway down the staircase and barrelling out of the front door, calling out instructions to her grandmother's driver as she dived headlong into the waiting carriage.

The streets were already busy as tradespeople went about their early-morning business, but thankfully the carriage made fast progress. It was only half an hour before she leaped out again, at which point it struck her that Hampstead Heath was a great deal bigger than she'd anticipated. Worse, it was shrouded in a thin, but impenetrable layer of morning mist.

'Where do they hold the duels?' she called up to the driver.

'I don't know, miss.' The man looked faintly startled. 'They're not exactly what you'd call legal.'

'Damn it!' She screwed her eyes up, but it was no use. A whole army of duellers could be standing twenty yards in front of her and she'd never be able to see them. As for going to look, it would be madness even to try.

She was just about to give up and go back to Mayfair in despair when a lone figure emerged from the haze, swaggering towards her with an instantly recognizable air of bravado.

'Jagger!' She curled her hands into fists, storming towards him. 'You loathsome cur!'

'Miss Craven.' He removed his hat with a flourish. 'Charming to see you, as always.'

'Don't you Miss Craven me!' She swung her arm back, reconsidered, and then lifted her knee forcefully instead. It was a manoeuvre she'd once witnessed while driving through Newcastle with her aunt and, although she'd never had occasion to use it herself before, the results were everything she'd hoped for. Jagger dropped to the ground with a heartfelt yowl of pain.

'That was for Caro!' She loomed over him. 'Now tell me where Aidan is or I'll do it again.'

'I don't know. He left.'

'Alive?'

'What do you care?' He flinched as she lifted her foot threateningly. 'Yes, alive.'

'If you're lying –'

'I'm not.'

'Good.' She felt her whole body sag with relief. 'Now promise me you won't breathe a word about Caro or I'll tell the whole of London what a despicable libertine you are!'

'Yes, your fiancé already gave me that speech.' Jagger staggered back to his feet. 'Tell away. It's no less than anyone expects.' A flash of his old impudent demeanour returned. 'If it's any consolation, I would have preferred you, but your cousin presented such an easy target.'

'You think I'm jealous?' Essie laughed incredulously and then kicked her foot out, catching him in the same spot as before. 'You're not a quarter of the man Aidan is. As for Caro, you don't deserve to breathe the same air!'

'Ow!' Jagger was on the ground again, hands clutched in front of him defensively, gasping for air. 'You might find the *ton* has a different opinion about that.'

'Then how about this?' She looked him over contemptuously. 'If you ever so much as *think* her name again, I'll make sure every tradesman in London calls in your debts. I've become quite good friends with my grandmother's butler recently and I'm certain he'll know just who to talk to.'

Jagger's face paled. 'You wouldn't. I'd be ruined.'

'Don't tempt me. In the meantime, I suggest you leave for the country before my grandmother gets her hands on you. You'll find that I'm a *lot* more reasonable than she is.'

She threw him one last scathing glare and then climbed back into the carriage, acknowledging the coachman's approving look with a nod before racing back to Mayfair. Where, unfortunately, there was still no sign of Aidan.

'I found Jagger.' She rushed back into the drawing room. 'He says Aidan's alive.'

'Oh, thank goodness!' The countess clutched at her hands. 'But where could he be?'

'Someone must have been his second for the duel. He'd be able to tell us. Could it be Mr Dormer?'

The countess considered for a moment and then nodded. 'Yes! I'll send someone to his rooms straightaway.'

'Send someone where?' Aidan's voice interjected from the doorway. 'Good morning, Mother. Essie.' He smiled nonchalantly, as if he wasn't remotely surprised to find the pair of them together, holding hands in the drawing room before breakfast. 'You're both looking very serious.'

'Of course we're looking serious!' Essie felt a powerful urge to grab hold of his coat lapels and start shaking. 'You've just terrified us half to death!'

'Have I?' He looked over his shoulder. 'Should I have knocked?'

'No, you shouldn't have – Aidan, I've been to Hampstead Heath.'

'When?'

'This morning! How could you fight a duel?'

'Oh, that.' He sprawled in a chair, still smiling his strange smile. 'Dormer just brought me home, good fellow. He wanted to come into the house, but for some reason I thought our business this morning was a secret. Out of interest, how *do* you know about it?'

'Have you been drinking?' His mother sniffed the air indignantly. 'Aidan, it's nine o'clock in the morning!'

'Yes. They gave me some whisky for the pain.'

'Pain?' Essie dropped into a crouch beside him, not entirely deliberately as her knees simply seemed to give way. 'Have you been shot?'

'Barely. It's just a graze across the top of my shoulder. Ruined a perfectly decent shirt and jacket too. Look, there's a hole.' He pushed a finger through and wiggled it in front of her. 'Damned nuisance.'

'Never mind your coat!' She clutched at his finger, reassuring herself that he was still in one piece. 'We thought that you were, that you might be . . . you know.'

'Dead?' He looked thoughtful. 'Yes, I wondered the same thing for a few moments. Fortunately not. As for Jagger, not even a scratch. I'm a terrible shot, although that worried me more than anything. I only wanted to scare the man, not kill him, but with my aim . . .' He shrugged and then winced. 'I had to shoot straight up in the air to be safe.'

'But when did you challenge him? Did you find him yesterday?'

'Actually . . .' He looked mildly shamefaced. 'When I told you that he wasn't in his rooms the other night, I wasn't being entirely accurate.'

'You lied to me?'

'I wasn't convinced he'd make it to the duel in one piece if you got your hands on him.'

'You still shouldn't have challenged him! You could have been hurt!'

'He dishonoured your cousin.'

'Exactly. *My* cousin! If anyone was going to aim a gun at him, it should have been me. *I'm* an excellent shot.'

'I don't doubt it.' His glazed expression appeared to focus suddenly. 'Why are you here, Essie?'

'Oh . . . right.' She let go of his finger. In all the drama, she'd almost forgotten her initial reason for coming. 'It's because of my father. He got your letter and as it turns out, our engagement isn't just based on a gentleman's agreement. There's an actual contract. So now he's threatening to sue you if we don't go through with it.'

'Ah. How unfortunate.' Aidan tipped his head back, letting out a low whistle as he stared at the ceiling. 'I'll be honest, I've had better mornings.'

'It's all right. We're not going to let him sue you. We're going to forget everything I've said and done over the past ten weeks and get married on the first of June like we were supposed to.'

'Was that a proposal?'

'No!' She sat back on her haunches. 'But if we don't get married then –'

'Then your father can do his worst. I don't care any more.'

'What?' Essie looked from him to his mother. Not once on her way over there, or on her way to Hampstead Heath and back, had it ever occurred to her that he might refuse her.

'Aidan.' The countess recognized her cue and stepped forward. 'I know you've had a trying morning, but if there's a contract –'

'We're still not getting married.'

'Yes we are. We have to!'

'Actually, we don't. Legally, your father might have cause to sue me, but he can't force me down the aisle. Or you either.' He gave a half-smile. 'Nothing's changed since the other night.'

'Everything's changed!'

'I doubt it. Not unless you've discovered some new-found burning desire to be a countess?'

'No, but –' She bit her tongue. Given the choice, she still didn't *want* to be a countess, but the thought of being without him struck her suddenly as ten times worse. And she couldn't have him without the title. The two were inextricably entwined. As for burning desire . . . well, that wasn't something she was prepared to discuss with his mother standing behind her.

'You're not thinking clearly.' The countess spoke up again. 'Think about what will happen if you don't marry. Think of Sophia.'

'Don't worry about me!'

'Eavesdropping again?' Aidan turned his head as his sister bounded into the room, looking as rosy-cheeked and cheerful as a milkmaid in a painting of some pastoral idyll.

266

'Coming down for breakfast actually.' Sophia smiled. 'I've no idea what you're all talking about, but whatever it is, Aidan should do whatever makes him happy. He deserves to be.'

'Thank you. You're rather a good little sister, do you know that?'

'I think so too. Hello, Essie, you're here early.'

'Yes, I came to discuss wedding plans.'

'Oh, goodie. Are you staying for breakfast? Can I be a bridesmaid?'

'I'd be thrilled –'

'No!' Aidan sat forward abruptly. 'Sophia, there isn't going to be any wedding.'

'What?'

'Yes, there is!'

'Enough, all of you!' the countess snapped. 'Aidan, this is serious.'

'I know.' He sighed heavily. 'But I've had enough. I'm sure that Father did what he thought was best at the time, but I'm not letting him define my life any more. This is too much to ask.'

'I see.' The countess subsided elegantly into a chair. 'Very well. We'll face the consequences together.'

'What's wrong with the two of you?' Essie put her hands on her hips. 'Don't you understand? I've changed my mind! For the first time in my life, *I've changed my mind*!'

'And I appreciate it.' Aidan pushed himself to his feet. 'Only, the thing is, I don't want to be someone you have to change your mind about. I think I deserve better. And I certainly don't want you to marry me out of pity. So thank you, but no thank you.' He reached for her hand, kissed it

267

and then yawned. 'Now if you'll all excuse me, I'm going back to bed.'

'No! This isn't just about you.' Essie twisted her fingers around his as he started to pull away. She wasn't going to stand by and let this happen, wasn't going to let her father destroy somebody else she cared about. At that moment, she felt as frightened as if Aidan were on his way to fight another duel, only this one would be death by a thousand cuts. 'You're not excused. We're engaged and I won't allow you to throw me over. It would be dishonourable.'

'Dishonourable?' His eyes turned from blue to grey in an instant, as if there were actual storm clouds brewing inside them. Big ones, full of rain and hail and thunderbolts.

'Yes, dishonourable!' She cleared her throat, uncomfortably aware that casting slurs on his character wasn't the most romantic way to persuade him. 'We're getting married and that's all there is to it.' She paused, bracing herself to sprint for the door. 'And Sophia's going to be a bridesmaid.'

'I need your help!' Essie burst through the door to Caro's bedchamber.

'Yes, we thought you might. We've just been discussing it.' Her grandmother was sitting on the edge of the bed, Mildred stretched out inelegantly beside her, paws in the air as she presented her belly for rubs. 'How's the earl?'

'He fought a duel with Mr Jagger!'

'What?' Caro lurched upright.

'Don't worry, they're both all right. Wait, you're talking again?'

'I had to. Grandmama started reading poetry and it was the only way to make her stop.'

'Not the poems of your suitor Mr Nightingale again?'

'Even worse. I thought that my ears were going to start bleeding.'

'I hold an artistic soirée once a month,' the dowager explained. 'I like to encourage the arts, although some of the attendees make it rather difficult. Fortunately, in this case, some of their efforts proved extremely useful. Caro told me exactly what happened with Mr Jagger and I told her some of the more salacious scandals of the past forty years. I thought it might put things into perspective.'

'Which it did.' Caro smiled. 'I feel ten times better already.'

'So on top of everything else, you're telling me I just missed forty years of scandal?'

'I'm afraid so. And Grandmama says it's on a need-to-know basis so until you do something equally stupid, I have to keep my lips sealed.'

'I've already done something stupid!' Essie wailed, flinging herself face-down beside Mildred. 'I made Aidan believe that I don't want to marry him and now he doesn't want to marry me!'

'Well, that's not *so* surprising. First you told him you didn't want to marry him, then you tried to embarrass him, then you stood on his toes, then you pushed him into the Serpentine . . .' Caro counted the items off on her fingers.

'And those are just the things we know about,' their grandmother interjected. 'Did he specify which precise straw broke the camel's back?'

'No. He just said that he deserves better than someone who's changed her mind about him and some stupid male pride thing about not wanting pity.'

'Ah.' Her grandmother sighed. 'I take it the wedding's still off, then?'

'No, it's back on.' Essie flipped herself over, earning herself a disgruntled canine grunt. 'At least I think it is. I told Aidan so and he was too much of a gentleman to contradict me. Even half-drunk, as it turns out.' Although, considering the speed with which she'd run out of the house afterwards, he hadn't had much of a chance to argue.

'You mean, you *refused* to end your engagement?' Caro opened her eyes wide. 'After all your scheming?'

'Yes. My father's going to ruin him otherwise.' Essie groaned. 'So now I have to insist on him marrying me for his own good. It's like I'm cod liver oil.'

'But you don't have to insist, do you?' Caro leaned forward. 'I mean, it's a shame about your father, but you didn't know there was a contract so you can't be held responsible. You don't have to be cod liver oil. You're free.'

'But I don't *want* to be free of Aidan, not entirely!'

'Oh, really?' Her cousin exchanged a swift, faintly smug look with their grandmother. 'Did you tell him that?'

'Not in so many words.' Essie pursed her lips. 'I just said that my father will sue him if we don't get married so we should forget everything that's happened so far and go back to the way things were.'

'How romantic.'

'It's the truth! Besides, his mother was there! What else could I say?'

'We can't tell you that, my dear. You're the only one who knows how you feel.' Her grandmother lifted an eyebrow. 'Presumably.'

'I feel like I don't want my father to ruin him.'

'Because?'

'Because he doesn't deserve it.'

'Because?'

'Because he's kind and honourable and good.' She adopted a virtuous expression. 'And he has a mother and sister to consider.'

'Very noble.' The dowager rolled her eyes at Caro. 'Honestly, it's like pulling a whole set of teeth at once. You try.'

'Essie.' Caro put a hand on her arm. 'Do you care for him?'

'Of course I do. We're friends now.'

'Is that *all*? Are you sure you're not just a *teeny-tiny* bit in love with him?'

'Love?' Essie threw her arms out, eliciting an actual growl from Mildred. *Could* she be in love? She'd been so busy thinking about whether she could bear to be a countess that she hadn't considered that particular emotion. She'd never had occasion to think of it before. She and Aidan were conspirators. Friends. Friends who'd kissed, but as for being any more than that . . . Her cheeks flushed as she remembered their night on the sofa at the inn. All right, maybe a little more than that. 'I don't know. How would I know?'

'How did you feel about him fighting a duel?'

Sick. Horrified. As if for the first time in her whole life, she might swoon.

'I was afraid,' she murmured softly.

'And when you found out he was still alive?'

Like she'd wanted to grab his face and cover it in kisses.

'Relieved.'

'How relieved?'

More than she'd ever been in her life.

'Quite a bit.'

'Because you love him?'

'Do I?' She swallowed. Did she? It seemed . . . *possible*. Whatever she was feeling at that moment was certainly different, although not completely new either. Now that she thought about it, the feeling actually went back a little further than that morning . . . She tried to pinpoint exactly when it had started, but it was too vague, as if it had been growing for a while. Possibly ever since the Smedley-Bullingdons' garden party when Aidan had first almost-kissed her. And she'd almost-kissed him. Or even earlier when he'd stopped her from throwing champagne over a duchess. When she'd started to think of him as a friend, someone she could rely on and trust, someone she might give up – or perhaps just slightly amend – her dreams for.

Could this be love? Romantic love of the kind that poets – *actual* poets – *Shakespeare!* – wrote about? Could she have fallen in love with Aidan without even knowing it? Was that why she was insisting on the marriage going ahead?

No!

She flung her legs out, using them to propel herself up off the mattress and causing a rippling effect that almost caused Mildred to bounce off with her. She didn't want to be in love and especially not now. The only thing worse than being contractually obliged to marry a man she *didn't* love was falling in love with one who'd just told her he deserved better and then insisting that he marry her anyway. No, she was absolutely, categorically, *not* in love with Aidan. She was marrying him as a friend, to repay him for what he'd done for Caro, that was all. She was being selfless and self-sacrificing and virtuous, dammit!

'That's the most ludicrous idea I've ever heard!' She rounded on her cousin and grandmother. 'I've spent the past ten weeks trying to get rid of Aidan. What kind of fool would I be to fall in love with him now?'

'So that's a definite no, then?' Caro tilted her head sympathetically.

'Yes it's a no!'

'Well then . . .' Their grandmother stood up. 'If we're all quite clear about that, I suppose I ought to go and liberate your father. He hasn't thrown such a tantrum since he was six years old. I'm rather afraid I shall need a new door, but he'll calm down when he hears there's still an engagement ball next week.' She paused. 'I presume that there *is* still an engagement ball next week?'

'Yes.' Essie paused. 'At least, I think so.'

'I'll write to the countess and check.'

Essie nodded, suddenly wishing they'd chosen a different theme. A masquerade struck her as horribly, ironically appropriate. If ever she'd needed a mask to hide the tumult of emotions raging inside her, it was now.

Chapter Twenty-two

(One Day before Wedding Day)

'It's a disaster! A total, unmitigated disaster.' Essie stared at her costume in horror. With its elaborate gold mask and matching tiara embellished with a dozen fierce-looking and fork-tongued protuberances, it had seemed like the perfect choice a month ago, but now . . . 'I can't wear this. Aidan's bound to call off the wedding if I have snakes on my head!'

'It's certainly dramatic,' Caro agreed. 'You insisted on being Medusa.'

'That was before! And I forgot what I ordered!'

'It could be worse.'

'How?' Essie tugged at one of the springy coils. 'I'll look cold-blooded!'

'Then we'll just have to swap costumes. Lucky for you, we're about the same size.'

'Oh, would you?' Essie spun around gratefully. 'Thank you! Who are you going as again?'

'Little Red Riding Hood. Remember how it was my favourite story when we were little?' Caro sighed. 'I just wish I'd paid more attention.'

'Why?'

'Never stray from the path of virtue if you don't want to be eaten by wolves, that's the moral, isn't it?'

'Either that or don't visit your grandmother.' Essie clucked her tongue. 'Whatever the reason, Red Riding Hood is perfect. Then if Aidan asks to end our engagement I'll have something to cover my head.'

'That's not going to happen. He's a gentleman, like you said.'

'Do you think that I ought to compromise him to make sure?'

'*Essie!*'

'I know.' She sank down on to the edge of her bed. 'It's just that he hasn't visited for nearly two weeks! It doesn't show much enthusiasm. And if he *does* ask me to release him then I'll have to agree. It would be hypocritical not to after everything I've done. And then my big bad wolf of a father will tear him to shreds.'

'You're mixing metaphors. The father rescues Little Red Riding Hood.'

'Not in my story he doesn't.'

'Essie . . .' Caro perched beside her. 'Are you completely certain that –'

'I *don't* love him. I *can't*!' She clamped her hands to her head in protest. 'This whole situation is such a mess. I feel sick.'

'That makes two of us.'

'Oh . . .' She dropped her hands immediately to reach for one of Caro's. 'I'm sorry. Here I am, thinking of myself again. Are you sure you're feeling up to a ball? Because if you're not, we could say that you're still feeling unwell.'

'No. I'm not letting you go through this alone. You were there for me when I needed you and now I'm going to return the favour.' Caro tipped her head sideways, resting it on Essie's shoulder. 'But this is going to be my last ball for a while. I've decided that I'm going home to Cleveland after the wedding.'

'Really?' Essie jerked in surprise. 'What about the rest of the Season?'

'The *last* thing I care about right now is finding a husband. I feel like I've just found myself and I've got so many things I want to do before I think about marriage! Grandmama says she'll sponsor me next year if I change my mind.'

'Then going home sounds like a good idea. Although I don't envy you telling your mother. Her ankles have only just recovered enough for her to come to London.'

'I'll think of some excuse.' Caro got back to her feet, reaching for the Medusa outfit and scrutinizing it at arm's length. 'You know, this might actually be a good look on me. I wouldn't mind petrifying a few men right now.'

'No one's going to recognize you with that mask and your new hair.' Essie smiled, admiring Caro's new cropped style. It gave her the look of an elegant, blue-eyed elf.

'Good. Then they won't see me coming.'

She blinked as the expression on her cousin's face transformed briefly into something almost unrecognizable, something vengeful – definitely more gorgon than elf.

On reflection, she wondered if switching costumes was such a wise idea, after all.

By the time they made their way down their grandmother's staircase three hours later, Essie was feeling self-conscious as well as sick, even more than when she'd first worn orange. Her borrowed costume was undeniably pretty, with a red skirt, white silk bodice and a scarlet hood draped around the neck, but as it turned out, she and Caro were the exact same size in every area except one, or more precisely two, and those two were bulging in a way that they'd never bulged before. She had to keep glancing down to make sure neither had escaped.

Her one consolation was that the expanse of bare skin also drew attention to the diamond necklace that Aidan had given her as a birthday present. Despite her objections, he'd left it behind at Redcliffe when he'd left and she'd brought it to London with the express intention of throwing it back at him a second time. Now, however, she wanted him to see her wearing it. Hopefully, he'd get the message. Honestly, with her cleavage thrusting so conspicuously, it would be hard to miss.

'You both look beautiful, my dears.' Their grandmother, dressed in gold with a black wig and chain of large pearls, abandoned her line of guests at the front door to greet them. Her father, Essie noticed, did not, throwing a mere cursory glance in their direction before turning to address somebody more important. Naturally, he hadn't bothered to wear a costume.

'So do you.' Essie thrust her chin into the air, refusing to let her father's behaviour bother her any more. 'Cleopatra?'

'Who else? I feel a sense of kinship.'

'Do you know what happened to the rest of her family?'

Her grandmother wafted a hand in the air. 'Details, my dear.'

'Is Aidan —?'

'Not yet, but don't worry, his mother assures me he'll be here. As for any rumours . . .' The dowager tapped a finger against the side of her nose. 'Not a thing. I believe that our secret is safe.'

'There's only one way to be certain.' Caro tugged on Essie's arm.

'One moment.' Their grandmother put a hand on both of their shoulders. 'Remember that whatever happens, you're my granddaughters and I'm proud of you both. I always will be.'

'Oh, Grandmama.' Essie felt tears start to well in her eyes.

'Now, now, that's enough sentiment. Go on and enjoy yourselves.'

'Yes, Grandmama.' Caro sniffed.

They went on their way to find that the lower floor of their grandmother's house had been completely transformed, with all but a few pieces of furniture removed, the carpets rolled back and the floors polished to a blinding high shine. Every room was also packed with guests, mingling together in costumes that ranged from the token effort to the downright bizarre. From the doorway to the dining-room-turned-impromptu-ballroom, Essie could see at least three Roman Caesars, a spattering of kings and queens, including one extremely corpulent Henry VIII, several sailors, a Minotaur, a chimney sweep and an assortment of ladies dressed as butterflies, flowers, birds and one particularly impressive unicorn.

To her immense relief, their own arrival was greeted with smiles rather than censure. Since it wasn't too hard to guess her and Caro's identities, even with all the cleavage and snakes, it had to mean that their grandmother was right and their recent adventures remained a secret.

'So far, so good,' she whispered to her cousin. 'How are you feeling?'

'Like I want to run back upstairs and hide under my quilt.' Caro took a deep breath and then fixed a smile on her face as the ancient Marquess of Bazley, draped in a toga and carrying an amphora and bunch of grapes – *Aesop?* – staggered towards them. 'But I can do this.'

'I know you can. Good luck.' Essie squeezed her arm before moving away, making a turn of the room as Caro stepped out on to the dance floor.

Three turns of the room and still no fiancé later, she was starting to contemplate hiding under a quilt herself when she finally spied Aidan standing in the doorway. He was dressed like a Tudor gentleman – a Tudor gentleman who appeared to have grown a beard in the almost two weeks since she'd last seen him, a black, slightly pointed one . . . She found it hard to breathe suddenly, assailed by a wave of longing. Robert Dudley? Queen Elizabeth's favourite, the man she'd supposedly loved, but never married in order to keep her independence. Was Aidan trying to give her some kind of message? Because if he was, then she was far too distracted by his beard to decipher it. Surely no man had ever looked so heart-stirringly handsome in a ruff?

She weaved her way across the floor, heart beating erratically, like a drum that couldn't find the right tempo.

For some reason, it made it hard to walk in a straight line too.

'Aidan.' She stopped a foot in front of him, though he seemed not to recognize her at first, his gaze dropping first to her cleavage before focusing on the necklace. He could hardly have looked more stunned if she'd actually worn her Medusa costume and turned him to stone. 'I was starting to think you weren't coming.'

'My apologies.' He shook his head as if he were trying to clear it. 'I arrived a little while ago, but I got waylaid by your father.'

'Oh dear, was he very offensive?'

'He was honest.' He gave a tight smile. 'Believe me, I've heard worse from my father's creditors. How's your cousin?'

'Better.' Essie glanced towards the dance floor. Caro was partnered with another of her suitors now, smiling as if she hadn't a care in the world, though in a way that didn't touch her eyes. 'At least, I think she is.'

'Good. Little Red Riding Hood?'

'Yes. Robert Dudley?'

'I thought you'd approve.'

'I do. I like this.' She gestured at the beard, feeling somewhat jealous of his fingers as they rubbed across it.

'Thank you. It wasn't intentional, but I didn't shave for a few days and then this evening . . . it just occurred to me.' His gaze dropped again, lingering on her chest for longer than was strictly polite. 'You're wearing your birthday present.'

'Yes. I changed my mind about that too.' She quirked an eyebrow. 'Why didn't you shave?'

'I had a lot of thinking to do. Alone. In an armchair. With a bottle of brandy.' His voice sounded rough. 'Essie, we need to talk.'

'Do we?' She gulped. 'I mean, we discussed everything the last time we met, didn't we?'

'Now I'm sober.'

'Oh.'

He glanced around. 'Is there somewhere private we could go? The library perhaps?'

'It's been turned into a card room for tonight.' She shuffled her feet. 'There's my bedroom, but if you want to call off the wedding then that's probably not a very good idea.'

His head jerked back around. 'I don't want to call off the wedding.'

'You don't?'

'No. You were right when you said it's not just about me. I have Sophia's future to consider. So . . .' He cleared his throat stiffly. 'Thank you.'

'Oh.' Her heart seemed to leap and plummet at the same time. 'You're welcome.'

'Would you care to dance?'

'No, thank you.' She shook her head, telling herself she ought to smile. This was their engagement ball, after all. Anyone looking at them might justifiably think they were planning a funeral instead of a future of conjugal bliss. Only her lips wouldn't do what she told them. 'I don't quite feel up to it.'

'Ah.' He nodded, as if he understood, his gaze sweeping the room again as if he couldn't bear to hold her gaze any longer. At this rate, he was going to know every nook and cranny. 'It was kind of your grandmother to do all this.'

'Yes.' She grimaced. 'It just seems a lot of fuss. For us. Considering.'

'Maybe we should elope to Gretna Green after all?'

'Then my father really *would* kill you.'

He gave a humourless laugh. 'In that case, St George's it is, as long as you're certain?'

'Yes . . . as long as you are?'

'Yes.' His expression became very intense all of a sudden. 'Essie, I wish that things could have been different. I don't want you – Dammit!'

'What?' She gasped in horror, vaguely aware of other voices increasing in volume around her. There was some kind of loud commotion in the hallway, accompanied by an announcement, but she was too mortified to make out the words.

'Get ready.' Aidan took hold of her arm.

'Why?' She stared up at him miserably, half-tempted to wrench herself away.

'It's the Queen.'

'What? She really came?' Essie started and looked towards the door, surprised to hear Aidan mutter something treasonous beside her.

'The happy couple.' Queen Charlotte smiled as she entered the ballroom and advanced towards them, bright brown eyes sparkling behind a jewel-encrusted mask. 'What charming costumes.'

'Thank you, Your Majesty.' Aidan bowed as Essie sank into a deep curtsey.

'Is everything ready for your nuptials?'

'I believe so, Your Majesty.' Essie forced a smile.

'I'm delighted to hear it. I wish you both great joy.'

Another curtsey and the Queen moved on. And that, Essie realized, was that. They had the royal seal of approval. It would be well-nigh impossible to stop the wedding now. From a practical perspective, it was most satisfactory. From an emotional one, she could feel a tight knot of misery forming in the centre of her chest, accompanied by a horrible echo in her head as Aidan's last words, *I don't want you*, rang over and over, confirming the worst. Aidan no longer wanted her, at the very moment she could no longer deny that she was hopelessly and headlong in love with him.

Chapter Twenty-three

The morning of the wedding was perfect, the kind most brides dreamed about. And that was despite an ear-splitting crack of thunder at dawn, followed by a two-hour-long deluge that Essie took for a sign but which had cleared completely by seven, leaving behind a pair of glorious rainbows to illuminate the newly blue sky over London and gild the pavements with a lustrous, golden sheen.

To Essie's surprise, the ceremony itself was similarly perfect. She didn't trip or stumble or drop her bouquet of carefully chosen marigolds or forget her lines. To be fair, two words hadn't posed much of a challenge, but she'd thought that *something* had been bound to go wrong. Instead, she and Aidan had both appeared suitably earnest as they'd said 'I do' at the appropriate moments, earning themselves a ripple of approving and, in several cases, relieved-sounding sighs from the collected wedding guests. Felix had been there among them, along with a proud-looking Uncle Charles and a tearful Aunt Emmeline and every single one of the candidates. Selina Birtwhistle had looked particularly happy, beaming on the arm of her new fiancé, Viscount Prowse. As it turned out, nearly the whole of the *ton* attended the ceremony at St George's, much to Essie's horror and her father's delight (or what she presumed was delight, since he was actually witnessed to smile, his chest puffed out like a proud yet completely insensitive pigeon). In short, the event was a triumph.

Unfortunately, that was where the perfection had ended. She and Aidan had left their wedding breakfast early in order to reach Middlemount before nightfall and the shower of rose-petal confetti that Caro and Sophia had tossed into the air on their departure appeared to have cast some kind of veil of silence over their carriage. Ironically, once they were safely ensconced and rolling away from Cavendish Square, it seemed that neither of them had anything to say. Every minute seemed to stretch for an eternity, making an already long journey seem to take ten times longer. Essie didn't have a timepiece, but at this point she estimated it had been three hours since either of them had last spoken and that had been about changing the horses. It wasn't the most auspicious start to married life. In three months, they'd gone from enemies to conspirators to friends to complete strangers, ones who just happened to be man and wife.

She stifled a yawn as she stared out of the carriage window. She'd slept poorly the night before – even worse than she had over the past two weeks – trying to navigate her way through a confusing fog of emotions, before finally coming up with a plan, a way to survive the situation she'd got herself in. She was nothing if she wasn't resilient. And just because she'd trapped herself in a one-sided and probably doomed marriage with a husband who'd already rejected her didn't mean that she was going to wallow in heartache and misery, no matter how tempting they sounded. And even though she'd broken the promise she'd made to herself on the morning of her eighteenth birthday, she wasn't going to let marriage destroy her the way it had her mother. No matter how numb she might feel now, she would find a way back to her old, independent self. In the meantime, she would take refuge in her new role as Celeste Craven, Countess of Denholm. She would immerse herself in all things *countessy*. The knot of misery in her chest was still there, only now it seemed to hang in a kind of void, as if there was a hole where her heart had once been.

Speaking of hearts ... She glanced surreptitiously towards Aidan, comparing his behaviour now with that on their nighttime flight after Caro. This time, they weren't touching at all. Instead, his freshly shaven jaw was turned slightly away from her, his expression so preoccupied that she thought he might actually leap out of his seat in horror if she tried to put her head on his shoulder. Definitely *not* the look of a happy bridegroom. In retrospect, she ought to have insisted that his mother and sister accompany them back to the country, but the now-dowager countess had wanted to give them some privacy, or so she'd told Essie *sotto voce* during the wedding breakfast, which had been arguably the crowning awkward moment in a morning full of awkward moments (and after starting the day with some well-meaning, but frankly disturbing, advice from her aunt about wedding nights, that was quite an accomplishment). Her new mother-in-law's meaning couldn't have been any clearer if she'd started suggesting names for her grandchildren.

Another yawn overcame her as she tried to think of some subject to talk about, if only to pass the time. She absolutely refused to discuss the weather, but maybe art? Hadn't Aidan once told her he liked painting? Maybe she could ask him whether he'd found any time for his brushes recently, in between thwarting elopements and fighting duels, that was. He'd probably tell her it was the most asinine question he'd ever heard . . .

'Here we are.' The sound of Aidan's *actual* voice jolted her back to herself. 'Middlemount.'

'We've arrived?' She stuck her head out of the window just in time to see the stone walls of a gatehouse give way to a long, oak-lined drive, at the end of which stood a sprawling Tudor mansion. In the gathering twilight, she felt as if the carriage had just jumped back in time. Unlike so many aristocratic families who'd torn down their ancestral homes to make way for modern neo-classical designs, the Ravells had kept the black and white, half-timbered original. She counted five overlapping gables, each featuring ornately decorated oriel windows over three floors, topped with a steeply pitched roof and at least a dozen large chimneys.

'Oh!' She sucked in a breath so violently that she started coughing. 'It's beautiful! Anne Boleyn could have lived here.'

'Coming from you, I take that as a compliment.' Aidan sounded pleased. 'Most people think it's old-fashioned. Not very elegant.'

'It's better than elegant. It has character.'

'I'm glad it suits you, but you might want to brace yourself. If I know my housekeeper, she'll have the entire staff lined up ready for your inspection.'

'Surely not at this hour?'

'I'm afraid so. Mrs Pugh is a stickler for tradition. She's been here for longer than my mother and knows everything about the house. If you have any questions, she's the one to ask.'

'I'm sure I'll think of something.' Essie gulped, wishing it were possible to sneak into the house under cover of darkness instead, preferably with a blanket over her head for good measure, but since that obviously wasn't an option . . .

She closed her eyes and slowed her breathing, focusing on getting into character. She was the Countess of Denholm and she needed to give the definitive performance of her life. She was going to be the best damned Countess of Denholm Middlemount had ever seen. It was time to pull back the curtain and perform.

Meeting every single member of the household took a considerable amount of time, so much that stars were visible by the time Essie reached the end of the line, but she was determined to start off properly. Everyone looked so serious that she was tempted to make jokes to put them at ease, only she couldn't imagine Aidan's mother doing such a thing. Besides, both the po-faced housekeeper Mrs Pugh and funereal butler Mr Rabbitt were following closely enough to hear every word and she had the distinct impression they considered laughing a capital offence.

'Thank you for the introductions, Mrs Pugh.' She stepped up to the front door finally with relief, glancing over her shoulder to where Aidan was deep in conversation with his steward. 'I'll do my best to remember everyone's names.'

'That won't be necessary, your ladyship.' Mrs Pugh looked alarmed at the very idea. 'Now, if you'd care to follow me, I'll show you to your rooms before dinner.'

Essie went inside to find the interior of Middlemount just as impressive as the exterior. The vast entrance hall struck her as gloomy at first, all dark oak panelling and flagstone floors, but there was a welcoming fire blazing in a large hearth in the far wall, above which was displayed a collection of fearsome-looking Medieval weaponry. The whole scene looked as if it hadn't altered for centuries. Even the chairs around the fireplace looked to be at least two hundred years old, with their high backs and intricately carved panels. There seemed to be carvings everywhere she looked. Of fruit, thistles, griffins and, in particular, oak trees. There were even oak trees on the tapestries that took up the two end walls, their branches home to a plethora of small birds and squirrels, none of whom looked remotely intimidated by the noble-looking birds of prey at the top.

'You did that very well.'

She spun around, surprised to hear Aidan's voice behind her. 'Did I?'

'Yes. It was kind of you talk to everyone. The scullery maids looked as if they thought you were the Queen.'

'You mean Kitty and Anna?' She smiled smugly. 'If I take on a role, I do it properly.'

'A role?'

She nodded, taken aback by the way his brows snapped together as if she'd just insulted him. 'I have to think of it as a performance. It's the only way I'll ever convince anyone that I'm a halfway decent countess.'

'You don't have to perform anything. I don't care what anyone else thinks.'

'Well, I do.' Essie pursed her lips, starting to feel nostalgic for the silence of the carriage. His scowl was showing no imminent sign of lifting. 'So . . . is it good to be back?'

'Yes. Even more than I expected.'

'You must be excited to get started with all your plans for the estate?'

'Very. There's a great deal to do. Speaking of which, I'll ask Mrs Pugh to have dinner sent up to your room. I need to consult some more with my steward.' He fixed his gaze on a point just past her shoulder. 'It'll probably be a late night.'

'I see,' she answered tightly. A late night. Their wedding night. After her conversation with Aunt Emmeline she'd been left feeling both curious and apprehensive about that, but now it seemed it wasn't even going to happen.

'If you have no objections, that is?' Aidan lifted an eyebrow.

'Why would I?' She started towards the staircase where Mrs Pugh was waiting, deciding she didn't want to spend any more time with him either. At least it was some consolation to know that her heartache shouldn't last very long. If he carried on like this, it would be easy enough to fall *out* of love with him. The next morning should probably do it. 'It's been such a long day, I'll say goodnight now.'

'Essie?'

'What?' She looked back around, surprised to catch a flash of uncertainty on his face. For a fleeting moment, he seemed on the verge of saying something else before he clasped his hands behind his back, looking more austere and distant and *haughty* than ever.

'Nothing. Goodnight.'

Chapter Twenty-four

The insufferable, stuck-up, cold-hearted prig!

Essie stormed up and down, tapping the back of her hairbrush repeatedly against the palm of her hand before muttering an expletive she'd recently learned from her mother-in-law and hurling it against her new bedroom wall. She'd sent her maid away after dinner so that she could fume more effectively in private, and after an hour in which she'd done little but strip down to her chemise, she'd worked herself into a furious, hairbrush-shattering lather.

How dare he! How dare he add insult to injury, acting as if *he* were the victim in all of this? As if being married to her was such a hardship and he hadn't just received the second half of her sizeable dowry to save his estate! When *he* was the one who'd pursued her, who'd insisted on them abiding by their fathers' ridiculous agreement, who'd been so infuriatingly honest and helpful and honourable that she'd eventually, unwillingly, fallen in love and then given up her independence to save him from her father's vindictive revenge! It wasn't as if she expected him to fall at her feet in gratitude, but some basic good manners would be nice.

Well, her performance as the countess might be over for today, but she wasn't going to retire to bed like some obedient wife *or* mope like a lovesick one. She still had her self-respect. And since it was impossible to feel any more wretched and unwanted than she already did, she was going to challenge her *husband* on his behaviour right now – and make a few things clear while she was about it.

She didn't bother with a robe, tossing her braid over her shoulder and storming through the connecting door to her new husband's bedchamber. Which was empty.

Drat! She started pacing again, wishing that she had another hairbrush to vent her feelings on. Apparently Aidan hadn't been exaggerating about a late night, but she could wait. She was far too hot-blooded at that moment to walk away.

She didn't know how long she paced up and down, only that she'd managed to traverse the entire length of the bedchamber sixteen and a quarter times before she heard footsteps approaching along the corridor outside.

Without thinking, she dived towards the window, concealing herself behind a pea-green velvet curtain a split second before the door opened. Which wasn't what she'd intended at all! She closed her eyes in exasperation. She'd come here to be seen, not to hide! And she could hardly step out again without looking ridiculous. Unless . . .

'Essie?' Aidan spoke before she could come up with a plan. 'It's a good thing I recognize your toes.'

'You do?' She glanced down at the digits in question. 'How?'

'You were barefoot that first night you came to my room.' He tilted his head as she emerged from her hiding place. 'And your ankles are unmistakable. For the record, you don't have to hide. You've every right to visit my chamber now.'

'I know. I forgot.'

His gaze flickered over her chemise. 'So what can I do for you?'

'I came to tell you something.' She folded her arms. 'No, actually that's not true. I came to shout at you.'

'I see.' He nodded slowly, as if he'd been expecting the words.

'Yes! I don't want to live like this, in silence, like strangers. We were friends before, weren't we?'

'We still are.'

'Not the way you're behaving we're not.'

His head jerked to one side as if she'd just slapped him. 'I'm sorry. To be honest, I wasn't sure how to behave today.'

'Smiling occasionally would have been nice. Or not making it quite so obvious how much you resent me! If this is the way things are going to be then, frankly, I'd rather go back to my grandmother's house tomorrow. Or my aunt's. As far away as possible!'

'Resent you?' He looked as if the words actually pained him. 'Essie, I don't resent you. How could I?'

'What?' She felt as if the wind had just been taken out of her sails. 'Then I don't understand. If you don't resent me then why are you acting so coldly? Why don't you talk to me like you used to?'

'Because what can I say except an apology? And then another? And another?' He sat down on a wooden coffer at the end of his bed and draped his arms across his knees. 'I thought that nothing could feel worse than marrying somebody for money, but I was wrong. Falling in love with the person you're marrying for money and then watching them abandon all of their hopes and dreams just to protect you is a million times worse.' He clenched his jaw. 'If it had been up to me, I would have let you go. If it hadn't been for Sophia, I would have taken my chances in court.'

'Falling in love?' There wasn't enough air in the room. That was the only explanation for why her voice had suddenly become so high-pitched. 'You love me?'

'Isn't it obvious?' He looked up at her as if it ought to be. 'I've liked you since that first night you crept into my bedchamber. Then I thought you might be a little . . . *unusual*, and then I knew you definitely were, especially that time you made us climb a tree, but then I fell in love with you. It occurred to me somewhere on the way to Gretna Green, and once I'd thought it, I couldn't *un*think it, no matter how hard I tried. But then we found your cousin and you talked about all the things you wanted to do together – travelling, acting, having a cottage with honeysuckle around the door – and I realized I couldn't hold you back any longer. I wanted you to have what you wanted and I couldn't bear the thought of spending any more time with a person who didn't love me in return. I knew I had to let you go straightaway.'

'So *that* was why you ended our engagement?' She gaped at him. 'Because of what I said to Caro? I was trying to make her feel better!'

'You were very convincing. Everything you've done to dissuade me from marrying you has been very convincing. You wanted all those things you said to her. I could see it in your face.'

295

'I did.' Somehow she nodded and shook her head at the same time. 'But it's not so straightforward. They're not *all* I want any more.'

'They're not?' He looked hopeful.

'No. I mean, it's possible to want several things at once, isn't it? Sometimes even things that contradict each other?' She frowned. 'But *you* said you deserved better! You said you didn't want me!'

'I meant that we both deserved better than a contract.' He stood up and advanced towards her. 'Essie, I wish that we could have met normally so I could have courted you properly. I wish that our fathers had never had anything to do with any of this. As for not wanting you, I never said that.'

'Yes you did! Just before the Queen arrived at our engagement ball, that's exactly what you said!'

A look of comprehension crossed his features. 'Only because I never got a chance to finish the sentence. I was going to say that I didn't want you to feel trapped. I would never have said that I didn't want you. Essie, I want you more than I've ever wanted anything in my life.'

'Really?' She swallowed. 'Truly?'

'Really and truly.' He reached for both of her hands, cradling them against his chest. 'Which is why I'll do everything in my power to make this up to you. To make you happy.'

She blinked frantically, mortified to find her vision blurring. If he was telling the truth then she'd misread the events of the past two weeks completely. He hadn't rejected her. He still wanted her. And she still wanted him.

'You don't need to make up anything to me. I chose this marriage. I chose you.' She sniffed and then thrust her chin up, unwilling to let him off the hook so easily after all her anguish. 'You should have told me you were in love with me!'

'Would you have wanted to hear it?'

'Yes, as a matter of fact, I would. Because I happen to be in love with you too.'

'You don't have to say –'

'I am!'

His gaze clouded with a mixture of suspicion and hope. 'Since when?'

'I have absolutely no idea. I didn't want to fall in love with you and then I was afraid to admit it because I thought you didn't want me, but then you grew a beard and I realized that I did.'

'Because of my beard?'

'It *really* suited you.'

He moved so fast that she barely had time to gasp before his lips were on hers, kissing her so passionately that she had to wrap her arms around his waist just to stay upright. 'So that's why you married me?' he murmured huskily. 'Because you loved me?'

'No.' She shook her head, struggling to get her breath back. 'I couldn't bear the thought of being married to somebody who didn't care for me either, but I knew that my father would ruin you otherwise. If anything, I married you *despite* being in love with you. I loved you so much I was even prepared to make him happy! That's pretty much the biggest compliment I can give you.'

'It never even occurred to me.' Aidan's mouth twisted into a rueful smile. 'All through the ceremony, I felt like the worst kind of villain.'

'Me too. I've hardly ever been so depressed.' She laughed in agreement. 'And everyone around us was so happy.'

'Everyone enjoyed it except us.'

'And it was supposed to be the happiest day of our lives!'

'You looked so beautiful.' He laid a hand against her cheek. 'I particularly liked the marigolds.'

'You could have mentioned it at the time. You could have mentioned *anything*.'

'I didn't know how to. I felt so guilty for trapping you.'

'That's ridiculous. *I* was the one who insisted we go through with it. I even thought about compromising you to make sure you couldn't back out.' She bit her tongue as his eyebrows shot upwards. 'It was a very brief thought.'

'It still sounds interesting.' His gaze heated. 'Out of interest, how exactly were you going to do it?'

'Something like what happened at Vauxhall.' She smiled wickedly. 'I might have removed your ruff too.'

'In your grandmother's house? With the Queen in attendance?'

'You have to admit, it would have been pretty hard to change your mind then.'

'Definitely. I'm starting to wish I'd held out a little longer.'

'It would have made things awkward.'

'Oh, undoubtedly.' He bent his head, sliding his lips down her throat in a way that sent a shiver of excitement shooting through her body. 'Although . . .' His mouth drifted lower, down to her collarbone . . . 'probably not any more than today?'

'No-o,' she conceded as the shiver turned into a definite throbbing. 'Probably not.'

'You know, today's not over yet. There are still a few minutes until midnight. Maybe we can make amends for the rest of it?'

'What do you mean?'

'Well . . .' He lifted his head. 'What would you have done *after* removing my ruff?'

'Honestly I'm not even sure how to do that. Are there buttons?'

'Ties, but theoretically speaking . . . what else would you have done?'

She cleared her throat, her imagination shooting off in all sorts of unladylike directions.

'Because I have a few suggestions.' He drew her closer, smoothing his hands leisurely over the curve of her spine. 'I could show you now, if you like?'

'Now?'

'Unless you're too tired?'

'No.' She'd never felt so awake in her life.

'Good.' He kissed her again, nudging her lips apart and dipping his tongue inside. For a moment, she hesitated, all of her misgivings rushing back in a panicked torrent before she told them firmly to go swivel and kissed him back, every nerve and sinew tingling with anticipation as his fingers drifted over her lower back, bunching in her chemise and tugging it slowly upwards.

'Essie . . .' He moaned her name, breaking the kiss just long enough to draw the garment over her head.

'No, don't look!' She lost her nerve as cold air touched her skin, throwing herself forward and burying her head in his shoulder.

'Why can't I look?' He staggered slightly under the force of her embrace. 'You're beautiful.'

'I'm naked.'

'That's what I meant. I only caught a brief glimpse, but trust me. Beautiful.'

'I still don't want you to look.'

'Would it help if I was naked too?'

She peeked up at him, intrigued. 'It might.'

'In that case, you'll have to take one step back.' He smiled lopsidedly, cupping her face in his hands when she looked dubious. 'I'll shut my eyes if you insist.'

'No peeking?'

'On my honour.'

'What about your valet?' She threw a suspicious glance at the door as she stepped backwards, folding her arms around herself just in case. 'He's not likely to come in, is he?'

'No.' Aidan unwound his cravat and tossed it aside. 'I have a man to look after my clothes, but I've always thought I was capable of dressing and undressing myself.' He stopped halfway through his waistcoat buttons and lifted an eyebrow, though his eyes themselves remained closed. 'Unless you want to help me?'

She didn't wait to be asked twice, brushing his fingers away and digging her teeth into her bottom lip as she unfastened the last few buttons. 'There.' She smoothed the waistcoat over his shoulders and tossed it into a heap on the floor. 'Now what?'

'Shirt.'

'Shirt.' She started on the next set of buttons, starting at the top and making her way swiftly downwards, resisting the urge to simply grab each side and rip the fabric apart. She was even prepared to sew the buttons back on afterwards – and she hated sewing.

It was a heady sensation, peeling each side away and feeling the heat rise from his skin, accompanied by the faint scent of bergamot. She breathed it in, her eyes drawn to the thump of the pulse in his neck. It made her own thrum harder and faster in response, a heavy pounding she could feel from the top of her head to the tips of her toes.

Instinctively, she swayed closer, hearing air hiss through his teeth as the tips of her breasts brushed lightly against his chest. Just a couple more buttons . . . At last she dragged the shirt over his arms and threw it in the vague direction of the waistcoat.

'Essie . . .' He made a guttural sound, something between a cough and a growl, as if he were forcing the words out. 'Are you certain about this?'

She took half a second to consider before nodding, then realized his eyes were still closed and touched her lips to his chest in answer.

'Was that a yes?' His voice was almost unrecognizable.

'It was a definitely.' She grinned and then spun away, leaping up on to the bed and diving under the covers. 'You can open your eyes now.'

'It's about bloody time.' He obeyed at once, charging straight after her and under the coverlet.

'Wait!' She let out a startled shriek. 'You're supposed to be undressing.'

'I'll get to it. There are a few other things I need to do first.'

'Such as?'

'This.' He grabbed hold of her legs so that she couldn't wriggle away, pulling her down the bed towards him and pressing a trail of kisses over her stomach.

'Aidan!' She stiffened and then surrendered as her insides turned to liquid, her inner organs all quivering while what felt like a torrent of molten hot lava poured through her veins. She stretched out, feeling heavy and weightless at the same time, struck with the vague impression that she was sinking into the mattress.

'Essie . . .' He paused with his lips halfway up her navel. 'If I do anything you don't like, tell me.'

'I will.' She traced her hands over his shoulder blades, heaving a long sigh that turned into a whimper as his mouth closed around one of her breasts. 'Is this debauchery? Am I being debauched?'

'We both are.' He swirled his tongue gently around the nipple before lifting his head and grinning at her from beneath the covers. 'I have to admit, I'm enjoying it so far.'

'Me too.' She heaved herself up on to her elbows in surprise. 'Does that mean you've never done it before either?'

'We were engaged.' He looked mildly embarrassed. 'It would have felt disloyal.'

'You're right, it would have been.' She nodded emphatically. 'In fact, now that I know what it is, I don't like the idea of you doing this with anyone else.'

'Then you don't need to worry.' He moved up the bed, holding his body over hers. 'Do you know why I couldn't

302

choose one of your candidates? It's because you're irreplaceable, Essie.'

She coiled her arms around his waist in response, pulling him down on top of her and kissing him harder and more insistently than before, harder than all of their other kisses combined. He responded just as eagerly, shifting his weight to one side so that he didn't crush her while one of his hands slid lower, over the curve of her hip and then inwards, delving into the curls between her legs. She didn't make so much as a token protest this time, wrapping her legs around him and pushing her body against his hand instead. And then he touched her more deeply and the molten lava in her veins flared and surged faster, as if it were building towards some kind of eruption.

'Wait a moment.'

'What?' She let out a wail of frustration, coming back from the brink of oblivion as he rolled away. 'Where are you going?'

'Not far.' He climbed off the bed and began to unfasten the falls of his trousers. 'I'll be back in a minute, I promise.'

She propped herself up on one arm to watch, indifferent now to her own nakedness and far more interested in his. Her skin was still tingling from the way he'd just touched her and the sight of him undressing somehow exacerbated the feeling. She liked the way the muscles in his chest rippled as he moved, she liked the way he threw his trousers across the room as if he couldn't wait to be rid of them, she liked . . . Oh.

Her arm slipped, sending her tumbling sideways on to the bed as he removed his drawers.

'Essie?' He came back to her at once. 'You can still change your mind if you're not ready.'

She lifted her eyes to his and felt a rush of love. He looked serious, honourable, and as if he were burning up at the same time. She had absolutely no intention of saying no, but she appreciated the offer. Ironically, it made her want him even more. Honestly, it made him irresistible.

'You know, I hardly *ever* change my mind.' She lifted her hands, threading them into his hair as he slid back into bed beside her. 'I'm very stubborn that way.'

'I've noticed. It's one of the things I love most about you.'

'Me being stubborn?'

'Determined.'

'Headstrong and obstreperous? That's what my aunt calls it.'

'You know . . .' He smiled against her lips. 'I finally did what you asked and thought about the qualities I might want in a wife and those two words were at the very top of my list.'

She kissed him. And by the time they were finished, she felt utterly, thoroughly, debauched.

Chapter Twenty-five

Essie woke up slowly, rolling on to her back and reaching an arm out to find the space on the bed beside her cold and empty. Which was odd because the last time she'd stirred in the middle of the night Aidan had been snuggled up beside her, one arm beneath her neck, the other curled around her waist, his breath warm and reassuring against her neck.

She opened her eyes, pleased to discover that the hollow feeling in her chest appeared to be whole again, and sat up, but there was no sign of him in the room either, only a random stranger stirring the coals on the fire. No, not a random stranger . . .

'Hello.' She rubbed her eyes sleepily and gave a wide, unladylike yawn. 'It's Beth, isn't it?'

'Yes, my lady. I'm sorry if I disturbed you.' The girl gave a shy smile.

'You didn't. Do you know where Ai – I mean, the earl has gone?'

'He went for a ride, my lady.'

Essie drew her brows together, surprised that he hadn't woken her up to join him. If he'd asked then she would have agreed readily, but perhaps he hadn't wanted to disturb her? Or perhaps he'd thought that she'd had enough activity during the night, which was certainly true. Or perhaps he didn't know how much she enjoyed riding? Had she ever told him? She couldn't remember, but headstrong and obstreperous aside, there was still a lot they had to learn about each other. Which meant that the best thing she could do now was go and tell him everything. 'How long ago was that?'

'About an hour, my lady.'

'Thank you.' She swung her legs over the side of the bed, keeping the sheet wrapped around her body for modesty, and shuffled through to her own bedroom. Most of her trunks were still packed, but fortunately she knew exactly where her riding habit was, wriggling into it hastily and tying her hair back with a ribbon before hurrying down the staircase, past the breakfast room and out of the front door before a shocked-looking Mr Rabbitt could stop her.

She drew in several deep lungfuls of air on her way to the stables. The morning was just as glorious as the one before, the early-morning sun gilding the parkland so that the grass seemed to glow orange. *Orange.* How fitting. A ride would be bliss. With any luck, one of the grooms could tell her which way Aidan had gone so that she could borrow a horse and ride after him.

She rounded the corner of the stable block and then stopped dead, taken aback by the sight of a naked man. Actually not completely naked, she realized after a few stunned seconds, although his buff-coloured trousers initially gave that impression. In reality, only his top half was bare, the muscles of his back rippling and glistening with sweat as he repeatedly lifted an axe and swung it downwards on to a large chopping block. Judging by the sizeable pile of logs lying beside him, he'd been busy for some time.

She snapped her mouth closed, about to retreat when she realized that it wasn't *just* any man. It was her husband.

'Aidan?' She took her time crossing the stable yard, appreciating the view for as long as possible. 'What are you doing? I thought that you'd gone for a ride?'

He turned at the sound of her voice, immediately dropping the axe and reaching, disappointingly, for a shirt.

'Good morning, Essie.' He inclined his head in a strangely formal gesture. 'I was about to, but then I saw these.'

'Don't you have gardeners to do that?'

'Quite a few, but I like getting my hands dirty.'

'Well, I like early-morning rides.' She gestured at her riding habit. 'I was going to come and find you.'

'Ah. My apologies. I couldn't sleep.' His gaze swept over her in a way that gave the bizarre impression he was checking for injuries. 'How are you feeling?'

'Very well.' She studied his face, beginning to feel uneasy. He was being distant again, as if the night before had never happened. As if he hadn't touched or caressed or kissed her in ways and places that had sent her pulse accelerating to ten times its normal pace and made her positively eager for nightfall so they could do it all over again. Unlike at the coaching inn, there was no doubt in her mind that what had happened between them had been real and not a dream. Her imagination could never have come up with anything quite so inventive. She hadn't even known that such sensations were possible. 'Aidan, what's the matter?' She took a step closer towards him. 'What are you really doing out here?'

He turned his head and stared into the distance. 'I needed some time to think.'

'What about? Last night?'

He gave a swift nod, his jaw clenched. 'Do you still want that ride?'

'Yes.'

'Then wait here.'

She frowned after him, tapping her foot while he went into the stable block and emerged after what felt like an hour but was probably five minutes with two horses, one bay, the other chestnut.

'These are Merlin and Nimue.' He smoothed a hand over the neck of the bay before passing her the reins. 'Your aunt told me how much you enjoy riding back in March. I thought Nimue would be a nice surprise when you arrived.'

'It is. She's gorgeous.' Essie scratched behind Nimue's ears. 'I wish I had a treat for her.'

'You can treat her later. Right now, I need to show you something.' He held the mare steady as Essie hoisted herself into the side saddle, then he mounted the chestnut. 'Follow me. It's not far.'

She trotted cautiously after him out of the stable yard, then broke into a headlong gallop as they reached open parkland. Ordinarily, she would have enjoyed the rush of wind in her hair and the bite of cold air on her cheeks, but this morning she couldn't shake a growing sense of disquiet.

After a few minutes, Aidan pulled on his reins, dismounting as they reached the summit of a gentle incline, topped with a small copse of trees. Essie followed suit and then caught her breath in amazement. The other side of the slope was steeper and ablaze with colour, a meadow filled with tall grasses and a multitude of vividly coloured flowers: campion, vetch, clover, oxeye daisies, corncockle, even some buttercups and cowslips left over from spring, each trying to outdo each other in splendour. There seemed to be butterflies everywhere she looked too, their fluttering dances accompanied by the low hum of insects and the sweet scents of the flowers themselves. The whole scene was a feast for the senses, so beautiful that she was tempted to lie down, spread her arms and legs out and breathe it all in.

'It's stunning.' She let her breath out finally.

'It is . . .' Aidan tied both sets of reins to the branches of an oak tree before resting his hands against the trunk. 'But *this* is what I wanted to show you.'

'The tree?' She tipped her head back, looking up. And up. The oak was huge, more than fifty feet tall and so wide that both she and Nimue could have easily hidden behind it. She had a feeling that she'd seen it somewhere before too, although she'd never been here. 'Are we climbing it? I don't see a cat.'

He gave a small, reluctant-sounding laugh. 'No cat today. This tree's been here for more than three hundred years. According to family legend, the first earl planted the acorn and our family will keep the earldom so long as the tree thrives.'

She clicked her fingers. 'It's the one on the tapestry, isn't it?'

'And coat of arms.'

'And those paintings in your office in London.'

'You noticed those?' He sounded surprised.

'Of course. They were good. A bit depressing, but very atmospheric.'

'I was depressed when I did them.' He sighed, though he still didn't look at her. 'My father used to bring me here at least once a week. It's where he told me about our engagement. I remember him saying that it was important for the estate, although I didn't understand why at the time. Not until –' He slapped a hand against the trunk before spinning around to face her. 'You asked me once why I wasn't angry about our engagement. The truth is, I was. I felt like you. Trapped. Powerless. I already knew I would inherit the earldom one day and I felt like everything in my life was being decided without me. You once called me defeatist, but that wasn't why I agreed. It was duty. That was the other thing my father talked about here, about being the earl, about our family history, about all our obligations and responsibilities. Week after week, year after year. It was exhausting. And it was all lies. The whole time he was lecturing me about duty, he was busy destroying this place. Not deliberately, but if he'd only told me how bad things were then I would have understood. I would have helped. Instead, he kept on lying and lecturing.' He lifted his hands to his head, raking them through his hair. 'I thought that I knew who my father was, but I didn't have a clue. It was all just an act.'

'Maybe he didn't know how to tell you the truth.'

'He should have tried. And then he died and left me to fix everything, and all that talk of duty made it impossible for me to walk away. I was angrier then than I ever imagined I could be. It took me the whole first year after I inherited to come to terms with it. If we'd met at Redcliffe then, things might have been very different.'

'Then I'm glad that we didn't.' Essie reached a hand out.

'Are you?' He met her gaze squarely. 'Because I can't go through that again.'

'Meaning what?'

'Meaning that I can't love somebody and not know who they really are again. I need us to be completely honest with each other. Essie, I need the truth. No pretence. Just our real selves.'

She dropped her hand again, offended. 'Who do you think that I'm being?'

His eyes flashed with some powerful emotion. 'Last night, you said you were playing a role.'

'Being the countess, yes. What choice did I have after you said you didn't want me? I was too miserable *not* to pretend to be someone else. Never mind the fact that I didn't have a clue what I was doing!'

'I never said that I didn't want you.'

'But I thought you did!'

'Essie . . .' His voice sounded pleading. 'I just need to know that when you're with me, it's the real you, not you making the best of things because you think there's no other choice.'

'Yes, this is the real me!' she exploded. 'And when have you ever *not* seen through my performances anyway? Either at that first ball when I wore orange or the second one when I was going to throw champagne over a duchess? Apparently I'm not that good of an actress because you saw through what I was doing each time!' She pressed her hands to his chest and shoved hard, sending him sprawling into a patch of wildflowers. 'I told you how I felt last night. I love you. *That* was the truth. And if you're suggesting that what happened afterwards was a performance then you can go straight to hell and stay there!'

'Wait!' He jumped back to his feet and came after her, catching her around the waist as she reached for the mare's reins. 'I'm sorry. I didn't mean it that way, but when I woke up this morning it all felt too good to be true. Three months ago, on my way to Redcliffe, I thought that the best I could hope for was to meet somebody I could like. I never dreamed you might be somebody I could love too, who might love me in return.'

She turned around in his arms, glaring furiously. 'Do you know what I always loved most about acting? It gave me an escape, a chance to be someone else with a whole new start, but last night, for just about the first time in my life, I didn't want to escape. I wanted to be *me*! And I already had a new start. Or I thought that I did.' She shoved him away again. 'That was a horrible thing to accuse me of!'

'You're right, it was. It can just be hard to trust happiness when so much in your life has gone wrong.'

'So your answer is to chop logs and be haughty and clamp down on all your emotions just so you don't get hurt again?'

He looked faintly stunned. 'You're right. I *do* do that.'

'I know. It's infuriating!'

'So let's start again. From this moment.' He moved closer, his gaze intensifying. 'Essie . . . will you marry me?'

'In case you hadn't noticed, we already *are* married.'

'But I never asked you.'

'So you're asking me to marry you *after* the wedding?'

'Better late than never. Will you be my wife?'

'Not after what you just accused me of, no. And don't expect to share a bed again any time soon either.'

'I'm *really* sorry. Tell me what I can do to prove it.'

She scrunched her mouth up, thinking. 'All right. First, I want you to include me in your discussions with your steward. It's my dowry that's supposed to save this place, isn't it? So I should get a say in how it's used.'

'You're absolutely right. I should have thought of that.'

'Second, I want a proper courtship. We never had a real one of those either and I want romance with a capital R. Flowers and music and champagne. I want you to write odes about my ankles and songs about my tea-coloured eyes and then serenade me outside my window and all of the other things that suitors are supposed to do.'

He nodded emphatically. 'I can do all that.'

'Good. Then, afterwards, you can propose to me again in the most romantic way you can think of – with a ring!' She lifted her chin. 'And then *maybe* I'll consider it.'

'I'll be very persuasive.' He walked her backwards until she was pressed against the tree trunk. 'When I'm done you'll be sick of romance.'

'No more being haughty and distant?'

'I promise. And if I forget, you have permission to push me all the way down this hill.'

'That's not far enough.'

'Then I'll find a bigger one. A mountain.'

'In Hampshire?'

'We'll go to Wales. As for playing the countess, you don't need to be anyone other than yourself.'

'You say that now –'

'Because I mean it. Half the time I don't know how to be an earl either, but we'll work it out together.' He tipped his forehead against hers. 'Just how long a courtship are we talking about? Because a wise woman once told me a week was enough.'

'She obviously had no idea what she was talking about. To romance me properly? Three months.'

'*Three?*' His voice sounded strangled. 'Two.'

'Two and a half. That's my final offer.'

'Ten weeks.' Aidan groaned. 'This is going to be torture.'

'It's not so long.' Essie rubbed her nose softly against his. She had a feeling it might be torture for her too, but now that she'd thought of it, she was looking forward to being wooed. 'I lost you in ten weeks. It seems fitting that we take another ten to find each other again. After that, *if* your proposal is good enough, we get to live happily ever after.' She grinned. 'I'm calling that Plan E.'

PLAN E: ESSIE EVER AFTER/EPILOGUE

This above all: to thine own self be true,
And it must follow, as the night the day,
Thou canst not then be false to any man.
Farewell: my blessing season this in thee!

Hamlet, Act I, Scene III, 78–81

Underlined and bookmarked by Anne Craven, Lady
Makepeace, 7th March 1806

Chapter Twenty-six

*(Ten Weeks after the Wedding of Miss Essie
Craven to the Earl of Denholm)*

Essie dropped the letter into her lap. She was sitting on the stone terrace that ran along one side of the knot garden behind Middlemount, one of her top three favourite places in her new home after ten weeks of exploring. The low hedges were planted in intricate rose-shaped swirls interspersed with neat gravel pathways that led to a tiered fountain in the centre, and the combination of beauty and symmetry, accompanied by the light trickle of water, made her feel soothed and contented. According to her husband, it was one of the few places where she would actually sit still for longer than ten minutes, which was why he kept seizing the opportunity to set up his easel in front of her, regarding her intently while dabbing at a canvas and then refusing to let her see the results. Today, however, she was all alone, looking and listening without either seeing or hearing, her mind preoccupied with what she'd just read.

'What are you looking so serious about?'

Not so alone, after all, she realized, as Aidan's voice brought her out of her reverie, the question accompanied by the gentle touch of a finger against the nape of her neck. She made a low purring sound as his lips replaced it and moved lower, leaving goosebumps in their wake. She'd never purred until a few weeks ago, but now she was becoming quite the expert. She and Aidan might not have literally consummated their marriage again since their wedding night, but they'd discovered plenty of other ways to pass the time together. The past ten weeks had been extremely educational.

'Just a letter from Grandmama.' She smiled as his lips continued their tour of her neck, drifting towards the front. He'd grown his beard back and the bristles chafed softly against her skin. 'She says Mildred's a brazen hussy.'

'Pardon?'

'Puppies. Grandmama is extremely displeased.'

'Ah.'

'She also says she's going to send us one.'

'Do we get a choice about that?'

'It's Grandmama.'

'Fair enough.'

Aidan nuzzled into her neck as Essie continued, 'She's worried about Caro too.'

'Why?' His lips stilled. 'Jagger?'

'Oh no, according to Grandmama's spies he's somewhere in Scandinavia, but apparently Caro's turned down another proposal, this time from a friend of Felix. At least *he* was already in Cleveland and didn't follow her all the way from London like the Marquess of Bazley or poor Mr Dormer or any of the others whose names I've forgotten, but that makes *twelve* refusals. Grandmama thinks she's trying to set some kind of record.'

'If she doesn't care for any of her suitors then it's for the best.' Aidan went back to nuzzling again. 'Besides, I had a letter from Dormer the other day. He sounded in much better spirits.'

'Thank goodness.' Essie nestled against him as he came to sit beside her. 'Isn't it funny how things work out? If someone had asked me at the start of the Season, I'd have told them that Caro would be a duchess by now.'

'And you'd be . . . ?'

'Playing Electra.'

'Mmm. Well, as brilliant as you'd be as an avenging Greek princess, I prefer you as my countess.'

'Fortunately, I quite like being her too.' She twisted her head to smile at him. 'Where have you been all day anyway? I had to eat luncheon on my own.'

'Sorry about that. The new threshing machines arrived so I needed to check everything was in order. Then I went to see how the repairs to the cottages are going.'

'And?'

'They'll be finished by the end of the month. We're making even faster progress than I'd hoped.' He pressed a kiss into her hair. 'By the way, I don't suppose you know what day it is?'

Essie stiffened, feeling her pulse kick and accelerate instantly. She'd been counting down the weeks and days with a growing sense of excitement, but instead of a proposal at breakfast like she'd expected, Aidan had spent the meal talking about crop rotation and then disappeared for most of the day. She'd been starting to worry that he'd forgotten their ten weeks were up.

'Not a clue.' She feigned a puzzled expression. 'Why?'

'Oh, no particular reason.' He reached for her left hand, toying gently with her ring finger. 'Although you'd make me the happiest man in the world if you would do me the very great honour . . .'

'Yes?' She prompted him as he paused.

'The considerable honour . . .'

'Yes?'

'. . . of dancing with me.'

'What?' She jolted her head around at the sound of a lone violin. 'What's that?'

'You said you wanted romance.'

Another second and a few more violins joined in, accompanied by the deeper strains of a cello.

'It sounds like an orchestra.' She gaped at him in astonishment.

'It is.'

'Where?'

'On the other side of that wall. As I recall, the last time I asked you to dance, you refused me. So . . . ?'

'Now?' She laughed and then nodded, allowing herself to be pulled to her feet and into his arms. A moment later and they were waltzing around the terrace, the way they had at Vauxhall.

'You know I never did get permission to dance this.' She tipped her head back, looking up at the sky. The sun hadn't yet dipped behind the horizon, but the moon was already high, almost full and luminously bright.

'I won't tell.' Aidan waggled his eyebrows. 'So how am I doing? Romantically speaking?'

'This is lovely.'

'On a scale of one to ten?'

'Eight.'

'Eight?' He looked offended. 'Where am I losing points?'

'Nothing specifically.' She lifted her shoulders, smiling mischievously. 'I'm just very demanding.'

'I know that. It's been a long ten weeks.' His voice had a ragged edge as he twirled her around in a circle and then caught hold of her hand, pulling her towards a gate in the wall. 'Which is why we need to hurry.'

'Why? Where are we going?' She caught at her skirts, struggling to keep up as he marched them briskly along an avenue of tall pine trees.

'Somewhere romantic, I promise.'

'I'm beginning to regret using that word.'

'And I'm just getting started.'

'Not to criticize –' she tugged on his hand – 'but we're heading *away* from the music.'

'So we are.' He didn't break his stride. 'Don't worry, you'll still be able to hear them.'

'But –'

'Trust me.'

'I do, but you're being very mysterious.' She looked about curiously as they took a path around the lake and up a slope on the other side. 'I thought you told me not to come this way because you were felling trees.'

'Not felling exactly, more like building something.'

'What?'

'You'll see in a moment.' He stopped walking abruptly and came to stand behind her, placing his hands over her eyes. 'Let's make this a ten, shall we?'

'If you think you can . . .' She shuffled forward, laughing. After a few steps, they obviously reached the crest of the slope because her legs straightened beneath her and her breath started to come easier again. And then Aidan took his hands away and she gave a small cry of astonishment. The ground dropped away immediately in front of them, revealing a dozen rows of benches leading down to a wooden stage with a low stone building behind it.

'It's an outdoor theatre.' Aidan sounded triumphant. 'I admit it's a bit of a gamble considering the British weather, but I'm being an optimist these days.'

'It's wonderful!' Essie pressed her hands to her mouth. 'I don't know what to say. It's the most perfectly romantic gesture I could ever have imagined!'

'I even hammered some of the boards down myself. And your first performance can be at our summer fair next month. I expect to be dazzled.'

'Next –?' She started to protest and then stopped. Considering what he'd just given her, a month was the least she could do. 'Challenge accepted.'

'Good. Now, it's time for dinner!' He gestured to a hamper on one side of the stage. 'I have candles and champagne too.'

'It looks like you've thought of everything.' She felt as if her face might split in two from smiling. 'You know, you're *very* good at romance.'

'I had ten weeks to plan.'

'I was starting to think that you'd forgotten.'

'I know. I thought it would heighten the effect. And I'm not finished yet.' He reached behind the hamper and held up a canvas. It was a portrait of her in a lemon-coloured dress, standing in a tree and holding a small tabby cat.

'Sir Purrsalot?'

'The one and only. After some deliberation, I decided that was the day I started to fall in love with you. Although it's possible that seeing your undergarments might have had something to do with it too.'

'And you say you're not talented? This is even better than the other one.'

'What other one?'

'That sketch you did of me at Redcliffe.'

'Oh.' He looked faintly sheepish. 'That might have been the first sketch, but there have been plenty of others since then. You've rapidly become my favourite subject.'

'Really?' She felt her face blossom with colour. 'I'm flattered.'

'I keep telling you, you're beautiful. Maybe this way you'll finally believe it.' He smoothed a hand across one of her cheeks and then winked. 'You make a refreshing change from landscapes too. Now, what's next?' He put the painting down and drew a piece of paper from his jacket pocket. 'A sonnet. So I admit, I had some problems finding rhymes for Essie. The only obvious word was messy, but —'

'Perhaps we should leave the poetry until after the proposal.' She made a grab for the paper, folding it up and tucking it neatly inside her bodice. 'Just in case.'

'That took me six hours!'

'And I appreciate it, but you know what Jane Austen says about poetry and love in *Pride and Prejudice*?'

'No.' He looked apologetic. 'I like the title, but I haven't actually read it.'

'You *haven't* read it?' She shook her head incredulously. 'From now on, I'm going to read you a chapter in bed every night.'

'When it comes to bed, I'm prepared to let you do anything you want at this point.' He spread his arms out. 'Now *please* tell me all of this is at least a nine?'

'It's a ten. A perfect ten.'

'Then there's only one more thing to do.' He bent down on one knee and held out a box, opening the lid to reveal a gold band decorated with a brilliant, solitaire diamond. 'Essie, will you –'

'Yes!' She climbed on to his lap, sending them both sprawling across the stage. 'Of course, yes! I thought you were never going to ask!'

About the Author

Jenni Fletcher is the author of more than fifteen romance novels, ranging from the Roman to Victorian eras because she has historical commitment issues. She teaches creative writing at Bishop Grosseteste University and her books have been nominated for four Romantic Novelists' Association Awards. She also won the Libertà Books Shorter Romantic Novel Award in 2020. Jenni grew up in Scotland and Somerset, and now lives in Yorkshire with her husband, two children and one extremely hairy dog. She likes to write early in the mornings and is easily distracted by Twitter, where you can follow her @JenniAuthor.